COMMON WELL

A NOVEL BY

STEPHEN E. MEYER

ISBN (Print): 978-1-66789-559-8
ISBN (eBook): 978-1-66789-560-4

For my daughters, Veronica and Ruby

CONTENTS

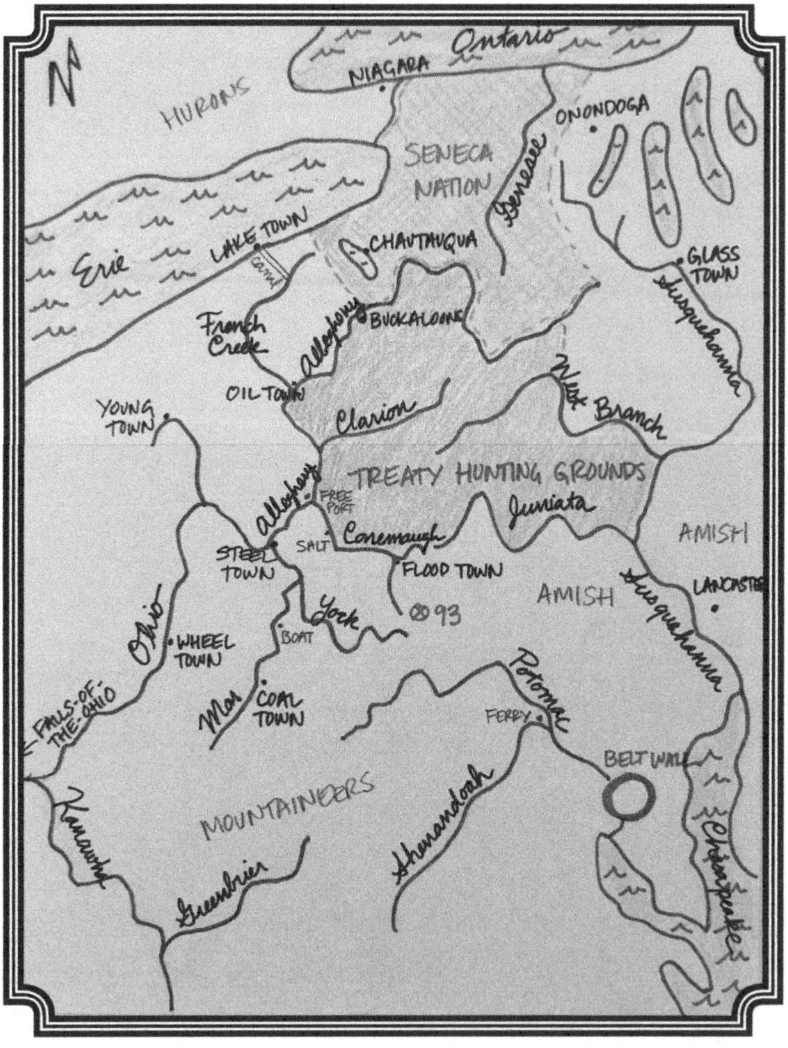

N
Ontario
NIAGARA
HURONS
SENECA NATION
ONONDOGA
Genesee
Erie
LAKE TOWN
CHAUTAUQUA
GLASS TOWN
Susquehanna
French Creek
Allegheny
BUCKALOONS
OIL TOWN
Clarion
West Branch
YOUNG TOWN
TREATY HUNTING GROUNDS
Allegheny
FREE PORT
Juniata
AMISH
STEEL TOWN
SALT
Conemaugh
FLOOD TOWN
AMISH
Susquehanna
LANCASTER
York
93
Ohio
WHEEL TOWN
BOAT
Potomac
Mon
COAL TOWN
FERRY
FALLS-OF-THE-OHIO
BELT WALL
MOUNTAINEERS
Shenandoah
Kanawha
Greenbrier
Chesapeake

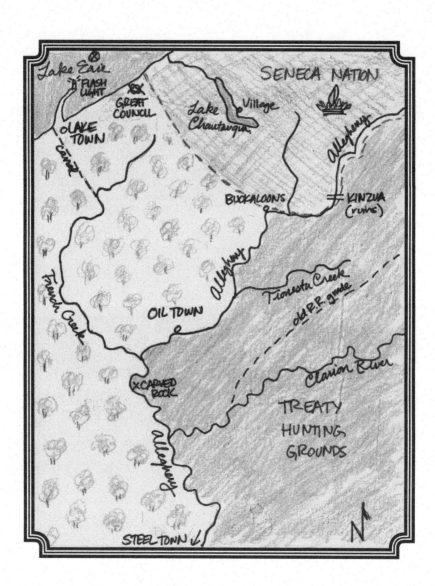

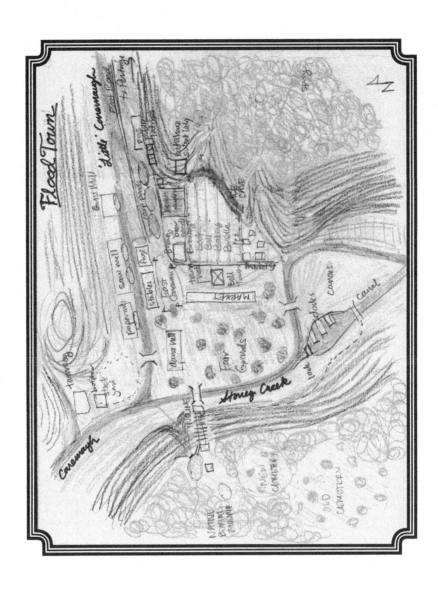

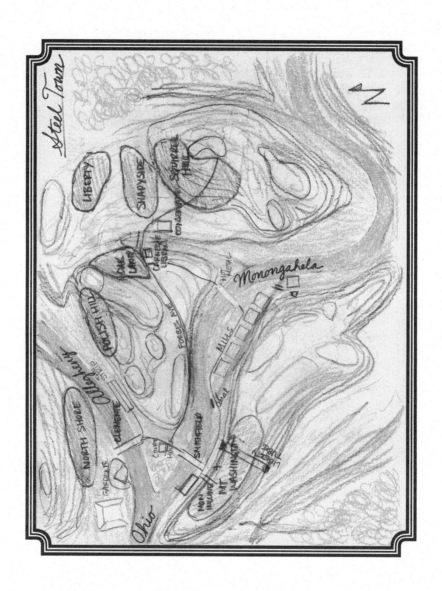

The colonization of Mars in the twenty-first century A.D. was a triumph of human progress and ingenuity. The achievement was marred by a single flaw—the water, sourced from the Martian polar ice caps, made the settlers sick. And even the most advanced AIs couldn't solve the mystery why.

A fleet of colossal tankers was built to transport fresh water from Earth, an engineering feat without parallel. But when the squabbling factions back on Earth threatened to interrupt that supply, Mars deployed a weapon that disrupted electrical power and communications, plunging the planet into darkness.

Now, centuries later, most Martians have long since forgotten about Earth, focusing their energies on genetic enhancements, and exploring the distant stars.

PART ONE

——

RETURN

1

A tiny clock appeared in the lower left corner of her field of vision, the digits colored orange, the seconds ticking down, the milliseconds—which seemed like overkill—cycling franticly. *Under an hour.* She drifted over to the tiny oblong plate of glass and was shocked at how vibrant the blue was this close up, the bands of clouds, the curved line of night. Beyond that, the arc of a shimmering green aurora. She exhaled and the little window fogged.

She had been in this modified maintenance closet for the past seventy-two hours, waiting for a weather window. It was so cramped her outstretched arms could nearly touch the four walls. The closet was a stark contrast to the spacious cabin they provided her in the fast packet ship out here, equipped with a state-of-the-art gym machine so she could keep up with her punishing routine, an actual shower, and a luxurious gel-pad bed.

Here she slept velcroed to the wall on a thin mat. But this ship was used to carry water, not people.

A long checklist hovered to her right, above icons for the different op sims. She had run through each stage hundreds of times, then out of sheer boredom moved on to the old vids, quizzing the name and use of every object in every scene. Now she dismissed the list with a mental flick, but it stubbornly slid back into view.

Enough, she thought.

She could sense the apologetic shrug of her mentor and somehow that annoyed her even more, but she kept her emotions in check. Not that it mattered, they would know.

With the slightest press of her fingers against the outer hull, she propelled herself over to the corner where a set of shelves stood. In among the jumble of odds and ends, one packing crate had been illuminated by her mentor, traced with a helpful yellow outline. She shifted the container over to her bed mat and strapped it to the wall. When she placed her hand on the flat panel, the locks sprung open with a hiss.

Inside, a black suit was folded neatly, its hex grid seams slightly raised, the herringbone mesh weave of the fabric glinting in the low utility lights. Next to the suit a hardshell backpack was nestled, almost ceramic to the touch—as well as a helmet, shiny and polished like a carapace. She hovered over the open chest for a long moment, frowning, and even peeked underneath the suit.

That's it?

Her mentor confirmed the contents were as expected.

Weapons?

Silence. Just the spinning clock, which she could have sworn had increased in font size.

She coasted across to the opposite corner and started removing her clothes, wrapping everything into a tight ball that she left floating like a balloon while she used the ancient negative pressure toilet. When finished, she removed the sealed waste bags, gathered up all the empty food tubes and water bulbs and med kits from the last days, and wadded them together with her clothes. To the right of the window, she rotated a circular hatch ninety degrees, slid out a cylindrical drawer, and jammed everything in.

A slight tug detached the circlet from the magnet mounts under her skin, one at each temple. All the displays immediately vanished as well as the constant, almost physical, presence of her mentor. The glow of the headband slowly faded to its default gray color.

She gently laid the circlet on top of her clothes in the cylinder, feeling a rush of mixed emotions. Going all the way back to her pod, she couldn't remember a time when her mentor wasn't present, right there alongside her—inside her—with a helpful nudge, suggesting a stream to follow, a playlist, a funny glif, monitoring her vitals, there when she woke up, providing white noise to help her fall asleep, even retrieving interesting dreams that they would then mutually analyze.

In mission training they had her go prolonged periods without wearing the circlet to see her unaided reaction in high stress, rapid decision scenarios. But afterward there was always the reassuring snap of the headband settling back into place on her brow, the immediate comforting flow of information.

She slid the drawer closed and sealed the hatch. After a moment, a green button lit up alongside, which she pressed, flushing the airlock clear.

Now she was truly alone, suspended in mid-air, naked, save for a pendant necklace that floated in a halo around her neck. Of course, not truly alone—there had to be cameras in this room somewhere—but alone where it mattered, inside her head.

Her thoughts raced while she methodically donned the suit. *Could this entire mission just be an elaborate ruse?* The cover story of inspecting lunar mining operations was a total fabrication. The manifest on the packet ship had been modified so there was no record of her on board, nor of her mid-flight detour and rendezvous with this tanker. But then, obfuscation was standard operating procedure for Audit.

Who knew about this mission? Wen Prime, of course. The Founders, and that meant their admins too. Which meant there were dozens in the orbit of the C-suite who had bits and pieces—*could they have assembled the fragments?* Even she didn't have the full picture.

She had been a curiosity in and around the Founder's Club this past year—training in their gym with all the machines set on max, swimming with a weighted suit in their pool, wolfing down massive portions in their private cafeteria. Wen Prime liked flaunting her in their faces, in the raw, shocking their sensibilities. But once they heard whispers she was from Audit, no further questions were asked. People stayed out of her way, avoided eye contact, projected neutral-shaded emotions from their circlets.

Possibly the AIs had run an updated scenario—one that shuffled Wen Prime out, pruned the org chart? It had happened before, a clean reboot. Easy enough to jettison her out here, no questions asked.

Yet there were so many simpler and direct ways to delete someone, not an elaborate staged drama like this. Taking them deep underground to the reservoirs, or driving them in a rover far outside the Dome. AIs controlled the feeds, could simply shift the narrative in real time and it was as if the person never existed.

She finished squirming her body into the suit, which took some acrobatics while weightless. The interior layer of gel padding was cold against her bare skin, the kevlar fabric tight around her shoulders. Apparently she'd put on more muscle since they had fit her. She exhaled deeply, fastened the last seal, pushed the doubts aside. The reality of what lay before her was daunting enough, and the most probable outcome was not much different than her paranoid fantasies.

A jarring rumble shook the room, signaling the two-hundred-kilometer-long intake hose was being deployed. This storage closet was part of a bracelet of mechanical rooms that fit like a cuff around the intake hose, located fifty meters above the suction nozzle—a remnant from centuries ago, when the ship was not fully automated and had to be manned by actual people.

She glided once more to the window. The tanker had traversed to the night side, and she stared down into the black void. In advance of the tanker's approach, one of the low-orbit satellites had blasted a powerful pulse of charged ions. An aurora of ghostly green ribbons rippled outward in concentric circles. The weapon was harmless to living things but completely disruptive to electrical circuits and radio signals. If she wore the circlet down there her brain would fry.

The planet once had been plagued by endless wars, but now was dark and silent. *The Founders had no choice but to put a stop to it.*

On cue, after the hull vibration had subsided, a green light began to blink above a larger, person-sized airlock door set into the outer hull. *It's time.*

She clipped the hardshell pack on her back and twisted the dials on the shoulder straps to lock it in place. Even though weightless, the pack altered her center of gravity and threatened to tip her, like it had in training, when she cracked her head against the hull. The helmet formed a tight seal to the hard collar around her neck and she felt it pressurize, took a few breaths. How she missed the instant feedback her mentor could have provided: oxygen levels, heart rate.

The green light over the airlock increased pace, more insistent now. *If I don't enter,* she idly wondered, *what exactly will happen?* Was there an operational unit positioned outside the entry to the mechanical room—*will they rush in and shove me in the hole?*

This sort of nonsense was exactly what her mentor helped prevent—or, to be precise, her mentor always being there provided plenty of motivation to never let these kinds of thoughts slip out.

She opened the hatch and crawled inside. A very dim light came on, so faint that it was almost imperceptible from complete darkness, dull red in color so it wouldn't affect her dark vision. The airlock was a cramped egg-shaped space bulging out from the hull, with nothing more than a fold down bench for her to sit on and two handrails to grip.

Inside the dome of her helmet were mounted three miniature analog instruments—a gyroscope, a compass, and an altimeter—old tech that wouldn't be disrupted by the electromagnetic pulse. The dials glowed fluorescent green and were magnified by glass bubbles, so she could read them at a glance. Stiffly, she bobbled her head side to side, up and down, confirming the horizon line on the gyro and the bearing on the compass moved accordingly.

The chamber shook as the hose skipped across the outer atmosphere and the hull began to glow translucently, pink-orange, the way a bright flashlight looks when shining through skin. She felt the heat radiating through her suit. But soon the nozzle had fully punctured through the mesosphere, and she heard the horizontal stabilizer fins extending along the length of the intake hose as it continued its descent.

The AIs had run endless sims on what would be the ideal altitude. Too high and the acceleration in the first sixty seconds would push her past the sound barrier and cause a sonic boom that could be heard for miles. Too low and the static built up in the charged atmosphere might trigger lightning. She was little more than an input variable in their probability equations. They had settled on thirty-one kilometers.

After a couple of minutes, the dull red interior light blinked a few times and then switched off, leaving her in complete darkness for what felt like an eternity as the chamber decompressed.

Then without warning the outer sphere cap pivoted open and upward, exposing her, perched on the narrow seat ledge, squeezing the handrails tightly, feeling the first faint tug of gravity. Countless hours in the wind tunnel wearing the full haptic rig could not replicate this view of staring straight down into the void. The sims always supplied some texture, a faint sketch of landscape far below, but this view was total black. She would've been better off training blindfolded.

Now or never.

The motion was simple—standing up, leaning forward and letting go, like slipping from a ladder into a pool. One microsecond she felt the support of the railing, the next she was in full freefall.

There was no sensation of falling or speed or acceleration, the atmosphere was so thin at this height. Just the altimeter dial spinning faster and faster. No sound, other than her ragged breathing. In her head she was counting to herself—an absurd task best suited for her mentor.

40 .... she felt the air pressure starting to build up in front of her.

55 .... she noticed the compass bearing was circling around, the horizon line on the gyro wobbling. She blinked in disbelief. *How did both crash simultaneously?!*

60 .... she realized there was nothing wrong with the instruments. *I'm the one spinning!*

65 .... the monochrome black that surrounded her took on a reddish hue around the edges. A very bad sign—blood was rushing to her head.

She lost count. In a few moments she would be unconscious.

Straining with effort she lifted her head skyward, puffed out her chest, scissored her legs together, locked her knees and squeezed her glutes tight, pulled one arm into her side while extending the other out, off to the side—which caused her body to flip and roll and spin into a heads-down corkscrew dive. She quickly splayed her limbs out again, arched her back and the wind caught her like an outstretched palm, the instruments stabilized, the roaring of blood in her ears subsided.

That was close.

With her eyes now fully adjusted to the dark, the landscape below began to take form, illuminated by a full moon and the glowing aurora overhead. To both the east and west, regular deep shadows, almost like waves, demarcated the parallel ridges and valleys typical of this region. Directly below her, a high flat plateau stretched like a ribbon. The ground cover was heavily forested everywhere she looked—except for one tiny carved-out circle, glinting silver in the moonlight, like a flat battery disc lying on a black carpet. Directly in her line of flight.

If they had sent an advance team to prepare a landing zone, they could hardly have chosen a more ideal location. At nearly eight hundred meters elevation, it was the highest point for miles. Orbital scans revealed the site had once undergone surface mining, a whole hilltop removed to expose a seam of fossil fuel, and then backfilled so the terrain was flat.

A near perfect circle, nearly a kilometer in diameter, had been cut from the surrounding trees and in the clearing stood a field of grass. A stone wall was located at the southwest corner, seeming to serve no purpose. But otherwise, no sign of habitation.

The site had prompted a lot of questions, but the evasive way her mentor answered—obviously coming at the direction of the AIs—was a subtle way of suggesting, *best not to press*. Just add it to the list of a thousand other questions with no answers forthcoming.

Her thoughts had drifted—something her mentor would have never permitted—and her focus snapped back to realize the altimeter was down under two kilometers. *Now comes the tricky part*. She'd watched every possible vid from the archive, rehearsed the motions in the haptic rig, but it was impossible to conduct a live trial in advance. *So this had better work*.

She put her left arm forward to balance herself in the air stream, felt along the edge of the hardshell pack until locating the handle, gave it a yank, and with great relief felt the parachute deploy above her, suddenly jerking her shoulders upright, arresting her freefall.

Grabbing the steering toggles, she brought the chute under control and approached the clearing in a wide spiral. She glanced up, the chute itself and the lines were practically invisible by design, made of translucent microfiber. The only way for her to be observed would be if she passed in front of the moon at the precise moment someone was looking at it.

The ground rushed up at her, she pulled down hard on the toggles to level the chute as she swished through the grass. Her boots chunked into the dirt and her momentum carried her jogging a few steps forward.

From when she had first jumped, only about five minutes had elapsed.

It had been over eight hundred years since a Martian had last set foot on Earth.

She immediately unsealed the helmet and inhaled deeply, breathing the night air. The smell of grass in the meadow hit like a physical shock—crisp and cold and damp—like fluid pouring into her lungs. She struggled for a moment to exhale, could feel the rush of rich oxygen in her blood. *Better than any drug Wen Prime gave me.*

She had expected something like the humid dank air in the greenhouse levels—but nothing on Mars smelled, tasted, felt anything close to this. She stood there for a moment just drinking it in.

Here at ground level, the meadow was not level as it appeared from above, but instead was tilted on an incline with a curved rim rising to the north. The trees encircling the field were massive, easily thirty meters tall, the treetops against the night sky creating the impression of standing in the center of an arena.

Already the aurora from the satellite pulse was beginning to fade and the bright moon once again dominated the sky. The long slant of her shadow was visible in the silvery light. Up near the ridge, four deer were out in the field grazing. One with antlers lifted his head, noticed her arrival, then returned to eating.

The wall was a short distance to her left, down in the lowest part of the field, a bright white line. Well over the horizon to the northwest, along the flight path of the tanker, lightning flashed, sparked by the intake hose dragging through the over-charged atmosphere as it descended to the surface.

Huron, she recalled with some difficulty. The name of the freshwater lake where this refill would be taking place, almost five hundred kilometers away. Her mentor would have immediately listed a dozen interesting facts, plotted the orbital path, displayed a running progress bar—instead she was left with a dull ache beneath her temples as she forced herself to concentrate on the task at hand.

The parachute lay in a crumpled crescent behind her. She wasted no more time, bunched the sheer fabric and gossamer ropes, retrieved the helmet and awkwardly dragged them through the wet grass toward the wall, to provide some cover. Just this small amount of physical activity in the higher gravity took extra effort.

She unclipped the hardshell pack and propped it on top of the tangled parachute. Inside, a pouch was nestled underneath where the chute had been stowed. She ripped the tab to break the vacuum seal and took inventory.

The clothing was the subject of a heated thread among the AIs, with opinions ranging from keeping the full suit on, to a crude frontier getup that seemed implausible, even in the old vids they were modeled upon, to having her be naked. The outcome—by no means a consensus—resembled the common jumpsuit worn by Essentials. But instead of being sleek and synthetic, this outfit was shapeless, save for a built-in belt at the waist, and was woven from raw natural fibers. *Linen*, she said to herself, remembering the word.

She removed the rest of the contents, examining each individually. Soft shoes—*mocassins*. A carryall bag for over her shoulder—*satchel*. Strips of dried and salted animal protein—*jerky*. A container of water—*canteen*. A folded page of *papyrus—no, paper*—that displayed an even grid pattern of plus and minus signs. *The most important item.*

She unpeeled herself from the spacesuit and once again was nude. Yes, she was at forty degrees north latitude, at higher elevation, only a month after the vernal equinox, at night, with clear skies. But all the sims had portrayed the climate as balmy and humid, not cold and damp. The thin cloth of the jumpsuit was barely an improvement over wearing nothing.

As she was dressing, she marveled at the attention to details, the smudges of mud, the tears and scuffs in the fabric. AIs were obsessive, believed the entire mission hinged on every trivial item, down to the molecular composition of the mud stains—which she bet was actual silt filtered from the holding reservoirs. That's the level they would go to. The reek of sweat from the jumpsuit seemed a little over the top until she got a whiff of herself after days holed up in that maintenance room. *Yep, they nailed it.*

The spacesuit and helmet went onto the pile, as well as the vacuum pouch, everything she had come down with, except for the pendant necklace, which she tucked underneath the collar of the jumpsuit.

One last foam-padded compartment in the hardshell pack contained a crude glass bottle filled with amber fluid. The top of the bottle was coated with a red sealant—*wax*—that she cracked open by tugging at an embedded string, revealing a *cork* stopper. *They had certainly outdone themselves.*

She doused everything on the pile with the liquid from the bottle, even the helmet and hardshell pack, then waited. Nothing happened. She sniffed the bottle: an alcohol smell. There was a slight flash of panic. *Wait—was that a bottle of... whiskey... that she was supposed to be traveling with? Was there a different vial hidden somewhere?* How tedious to not have her mentor there, instantly providing the correct course of action.

But as she stood there fretting, wispy blue flame began to curl up from the edges of the chute. The chemical reaction accelerated, the materials began to dissolve into a fine translucent ash that dissipated into the air. She looked at the empty bottle, shuddering to think what would have happened if it had cracked during entry.

The fire glowed ghostly blue, yet strangely did not throw off any heat. She slung the satchel over her shoulder, knowing she should get on the move, didn't have to wait for the burn to complete, no way to stop the chain reaction once it began. But her curiosity led her over to the wall.

It stood about three meters tall, constructed of white marble that flickered, reflecting the blue flames. An odd gap split the wall in the middle, through which the field continued a hundred meters to the tree line. To her left, the wall ended in a tall wooden gate, the same height as the wall. She couldn't make any sense of the geometry, nor the purpose— the wall did not enclose anything, the gate didn't lead anywhere, the whole structure just free standing out here in the field.

She noticed there was writing on the wall, a date engraved: *September 11, 2001.* She had spent months reviewing the historical events of the century that preceded the Severance and couldn't recall anything special about that date. *Is it astronomical, aligned with the sun—like the ancient stones at Stonehenge?*

There was more writing on the other side of the gap. This section of the wall was a series of vertical marble slabs, standing close but not touching, centimeters apart, aligned in a subtle zig-zag pattern. On each section was inscribed a name.

This is a tomb, she suddenly realized.

She walked down the line, reading each name, counting as she went, forty slabs in total. *Who were these people?*

She wished her mentor were here to clear everything up.

"Hey!" a voice shouted.

She spun around, startled, and saw a figure standing out in the field at a distance.

"Hey! You can't be here!" A male voice, nervous and high-pitched. "What are you burning?"

Without even acknowledging the calls, she immediately ran to the wooden gate, seeing open field and the tree line beyond. *It was locked!* A metal latched peg, inserted into the ground—*on the other side*! She grabbed the wooden slats and rattled the gate to see if it could be dislodged, with no luck. And it was too tall to climb.

"Hey you! Stop! You are trespassing!"

The person in the field was starting to move in her direction. She looked back along the wall, gauging the distance past the forty slabs to the gap, and made an instant decision. She broke into a full sprint.

All those hours in the swimming pool at the Founder's Club wearing the weighted resistance suit were nothing like actually running in this gravity. Her legs felt full of sand, like a giant hand pressing down on her. She passed the smoldering remnants of the blue fire, the last items crumbling into dust. About two-thirds of the way her lungs began to burn, but she dug deep and focused her eyes on the gap in the wall, growing bigger with each step.

And then she reached the opening. She twisted her body to glance over her right shoulder—noted with satisfaction the person was still a good distance away, not even chasing after her, just standing there, watching her. Raising some kind of long stick or pole....

A sudden flash and bang and smoke and instantly her right shoulder was yanked all the way around, spinning her and dumping her on the ground hard on her back.

She blinked, looking up at the night sky and full moon, stunned. Her right shoulder felt like it was on fire. When she touched it, her left hand came away dripping with liquid that looked black as oil in the moonlight. *Blood.*

I've been ... shot?!

Bows and arrows were risks she had trained for. *But a gun?* Nothing in any sim suggested this was even a remote possibility. They had assured her ballistic firearm tech had vanished centuries ago—along with everything else after the Severance.

A deeper, instinctual part of her brain snapped her back to the present and the immediate danger she was in. She managed to prop herself up on her left elbow and saw the man was bounding toward her through the grass.

She struggled back to her feet, made a fist with her right hand and flexed the muscles in her arm. *They still work,* she thought with relief, trying to ignore the screaming pain in her shoulder.

And then he was upon her, holding the long gun like a bar across the front of his body, attempting to use his momentum to knock her prone again. She widened her stance, caught the gun barrel and stock with both hands and braced herself, sliding backwards in the slick grass but remaining upright.

The face of a teenaged boy opposite her, mouth set with determination but fear in his eyes. She was physically larger than him, easily ten centimeters taller and more muscular—he was scrawny, dressed in a checkered shirt, denim pants and tall boots, a cloth headband holding his long hair back.

But his center of gravity was lower, she felt his wiry strength winning out, almost toppling her over backward. They both grunted, struggled, she dug in her feet, gathered herself and made a full-body lunge forward—and as she did, a searing pain lanced from her shoulder down through her right arm all the way to her fingertips. She lost her grip and her arm buckled, the barrel of the gun swung forward and crashed into her head above her temple.

Everything exploded into stars and then went dark.

2

As she regained consciousness, she became aware she was still lying in the field. Cracking open her eyes, she glimpsed the teenage boy beside her, hovering over her, his long hair hanging down around his face. His bandana was bunched up and pressed down into her shoulder, where all his attention was focused.

"Don't die, don't die, don't die," he was whispering.

She remained motionless and kept her eyes shut.

"Jace!" another voice called out. "Where are you?"

"Over here!" the boy Jace shouted back, so loud and close to her ears it almost caused her to flinch.

She listened to the swish-swish-swish as someone approached at a jog. *One person.*

"I heard a shot, came out, you'd disappeared—" Out of breath from running, voice cracking. *Also a teenaged male.* Then suddenly a cry, "Oh my!"

"Shut up and help me, Benjy!"

The boy named Benjy came alongside and crouched down, voice dropping to a concerned hush, "What happened?"

"I'll tell you in a moment, but first we gotta stop the bleeding," Jace hissed—then, after a pause, urgently, "Give me your belt."

"Wha–"

"Just do it, Benjy," Jace said with force. "Now!"

It took all her willpower not to yelp in pain as they lifted her shoulder to loop the belt underneath and then knotted it tight, pressing the wadded bandana into the hollow of her shoulder, forming a tourniquet. *Quick thinking, this Jace.*

"There, I think that should hold for now," Jace exhaled deeply.

Both stood up, stepped a few meters aside.

"Listen. I couldn't sleep," Jace started. "I don't know, first night up here. I saw the full moon plus the aurora—bright as day—and thought, well—maybe there's some deer out in the field. And if I got one, we'd feast like the ancients during our stretch. You were fast asleep. So I grabbed my rifle and kit and snuck out of the cabin—"

Cabin? There wasn't supposed to be any structure for kilometers.

"I saw this blue glow over at the Wall of Names. At first, I thought it was a ghost and just about crapped my pants. Then I saw it was fire burning—so I ran over. And then I saw her."

"What is she doing here?" Benjy asked.

"Heck if I know. I shouted at her to stop. First she tried to jump the fence right into the sacred ground, then ran back toward the opening in the wall—"

"And so you shot her."

"Well what else was I supposed to do? I thought she was burning down the Memorial! We're the Ninety-Three Guardians. Guarding is right there in the name."

"We're not in Ninety-Three yet, Jace! And looks like you just screwed that chance. For both of us!"

Silence stretched on to a point where she wondered if they had left.

"Hey, what's with that outfit she's wearing?" Benjy finally asked.

"I dunno, never seen anything like it before…"

"And where is this fire you saw?"

"It vanished. I don't know how, Benjy. But I swear there was a fire burning right there when I came over."

"All I see here is an empty bottle." The sound of the cork being pulled. "Smells like whiskey... Please tell me you aren't drunk, Jace!!"

"Take that back or I swear I'll—"

"What, shoot me?"

More silence, even longer than the last time.

"Benjy, look. What's done's done. We gotta get her inside right away and see how bad it is." Then the direction of Jace's voice turned.

"And you—yeah you, lady. I know you're lying there listening."

She remained motionless, at first trying to maintain the bluff, but then decided to open her eyes and glare directly at the two boys.

"Oh she's pissed at you, Jace!"

"Can you stand up and walk?" Jace asked, ignoring Benjy. "Our cabin is down there in the gully, just past them hemlocks. It's not far. We can help you, if—if you need help."

"I can walk," she said hoarsely—surprised at the husky sound of her own voice, much deeper here at the planet surface. Slowly she rolled onto her side, pushed herself up onto one knee and staggered upright— waves of pain radiating from her shoulder at every movement.

"Just don't run," Jace said.

As they crossed through the field, with Benjy in the lead and Jace following behind her, no one talking, she played out different scenarios in her head. The gun was a primitive single-shot flintlock rifle—a *muzzleloader*. Could Jace have reloaded while she was out? *Unlikely.* But could she outrun them in unfamiliar terrain? *Doubtful.* Would they try to overpower or take advantage of her? *No—they won't. They're scared.*

So am I.

What troubled her the most was the fact a cabin was even here. *No way the orbital scans could have missed it.* Which meant the AIs

21

were fully aware, also had to know it was inhabited. So they must have anticipated some kind of encounter shortly after landfall. *Why didn't they tell me?*

They crossed the boundary of the field, entering a stand of hemlock pines so dense the moonbeams didn't penetrate, plunging them into darkness like entering a cave. The ground underfoot was pine straw, muffling all sound. She stumbled on an exposed root, almost lost her balance, and moaned from the shock wave of pain. Jace reached out a hand to steady her.

Ahead the canopy parted and in the middle of a clearing a small cabin stood, lit by a shaft of moonlight. A steep thatched roof perched like a giant fuzzy cap atop the structure. The mortared stone walls were whitewashed, a chimney rose at the far end with a wisp of smoke rising. *No other signs of people.*

Split firewood was neatly stacked alongside one wall, an iron pump handle, trough and wooden bucket were situated out front. From the trees came the soft gurgling sound of a stream. At the far edge of the clearing, an elevated platform stood on a tripod of poles about five meters above ground, a rough-hewn ladder propped nearby against a tree.

Noticing the direction she was staring, Jace offered, "Keeps food away from the bears."

Benjy opened the front door and they entered, dark inside save for the dull orange glow in the fireplace. He lit a long wax taper in the coals, then used that in turn to ignite a kerosene lantern. The interior was a single room with exposed wooden trusses overhead, the back wall dominated by an enormous stone hearth. Double bunk beds were not far from the fireplace, over which hung a wooden sign, emblazoned with the words: NEVER FORGET.

Every available centimeter of wall space by the entry was covered by tools hanging on pegs—trowels and shovels, rakes and mallets, saws and mauls, hatchets and pickaxes, ropes and pulleys, hand clippers and knives, sickles and two-handed scythes. Jace racked his gun next to a second rifle by the door, hung his powder horn on a hook, then yanked out a chair from the table in the center of the room and asked her to sit. Benjy cleared away the remnants of a meal and a game of cards to make room for the lantern, while Jace dug through a backpack at the foot of one of the bunks until he found a clean cloth.

As he undid the belt knot around her shoulder, she was stunned by the amount of blood, the whole front of her jumpsuit stained crimson. Her right arm was numb.

"Open your top," Jace said. Then immediately stammered, "I-I don't mean anything funny. I just need to see the wound. Benjy, get me the pitcher."

While she undid the top buttons and shrugged stiffly, exposing her shoulder, Jace ripped the cloth in two, dipped one half into the pitcher and used it to gingerly sponge away the blood around the wound, concentrating yet struggling to avoid looking down at her breasts. Benjy stared wide-eyed from across the table.

Jace examined her back near the shoulder blade, probing with his fingers. Then he wadded the other half of the cloth, retied the belt knot, a little looser than before, but still holding the bandage firmly in place over the bullet hole. He helped re-button her jumpsuit, then exhaled a held breath.

"The bleeding is under control. But the ball is still in there," he said.

"What does that mean?" Benjy asked, confused.

"We have to get her to my dad," Jace said flatly. "Or she'll die."

"That is a full day's hike—you know because we just hiked it! Over the mountains!" Benjy looked at her and shook his head. "She'll never make it—"

Jace, who had been staring at the wall of tools, suddenly exclaimed, "There's a canoe stashed down on the Stoney Creek!" He pointed to a pair of long handled paddles stowed up near the rafters.

As Benjy was thinking of an objection, Jace turned to her. "It's straight down at the bottom of the hill, we just follow the stream out back." He looked her in the eye. "Do you think you can make it?"

"Water," she whispered.

Benjy filled a ceramic cup from the pitcher, and she took a sip. The water was cold and crisp with an undertone of minerals and metal— nothing like the stale filtered water she was used to. She took a drink and then another, sat quietly for a moment, savoring it.

"I can make it," she finally said.

But when she stood up, the room started to spin on her and she had to sit down again. They both looked at her in alarm. She blinked and slowly stood, this time steady on her feet.

"Let's go."

Jace stood on a chair to reach the paddles. At the door, both boys took a moment to sling their rifles, powder horns, kit bags over their shoulders—reflexively, like she would when donning a suit before exiting the Dome. Benjy extinguished the flame in the lantern and they headed back out into the night.

This time Jace took the lead, walking single file with Benjy close behind her. The forest was dark as ever, but Jace had no problem locating the little stream and they followed a footpath running alongside it. The rifles and powder horns clinked together, the stream murmured, otherwise the woods were completely silent.

The terrain quickly grew steep and rocky as the stream tumbled down a narrow channel in the hillside. The footwork and balance required to navigate the winding trail was challenging, the relentless press of gravity felt like she was carrying sacks of concrete. She repeatedly stumbled and almost pitched headlong down the slope. Benjy came alongside and took her arm. At first she brushed him away, but then draped her good arm over his shoulder, her right arm dangling useless. She felt him stand straighter to support her weight.

As they descended, the forest transitioned from dense hemlocks into a stand of giant maple and beech trees. The moon filtered through the towering canopy, lighting the way ahead. The stream passed through a grove of stunted evergreen shrubs, bursting in bloom with large silvery-pink flowers that glowed in the moonlight. It was like crossing through a pristine snowfield.

"What are these?" she murmured.

"Mountain…" Benjy grunted under the weight of her, "…laurel."

She had an overwhelming urge to sit down and rest for a moment among the flowers, but Benjy tugged her forward.

Finally they reached the base of the hill, where the stream tumbled into a small river flowing north. The ridgeline on the opposite side loomed above them like the rim of a canyon. She stood on the bank, transfixed, watching the rippled surface of the river flowing past and away, curving around the bend, glimmering in moonlight.

So much water. And so much effort to get it to Mars.

"Found it!" Jace cried out, dragging the long hull of a canoe out from behind a boulder above the flood line. Benjy left her leaning against a large tree that overhung the river bank, and assisted Jace bringing the canoe down. They rattled the oars around the inner hull and under the plank seats, scattering cobwebs and spiders.

"No wasp nests," Jace declared.

Benjy burst out laughing, "I'll never forget the look on your face when you sat down on top of that nest. You jumped straight over the side and tipped the canoe!"

"I hate wasps," Jace muttered.

As the boys were talking, she stared down into the dark still pool beneath the tree roots. It reminded her of the view right before she jumped out of the airlock, that same irresistible tug of gravity—

"Hey! Don't fall in!" Jace shouted, snapping her back to the present.

At a shallow section of the river, they had her sit in the midsection of the canoe, leaning against one of the thwarts, and stowed their rifles alongside her within easy reach. *They don't see me as a threat anymore...*

She tried to shift her weight and grimaced. *They're right.*

They tossed in their boots, rolled up their pants, and slid the boat into the river. Benjy hopped in the front, Jace in the rear, and the boys started paddling downstream.

As they rounded the first bend, a flock of ducks nesting on the shore burst into the air and flew away, following the course of the river ahead, their wings beating in unison, catching the rays of the moon, then glided and skid onto the water surface, where they swam in lazy circles. The ducks had a curious spiky crest of feathers on their head, eyed the canoe quizzically as it passed.

"Mergansers," Jace observed.

"Or maybe grebes?" Benjy wondered.

Finding it hard to remain sitting upright, she slowly slunk backwards until she was laying down in the bottom of the boat, her knees propped up, looking up into the starry sky. The ribbon of the galaxy seemed to flow in the same direction of the river, the bright stars of nearby Vega and distant Deneb glinting brightly directly above.

The AIs would be captivated by everything she had encountered so far—naming all the tools in the cabin, pondering where the kerosene had been sourced, cataloging the various flora and fauna. She was struck by one common thread: *No electricity of any kind.*

So why did they even need the satellite blast before I jumped?

Centuries ago the weapon achieved its purpose—taking out the electrical grid. Yet still the network of satellites orbited, still bombarded the planet whenever a tanker refilled, plus fired at randomized intervals in between, to disguise any pattern.

Jace interrupted her thoughts by clearing his throat, asking "How are you doing up there?"

She didn't respond.

"Hang in there. We should make it by dawn."

After another pause, "Can I ask what's your name?"

"Taurii," she said.

"Tory," he repeated back to her.

Close enough. She didn't have the energy to correct him. She closed her eyes and listened to the sound of the river flowing past, the steady rise and dip of the paddle stokes, and as she drifted off to sleep she pictured the hillside of mountain laurels in the moonlight.

She jolted awake to the sound of the hull scraping across rock as the boys pulled the canoe ashore. She gripped the gunwale with her good arm, pulled herself up and lurched out of the boat onto the gravel. Another pair of flipped-over canoes were stowed nearby on the grassy bank. A layer of fog had formed over the river, causing her to shiver from the damp cold. At the same time her shoulder throbbed, burning hot.

In the first twilight, everything appeared in monochrome shades of indigo. Venus had risen, gleaming like a spark in the brightening east sky. Above them, atop a bluff overlooking the river, the dark outline of a house was silhouetted against the pale dawn, flanked by a pair of grand trees. Steep stone steps ascended to the house. The idea of climbing them seemed impossible. *Might as well be Olympus Mons.*

At the foot of the stairs stood a pole with a brass bell mounted on top and Jace rang it loudly once, twice, a third time. Somewhere up the hill a dog barked in response.

"I'll be right back," Jace said and sprinted up the stairs, taking them two at a time. A short while later he reappeared, wheeling a creaky cart down a footpath that bordered the riverbank. The cart was a strange contraption, a flat platform constructed around a single middle wheel a meter in diameter, propelled by Jace pushing two long poles at the back. She'd never seen anything like it in any of the vids. *A ...wheelbarrow?*

Jace rested the wheelbarrow on two rear prongs, pointed to one side and said "Sit here, Tory, if you can." She eased herself onto the planks of the platform which acted as a bench seat, her legs dangling, facing sideways. Benjy placed the guns down and then hopped on the other side. Both their weights were balanced on the center axis of the big wheel—requiring almost no effort by Jace to lift the wheelbarrow by the handles.

He fluidly spun the wheelbarrow around, put his back into it to get the wheel in motion, and propelled them down the little footpath, the wheel tracing the narrow track. The footpath curved around the front of the bluff and then ascended a series of switchbacks up the side hill. At each turn, Jace simply pivoted the cart on the wheel to change direction. Blackberry bushes alongside the path snagged the pants of her jumpsuit, scratched the bare skin of her ankles. She didn't even notice.

Halfway up, Benjy offered to take turns pushing, but Jace waved him off. At the top they passed through an open gate set in a stone boundary wall and entered a grassy yard. Jace rested the wheelbarrow on its back legs and put his hands on his hips, breathing hard. A dog came bounding across the yard, jumped up on Jace with its front paws, tail wagging, trying to lick the sweat off his skin.

"Down, Pickles!" Jace hissed. The dog wandered over and began to sniff at her clothes, engrossed in the new smell.

A side door in the house opened and a man dressed in pajamas came out. "Jace, is that you?" he called, still half-asleep.

As he approached he saw Benjy there too. "What are you boys doing back? And Jace, how many times have I told you, three bells is only for an emergency—"

He stopped short when he saw Tory slumped over on top of the wheelbarrow. "Who is she?"

"Her name is Tory," Benjy blurted out. "Jace shot her!" Then, seeing the glare Jace cast at him, added, "—by accident."

"*Shot?!*"

"Dad, I thought she was trying to burn down the Memorial ..." His pleading voice trailed off.

Jace's father raced over to her. While he examined the bandage and makeshift tourniquet, she observed him up close. He had a high forehead, hair cut short on the sides and graying at the temples, a beard of stubble, also streaked with gray. Mouth set in a line. Puffy bags under sharp blue eyes.

"Bleeding's under control ... but no exit wound," he said to himself, then noticed her staring. The corner of his mouth turned up in a kind smile, but his eyes remained serious.

"I'm going to take your pulse now, Tory," he said to her quietly, flipped over her left hand, placed two fingers on her wrist. After a few moments, he exhaled, his breath clouding in the chilly morning air.

"It's weak. You're in shock."

To the boys he said, "Let's take her over to the workshop."

Benjy eagerly took up the handles of the wheelbarrow, tilting the wheel at an angle away from her, to maintain balance with just her on it, while Jace's father walked alongside, keeping a protective hand on her knee. Jace trailed behind, staring at the ground, the dog following alongside him, looking up, trying to figure out what was going on.

In the back of the property, inside the enclosing wall, a barn and bird coop stood. Beyond lay an open pasture, a fenced-in garden, and an orchard of fruit trees. Jace ran ahead and opened the gate. A path led a short distance to a small outbuilding at the edge of the woods, constructed of logs, with a mossy wood shingle roof and stone chimney. Jace opened the double doors in the front and Benjy brought the cart in as close as he could.

Jace's father offered her his hand, but she whispered, "I can get up."

But when she tried, she found she couldn't move, like a giant pin running right through her shoulder, fixing her in place. So Jace's father gently lifted her up and carried her across the threshold.

The interior was a long narrow room, the wallspace opposite the door filled with shelves, a small stone fireplace at the left end. On the right, fishing poles stood side by side next to a desk littered with an odd assortment of equipment—a tiny vice grip and magnifying glass on a stand, cubbyholes stuffed with various feathers, scraps of cloth, spools of thread, barbed metal hooks. Over the desk, a window provided a view through a gap in the trees down to the river bend shrouded in fog.

The center of the workshop was dominated by a long table made from solid planks of wood, with stools and benches tucked in underneath it. Jace's father put her up on the table and helped her lie down, found a wool sweater hanging on a hook inside the door and bunched it into a pillow for her.

"Get a fire going, boys," Jace's father said.

Jace crumpled up a bunch of dry hemlock twigs and scrap paper from a bin near the fireplace, while Benjy brought in some split logs from outside and stacked them around the tinder. Jace removed some tools from a leather pouch on the mantel, wrapped a strip of charred cloth around a shard of rock, struck it a couple times with a steel tool, paused to blow on the cloth, then slid it under the nest of tinder. Within minutes a full blaze was roaring in the fireplace.

In the meantime, Jace's father brought over a carved pipe with a long wooden stem and stone bowl. He pinched a dried plant bud from a clay jar, packed it into the bowl. "Now I'm going to help you turn onto your side."

He brought over a wax taper lit from the fire and ignited the pipe, held it up to her mouth. "Don't inhale too deeply. Trust me, you don't want a coughing fit right now."

After she had taken a few puffs, he eased her onto her back. She was no stranger to drugs—one of the main functions of a mentor was to constantly regulate the wide spectrum of chemicals and hormones nearly every Martian used daily. This feeling was much different, a calming rush that chased the creeping panic away.

It was brightening outside and the window illuminated the room. She let her eyes wander along the shelves: empty glass jars with metal lids, clay pots painted with the names of plants and herbs-—*sage, rosemary, peppermint, marjoram, lavender, sweet violet, marijuana, chamomile, comfrey*—dried bouquets suspended by twine from the ceiling, jugs of kerosene lined along the bottom shelf.

When she turned her head to the other side, she locked eyes with a young girl peeking in through the open doors.

The girl's hair frazzled into a halo around her head. She idly chewed at her lower lip while her big owl eyes observed the scene in the workshop. She wore a nightdress, and below the hem her knees and shins were bruised and scraped, her feet bare, ankles grimy with what looked to be a ingrained layer of dirt. She glared back at Tory fiercely.

Eight, Tory guessed.

"Sara, please help your brother out. Fill the pail and set it to boiling."

"O Captain! My Captain!" she exclaimed, then darted away.

She returned a few minutes later with a sloshing bucket, filled a cast iron pot, hung it by its handle on a metal yard arm extending from the side of the fireplace. She used a pair of iron tongs to swivel the arm so the pot was suspended directly over the fire.

She stood up, smoothed the front of her nightdress, dramatically swept her hair back and tucked it behind her ears, then turned to the boys who were milling about. "Hel-looo Benjy," she said, "Aren't you boys supposed to be camping at Ninety-Three? And who is this woman?" jabbing a finger at the table.

"Her name is Tory," Jace said, already showing annoyance.

"We don't know anything about her," Benjy whispered, as if Tory couldn't hear in the small room.

Sara continued dramatically, like a prosecutor, "And why, may I ask, is she wearing those strange clothes?"

"I've never seen an outfit like this before," her father said, "but I have read a description that resembled this. A *jumpsuit* they called it. And the people who wore it lived inside the Belt Wall—"

"That's correct."

Tory finally spoke, surprising everyone.

Sara's eyes widened and Jace exclaimed, "I knew it! So she *was* up to no good!"

His father wheeled around and scolded, "I will hear none of that, Jace Anders! You forget the Basic Rule—"

And there was a tense moment as the two stared at each other. Finally, Jace recited in monotone, "*If you don't want it done to you, then don't do it to others.*"

"Exactly," his father said. "We send you boys up to Ninety-Three to learn how to look out for your buddy, how to survive. Service to the community. A sense of history. Not to play at being a—a *policeman*." He spat the word out with scorn. "I swear, you'll be the death of me."

The look that crossed Jace's face was as if he'd been physically slapped.

His father immediately changed his demeanor, said "Jace, I didn't mean—" but it was too late, the boy had dashed out of the door. Benjy looked around awkwardly and mumbled, "I'll, *um*—go check" and quickly exited too.

Jace's father ran his hand through his hair, thought for a moment about following, then shook his head. "I am truly sorry for that, ma'am."

He sent Sara running to the house for a blanket and clean towels and her sewing kit. While Sara was gone, he used scissors to awkwardly cut away the top of the jumpsuit, neither of them saying a word throughout. He started to remove her pendant necklace, but she pushed away his hand, so he just shifted it off to the side.

By the time Sara returned, the water in the pot was boiling. Her eyes goggled at the sight of Tory on the table, though it wasn't clear if because of all the blood or that she was topless. Her father unrolled a leather folio filled with metal tools, put a few in the pot of bubbling water and swiveled it back over the fire. He plunged his hands into the remaining water in the pail, scrubbed vigorously with a bar of soap, rinsed.

"Please get the bottle of whiskey, Sara. Bottom drawer of my desk."

"Are you a doctor?" Tory suddenly interjected.

He looked startled, more than anything that she had spoken. "No one's used that word to describe me before! That's something the ancients would say. People around here generally call me Tec."

"His real name is Tecumseh!" Sara announced.

He nodded patiently, continued, "—but to answer your question, the natural healing craft has been taught in our family for generations. Though I must admit—a gunshot wound is a new one for me."

Even with the relaxing drugs, she felt a sudden stab of panic.

"Sara, please bring the pot over here and set it on the end of the table. Be careful." A colander basket inside the steaming pot held the surgical tools. She dumped the instruments onto a clean towel.

"Now please bring a stool over here, yes—right there. And my glasses on the desk." She put them over his ears to rest on the bridge of his nose. "OK, now go wash your hands."

While Sara scampered over to the pail, he poured whiskey on another towel and dabbed blood away from the wound. Searing pain shot through Tory. The two boys had returned and watched silently from the doorway.

Using a sharp penknife, he said, "I've got to make a cut to open it up…" Another sharp bite of pain. "Sara, please wipe away the blood with the cloth." The alcohol burned. She fought an overwhelming desire to squirm as he used a clamping tool shaped like a pair of scissors, inserted it into the wound and opened it wide.

"I see the bullet!" Sara exclaimed, leaning in close.

"Yes, I do too… Tory, please brace yourself," he said calmly. "This is going to hurt."

With another set of clamps, he reached in. A burst of agony well beyond anything she'd ever experienced before—her mentor, if here, would have induced unconsciousness immediately. She heard someone screaming. *Is that me?*

She could feel the metal ball deep inside her pectoral muscle move and become dislodged as he gripped and pulled it out.

"Sara, press down hard with the cloth to stop the bleeding!"

He examined the bullet closely, holding it a few centimeters away from his glasses. "Intact!" he sighed with relief.

"OK, Tory I've got to go back in and make sure I get all the cloth scraps." Another round of pain, even worse than the last. She could feel the clamps moving around, searching, scraping.

"Got it!" Tec exclaimed.

"Jace, bring her clothes over." Tec located the entry hole of the bullet, smoothed out the bloody patch of fabric. "It matches!"

Sara hugged Benjy, and Jace placed a shaky hand on his father's shoulder.

The room was spinning.

Tec took a needle and spool of thread from the sewing kit and said, seemingly from a far distance away, "How are you doing, Tory?"

There was no reply.

3

In her fever dream, she was back on Mars riding the express elevator up the exterior of the Central Axis tower. Wen Prime towered over her, well over two meters tall, with their crest of ram's horns making them seem even taller. As the two ascended, the city of Nubai spread out below, glittering as lights came on in the twilight, curved radial arches extending outward in every direction from the top of the Central Axis. The bluish glow of sunset was visible through the transparent Dome.

Wen Prime turned their eyes away from the view and towards her, their oblong goat pupils always giving them a sleepy look, their circlet projecting a soft pink that signified, *I'm calm*. Despite her efforts to suppress her emotions, her circlet glowed green, projecting for all to see, *I'm nervous*. Her mentor, keying off her mood, flashed her a silly glif of a cuddly cartoon dog making a heart shape with its paws.

"You may be expecting some sort of pep talk—*Just be yourself and you'll do fine*," Wen Prime said, breaking the silence. "Well, don't. There is no possible way to outthink, convince, influence, or alter any of their thoughts or positions—on anything. The only objective when you walk into that room is to walk out of it after."

"If everything has already been decided, then why are we even having this meeting?"

Wen Prime allowed the slightest flicker of orange irritation to flash across their circlet. "Because they are bored. This is a form of entertainment for them."

The elevator decelerated as it approached the summit of the tower and imperceptibly came to a stop. Minutes passed. Nothing changed in Wen Prime's demeanor as they waited. The long sunset shifted from blue to amber. Finally, without warning, the glass cylinder of the elevator resumed its ascent, emerging from the floor into the center of a disc-shaped chamber built entirely of glass.

A narrow walkway extended from the elevator, and as she followed Wen Prime, she tried not to look over the side, a vertigo-inducing view straight down to the gleaming web of city streets a kilometer below. Five high-backed chairs—practically thrones—were arrayed in a semicircle, lit dramatically from some unseen source and set slightly higher, so the occupants looked down on the two of them standing in the center.

She had seen countless vids and streams of the Founders but never had seen them up close in real life. It was unknown whether these were in fact the original Founders, their lives extended across centuries, or clones, or a carefully cultivated line of descendants—not that it really mattered. The outcome was the same, the Founders held a controlling interest in Nubai and had since the original ships departed Earth long ago. While they were not as bleeding edge as some of the Influencers, they were each expected to be state-of-the-art in terms of genomic expression, and did not disappoint.

On the farthest right chair sat Gamma Founder, their body elongated to nearly three meters, with spindly limbs and spidery fingers, their skin a ghostly green hue, their head stretched into a big oblong cranium, their face composed of large jet-black eyes with tiny nostrils, mouth and chin below—a comic nod to the fact that Gamma Corp led the starship project.

Next to Gamma sat Beta Founder, taking the form of a half-human, half-cat, with orange striped fur, cat eyes, ears and whiskers. They dressed in an elaborate regal costume with puffy sleeves, pantaloons, stockings, and buckled shoes that were entirely encrusted with gemstones.

In the furthest left chair was Omega Founder, whose skin was transparent, revealing all the muscles and tendons underneath, their eyes bulging in their sockets, teeth smiling in a fixed grin. Omega wore a black top hat and a matching bowtie and nothing else. In the chair beside Omega was a cylindrical tank of murky green water and inside something amorphous and tentacled moved languidly—Delta Founder.

And in the center chair sat Alpha Founder, breathtakingly beautiful, like the ancient statute by Michelangelo brought to life, but sexless, their skin colored deep crimson red, with giant black bat wings extending from behind their shoulders, a long pointed tail, two sharp horns on their brow, glittering gold eyes and a forked tongue that idly licked their perfect lips suggestively.

Beside each of the Founders hovered their AIs, manifesting as holograms of the corresponding Greek alphabet letter, limned in the customary silvery glow that signified *No emotion*—which she always found humorous. In her experience, AIs were prissy, obsessive, petty, insecure—and above all, vindictive.

The Founders' circlets all projected shining gold—*I'm leading*—with Delta's circlet forming a ring around the top of their jar, and Beta's shaped like a tiara. Wen Prime somehow maintained their calm pink. She tried not to think about what emotions her circlet might be signaling—and her mentor was of no use, having apparently fled somewhere.

"Our dear friend Wen Prime," Alpha said, "what are you here to crow about today—countering a misinformation feed, the heroic disruption of some seditious plot?"

Gamma Founder let their AI do the speaking for them. "On the agenda today is a discussion of Forward Simulation Branch 2833-C—"

"Ah, good old 2833-C," Omega said drolly.

"It's still a hypothetical …" Beta said in a mewley cat voice.

Gamma's AI interrupted in a shrill tone, "Need I remind the Founders that in the fifty-eight years since first identified, the probability has increased from the threshold 0.01 to currently stand above 1.0 percent—the highest acceleration of any branch in the Forward Simulation."

"Yes, yes, we are well aware of all that," Omega said impatiently. "The question for today is what we're *doing* about it."

"So this is the Operative," Delta spoke through a projected speaker. Eyes peered out from inside the dark swirl of the cylinder.

Wen Prime spoke for the first time. "Yes, may I introduce Taurii 636—"

"Do you expect us to call your Operative … *she*?" Beta interrupted.

Gamma's AI said evenly, "As the pre-read materials outlined, the Operative is base human genotype, biologically female sex—"

"And do you propose letting your Operative in the Founders' Club, walking around, looking like *that*?" Beta cried. "There must be something that can be done."

Gamma's AI continued, "The Operative was categorized as Variant while in pod. To enhance a Variant genotype in any way poses a risk—if ever becoming a carrier of a virus, there is a chance of mutation—as much as 100X."

"Wen Prime is enjoying this," Omega chuckled. "Shocking us with a pair of tits."

Wen Prime was unphased, took the opportunity to continue. "Taurii 636 has been in Audit for ten years, a period of exemplary service,

40

most recently working undercover in Reservoir No. 3, disrupting a plot to sabotage the project."

"Couldn't possibly delay Reservoir No. 3 any further than it already it has been," Omega said. "Might actually have sped the damn thing up." Omega's goggle eyes glanced over at the tank, but Delta did not take the bait.

Alpha Founder leaned forward in their chair, golden eyes glittering. "I would like to hear the Operative explain the mission to me. In *her* own words."

Wen Prime gestured for Taurii to step forward.

Taurii cleared her throat and said with as much confidence as she could muster, "I'm going to perform a reentry to Earth via a tanker refill operation."

"And–?"

"Once on the ground, I'm going to embed myself in one of the human clans."

"What is your cover story?" Omega asked.

"I'm from inside the Belt Wall. Escaped, carrying a message."

"Why the Belt Wall?" Beta rolled her eyes and sighed. "They are so tedious, huddling in their little underground tunnels, *aping* us as best they can, waiting all these years for a ship to come and transport them to Mars!"

All the Founders laughed at that. Even the water in Delta's tank sloshed around.

Gamma's AI eagerly shared, "Because the inhabitants of the Belt Wall have attempted, however poorly, to model their way of life on ours here in Nubai, plus have isolated themselves from the outside for so long—we project low probability the Operative will get tripped up speaking on background, nor that an outside audience would be able to detect any inaccuracies."

"The small lie that hides the bigger truth," Wen Prime said.

Alpha nodded. "Please continue, Taurii."

She felt her heart begin to race under Alpha's steady gaze. "The message is a means to get an audience with the leader of one of the largest tribes, named John Cornplanter."

Alpha's forked tongue flicked out, their sharp fangs bit their lower lip seductively. "And tell me, what are you going to do when you meet this John Cornplanter?"

"I'm going to kill him."

Tory woke from the dream to find herself lying in a feather-stuffed bed with four tall posts, a canopy overhead and heavy embroidered drapes tied back at the corners. She was bathed in sweat with soaked linen sheets twisted around her body. Her right shoulder was bandaged and her arm was in a sling, pressed tight against her chest.

The small room was sparsely furnished with a chest of drawers, a washstand, and a bedside table. Sunlight slanted in and cast long shadows across the wooden floors and against the wall, where a sunbeam illuminated the framed portrait of a smiling woman. Sara, who had been sitting in a chair by the open window, sewing quietly, sprang up.

"She's awake!" she shouted, then raced over to the side of the bed, placed a tiny hand on Tory's forehead and proclaimed, "The fever is gone!"

"Water," Tory croaked.

Sara helped her struggle into a sitting position, poured a cupful from the pitcher on the bedside table and Tory gulped it down. Sara fetched her a second cup. As she was drinking it, the girl asked, "Who is John Cornplanter?"

Tory almost dropped the cup.

"You were talking in your sleep—"

Just then Tec strode into the room, a look of worry giving away to relief. "You're up—!"

He paused at the sight of the white nightdress clinging to her body, but an instant later continued. "I've never seen a fever like that. Like every virus attacked you at the same time! But not from the wound—that's clean, no infection, healing well." He shook his head gravely. "It was touch and go there for a while."

"How long was I asleep?" she asked, still groggy.

Sara counted on her fingers, "Three whole days!"

Tec leaned over, gently placed a hand on her wounded shoulder. "How are you feeling?"

She had to think about it for moment, used to having her mentor supply an instant assessment to questions like that.

"Hungry."

That made Tec laugh, "I'll bet! Well, I think I know the cure. Sara, how about getting things started on a special dinner for our guest? I've got to talk to Tory for a little bit. In private."

Sara rolled her eyes and left, thudding down the stairs. Once Tec heard the back door open and shut, he began to pace back and forth, working himself up to speaking.

"Jace is a good kid," he finally said. "I truly don't believe he meant to harm you. You know boys his age, he reads these ancient adventure books, with swords and armor, protecting the village from bandits." Tec glanced at the picture on the wall. "And it's been hard on him." His voice faltered for a moment.

Then he turned and locked eyes with her. "What I'm trying to say is, while Jace is responsible—he's my son, and I bear responsibility too. So, I'm here to beg your forgiveness."

She was quiet for a few moments, then said. "Can you help me up?"

"Of course."

He assisted in shifting her legs over the edge of the bed, the night dress sliding up above her knees in the process, then sat down beside her. She placed her left arm around his broad shoulders, he slipped his hand around her waist, and they stood up together.

For a moment she was lightheaded, but then nodded that she was okay to stand on her own, and slowly walked over to the window. Her satchel bag was draped over the back of the chair, her jumpsuit strewn on the floor among Sara's sewing materials, scrubbed clean of blood. The places that Tec cut had been jaggedly sewn back together, the bullet hole patched with a colorful swatch of striped cloth.

"Do you have any other clothes?" she asked.

"There are some clothes in the dresser that might fit," he replied. His eyes flicked over at the portrait. "There's a pitcher of fresh water for the washbasin and clean towels, if you want. Come downstairs whenever you're ready."

And he quickly vanished from the room.

She sat down heavily in the chair, her muscles stiff and joints cracking from the motion, and fished around in the bag until she located the folded piece of paper. *Still there.* In fact, it didn't look like anything inside had been disturbed.

She looked out the window into the yard, where a dozen or so brilliantly colored chickens were grazing, heads bobbing, strutting about. As she watched, Sara stealthily emerged from the shadows of the barn, stalking them. The chickens weren't fooled and kept their distance. But then the dog arrived to join in, and while the birds were distracted, Sara swooped in and snatched one up into her arms.

The girl carried the chicken dangling by its legs to a wooden block by the side of the barn with two iron nails sticking up. She slotted the bird's head between the pegs and turned it sideways, so the beak was caught, then reached for a hatchet lying in the grass. In one motion she pulled the legs back, stretched out the chicken's neck, swung the axe down and chopped off its head. She tossed the body in a heavy wooden bucket and waited for a while as the bird flopped around inside. Then she retrieved the carcass and marched back toward the house.

Tory sat in the chair for what seemed like a long time, just looking out at the barn and the meadow and the forest beyond. The late afternoon sun bathed everything in a golden glow, a slight breeze rippled the grass and leaves, carrying the pleasant smell of woodsmoke.

Eventually she stood, gingerly removed the sling and wriggled out of the nightdress, examined her body in a circular mirror above the dresser. The skin around the shoulder bandage was dark and bruised. Another vivid mark was on the side of her head, and her ankles were criss-crossed with scratches. Her hair was a complete mess.

She filled the washbasin and did her best to sponge herself down. She sighed—nothing but a full bath would get rid of the smell. The dresser drawers were full of neatly folded female clothing. Each drawer contained a small cloth bag filled with dried lavender sprigs. She found a billowing pair of underpants and an undershirt, as well as a plain linen dress dyed blue with indigo that just barely fit over her shoulders and hips, and because of her height, only fell to mid-calf. It was painful getting her injured arm into the sleeves, which ended at her forearms, and she had to keep the buttons at her collar open, revealing her pendant necklace.

Anything's better than the jumpsuit.

She did her best to tame her hair, then donned the arm sling once again. She poked her head out of the room, and seeing no one, headed toward the stairs, glancing in the three other bedrooms on the way. The children's rooms were crammed with all manner of things, but what she guessed was Tec's room was completely bare, save for a book on the nightstand. The stair boards creaked as she descended.

The ground floor was an open room with a fireplace on the north wall, opposite the front door. The stair landing was lined with bookshelves, and in the corner, by a tiny window that looked out into the yard, a desk was filled with papers and writing instruments. On the other side of the room, a long table and chairs were set. Behind the table, a large landscape painting depicted a little town at the junction of two rivers, nestled in a valley between forested hills.

She scanned the spines of the leather-bound books as she walked past: *Leaves of Grass, Treasure Island, Last of the Mohicans, The Fellowship of the Ring, Pride & Prejudice.* None were familiar, which was not surprising, given she'd never seen an actual book before. Whole shelves were filled with books on farming and plants and preserving, as well as volumes of history. She wanted to pick one up and look inside but was too nervous to disturb them on their shelves.

A couple of comfortable chairs were placed in front of the main fireplace. She slunk down into one of them, already exhausted from her short journey. Her body felt like it was full of sand.

From the chair she had a good view through the open archway into the kitchen, a separate addition to the west side of the main house. The kitchen was dominated by a yawning hearth with a crackling fire burning. On the stone floor in front of the hearth, various cooking implements were scattered about. A lidded pot perched atop a pile of glowing coals that had been raked away from the main blaze. Another steaming pot hung from a yard arm like the one in the workshop. A cast iron basket on an axle was attached to a complex set of pulleys and a suspended weight—so as the weight slowly dropped, the basket rotated above the flame, evenly roasting the chicken inside.

Tec and Sara were side by side at a work table, busy in preparation, and didn't even notice her arrival. Tec lifted a trap door in the floor revealing a ladder down into a cellar and Sara shuttled up and down, retrieving various items. The smells from the kitchen nearly overwhelmed Tory's senses.

Tory noticed large framed panel hung between the fireplace and the writing desk, finely embroidered, the letters stitched in needlepoint:

FALSE PATHS	SIMPLE PATH
Cities	Towns
Technology	Tools
Corporations	Crafts
Banks	Barter
Data	Observe
Media	Books
Universities	Libraries
Military	Militia
Bureaucracy	Consent
Science	Faith

THE BASIC RULE
If you don't want it done to you
Then don't do it to others

Just then Tec came out of the kitchen, smiling broadly, untying the apron from around his waist. "Dinner's just about ready" he said. "Come and have a seat at the table."

Sara opened the back door and furiously rang a bell, accompanying it by shouting "Di-i-i-nner!" as loud as she could.

They brought out plates and cups and cutlery, a pitcher of water, freshly baked cornbread and a ball of salted butter in a dish, slices of cheddar cheese, pickles, spears of asparagus, and the chicken carved up into pieces. The sun dipped below the trees and the room was growing dark, so Tec lit a lantern and hung it on a chain suspended from the ceiling beams.

Just as they sat down, Jace tramped in through the kitchen door, and hung his hat on a hook. His jaw set when he saw Tory. He frowned, noticing she sat directly across from Tec at the table, which then deepened into a scowl when he noticed the dress she was wearing.

"Let us say thanks," Tec said, and the three of them bowed their heads and observed a moment of silence. Tory looked around. *Who are they thanking?*

Sara, who sat to Tory's left, helped fill up her plate. "These make your pee smell funny," she whispered as she gave Tory a big serving of asparagus.

"Sara, not at the dinner table," Tec said sternly.

They ate in silence, just the sounds of the utensils scraping against the plates, chewing. For Tory, every bite was an explosion of flavor, the crisp crackle of chicken skin rubbed in salt and rosemary mixed with the juicy meat, creamy butter and crumbly sweet cornbread, the tangy bite of the pickles, the infusion of smoke in the cheese. She couldn't even identify the taste of asparagus—*metallic?*—but her initial revulsion quickly subsided and she eagerly ate more. She never had paid this much attention to food before, it was just a bland part of the daily routine that her mentor would conveniently distract her from.

Soon she realized they were all staring at her as she finished.

"Well, aren't we going to ask her?" Jace said, breaking the silence.

Tec sighed. "Tory, there have been a lot of questions—"

"Like, are you really from the Belt Wall?" Jace asked, his eyes flashing.

"Is it really haunted?" Sara wondered.

"Now just hold on," Tec waved his hands. "When you said that the other night, Tory, I thought maybe you were delirious! My grandma told us the old stories about the Belt Wall, which she heard from *her* grandma. Living underground, experiments. Some folks think its abandoned."

"Oh, there are people inside the Belt Wall," she said.

They all stared at her, expecting her to continue, and so she took a deep breath, recalling as best she could the narrative she rehearsed with the AIs. *Here goes.*

"I was one of them. Until a month ago, when I escaped."

Sara gasped. "Escaped?"

"The Belt Wall is like a prison. Once upon a time, the walls may have kept rebel armies out, but now they are used to keep people in. Soldiers guard every exit. Everyone lives in tunnels deep underground."

"Like worms?" Sara said, puzzled.

"But why?" Tec asked.

"The Speaker and her inner circle are all mad. Everyone is waiting for a ship to come and whisk them away to Mars. Have been waiting for centuries, always excuses, always delays. Everyone's life revolves around cryptic transmissions received from the Martians."

She paused to gauge their reaction. They were engrossed.

"They don't even think about the outside world anymore. There are neverending plots, intrigues—and purges."

"But somehow you escaped." Jace was skeptical.

"Do you have family still trapped there?" Sara asked, alarmed.

She remembered Wen Prime's maxim: *The best cover story is a true one.*

"I don't have any family—" which brought another gasp from Sara. "I was raised in a *pod* of other children. When I was old enough they sent me to work on the water systems, which are constantly failing, constantly in need of repair, very dangerous work. They call us *Essentials*. Among the Essentials there are many factions, secret organizations planning a rebellion—so naturally I joined one."

Then, insert the lie.

"The leaders of our ring came to me, said they intercepted an important transmission, and needed someone to smuggle it outside the Belt Wall. I knew the water system, knew the repair schedule, picked a day when water was diverted from a tunnel that led outside, and escaped."

"What was the message?" Jace pressed.

"Is it meant for John Cornplanter?" Sara asked.

All eyes—including Tory's—stared at Sara, who simply shrugged. "What? Tory said his name while she was sleeping," she said as a matter of course. "I put two and two together. But who *is* he?"

"John Cornplanter is the leader of the Senecas, who live far to the north, over the mountains, on the other side of the Treaty Hunting Grounds," Tec explained. "Why would the Belt Wall be interested in him?"

She reached into the pocket of her dress, removed the folded sheet of paper from the satchel and handed it to Tec. He examined it, and Jace leaned over as well.

"What is this? I can't make any sense of it," Tec said, handing the paper back.

"I can't either," Tory said. "It's in some kind of code. I was told John Cornplanter would have a scientist who can decipher the message."

"There very well might be a *Scientist* preaching among the Seneca." Tec said the word with scorn. "I've heard Cornplanter's a tolerant man. Though any time a *Scientist* wanders into our town, folks tend to chase them out."

"But how did you end up at Ninety-Three?" Jace continued his interrogation.

"When I emerged from the tunnel system, I traveled upstream along a river and reached a small town…"

"The village of Ferry, on the Potomac," Tec guessed. "About the closest of all settlements to the Belt Wall."

She nodded. "The people there gave me a bag of supplies—a canteen, some jerky, a bottle of whiskey."

Jace's eyes narrowed when he heard that.

Is he on to me? All the details the AIs asked her to memorize were becoming jumbled.

"They told me to follow the river upstream, where I could find an old path that led north over the mountains to the nearest town, where I might find help for the next part of the journey. But they wouldn't come with me, afraid of bandits in the hills."

Inwardly she cringed, certain she'd botched the narrative.

But Tec simply nodded. "The Mountaineers," he said. "I don't blame them. Did you come across any on your journey?"

"No, I guess I was lucky." Thinking quickly, she improvised. "That night, when Jace surprised me—I thought it was bandits— *Mountaineers*—and so I ran."

Jace wasn't convinced. "The bottle we found was empty. So who drank all the whiskey?" Jace asked with a smug look on his face.

She laughed, trying to make it sound natural, not forced. "I had some the first night. I never had whiskey before. I got sick, and threw away the rest. It was a nice bottle, thought it might be useful, so I kept it."

"B-but what about the fire?" Jace spluttered.

There's always one detail you can't explain away. Deny it.

"I don't know what you're talking about, Jace," Tory said cooly.

"There was a fire! A glowing blue fire—at the Wall of Names."

"There was a full moon that night," Tory said. "Could it have been that, reflected in the stones?"

"Sounds reasonable to me," Tec said quickly, shooting a glance across the table at Jace, who frowned, went silent and looked down at his plate.

"I'm going to need help. I have no idea how to find John Cornplanter."

"Well, you aren't going anywhere right now," Tec said firmly. "You need time to heal that shoulder, recover." Tec looked at each of his children in turn, "I'm speaking for all of the Anders family when I say, you are welcome to stay here."

"And Jace," he continued. "I've been thinking, with you being back….earlier than expected, that maybe now is a good time for you to take up my rounds." He added, "On your own."

Jace's face brightened at that. "Really?"

Tec nodded. "I will stay here. Sara and I will help Tory get better. And figure out what to do next, about," he gestured around the room, "well, everything."

"Yes! I can do it, Dad," Jace said.

"Good. We can talk more after we clean up from dinner. I'll get out the map and show you the route."

Sara, who had been sitting squirming in her seat, looking for an opening to speak, urgently asked, "Can I please be excused? I've got to go."

With her stomach full of food, Tory suddenly realized she did as well. "I do too," she said, embarrassed.

"I'll show you the way!" Sara said. She took Tory by the hand, led her through the kitchen and out the rear door.

Outside the evening was settling in, a slight chill in the air but still pleasant, the sky glowing orange in the west and overhead dark blue, the first twinkling stars appearing. She led them past the chopping block, behind the barn, and through a swinging door in the stone wall. A footpath followed the edge of the meadow where fireflies were winking, then turned into the forest and ended at a tiny hut.

Sara raced ahead and ran inside, the door on springs banging shut behind her. Tory stood there alone in the woods, feeling the cool dirt under her bare feet, breathing in the fragrant air, listening to the sound of frogs trilling down by the river. She looked back toward the house, little squares of light in the windows and a thin trace of smoke rising from the chimney.

Sara came out. "Your turn!"

Tory stepped into the cramped dark room. There was a horizontal opening at the top that let in the faintest trace of light, and her eyes quickly adjusted. As she sat down and started to go, the sound of water trickling in the pit far below, Sara called out, "See I told you it would make your pee smell!" and started giggling uncontrollably.

Tory couldn't help but laugh as well.

4

The next morning dawned gray and overcast, and rain pattered on the thatched roof and window panes. The house was quiet as she got up, dressed and headed downstairs. A plate was set out for her on the table—a fried egg gone cold, some of the cornbread from the night before, and a lukewarm mug of herbal tea. She ate it and didn't know the difference.

As she was finishing, the kitchen door opened and Tec entered, stomped his feet on the flagstones to clear off some of the mud, smiled upon seeing her. "We're out by the workshop," he said. "You're welcome to join us." He retrieved a stack of colored bills from a drawer in the writing desk, counted out a few, folded them into a shirt pocket. "See you in a bit," he said and exited through the kitchen door again.

A few minutes later, she stepped outside. The rain fell lightly on her skin and hair, feeling cool, almost ticklish. The mud in the yard squelched as she walked, her soft shoes sank in, her feet quickly became soaked by the puddles. At the workshop, the double doors were open and the one-wheeled cart was parked beneath the eaves.

Tec and Jace were busy loading wooden boxes filled with clay pots and glass jars, padded with hay. Once all the boxes were secured on the cart, they wedged in a duffle bag of clothes, a bedroll and blanket, a pack of food and a jug of water, and lastly, Jace's rifle and kit. An oilcloth tarp was draped over top it all and lashed down. Tory watched the rain drip from the edge of the eaves onto the fabric, bead on the surface, trickle off in unpredictable rivulets. She thought about the giant water tankers, the colossal underground reservoirs of Mars. *Here water just falls from the sky.*

Then she realized Jace was standing beside her, looking anxious. When she turned to make eye contact with him, he stammered, "Tory, I'm so sorry for what happened. For—what I did to you." He was close to tears. "Can you forgive me?"

She smiled as best she could and simply said, "Yes, I do."

He lunged forward, hugged her tightly to the point her shoulder hurt, and then started to cry, his whole body heaving. She didn't know exactly what to do, but putting her arms around him felt natural.

After a moment he regained his composure, wiped his eyes.

"What did I miss?" Sara yelled, leading a donkey down the footpath toward them, coaxing the animal along with a carrot.

"Nothing!" Jace yelled back.

Tec came over to his son and handed him the wad of paper bills. "This adds up to five dials, that should cover any and all expenses. And if anyone can't pay, just get a note from them, OK? We'll settle it later."

Jace shoved them into his pants pocket.

"Stop at Aunt Saki's first and make the deliveries in town. Let her know I'm here, so she won't need to send Grandma to look in on things—"

Jace nodded.

"When you head east you can spend a few nights at the Hildebrand's, and make day trips from there. They've got a spare room. But please make sure to help them out with chores, they are getting on with age—"

"I will, Dad."

"When you arrive at the Portage Inn, a bed, two meals and stabling costs one dial per day—don't let anyone tell you otherwise. Now there's some rough characters that hang around the Inn, especially when the East Caravan is due to arrive, which may be any day now. So whatever you do, don't get talked into playing a game of chance—"

"Dad. I can take care of myself."

Tec smiled, patted him on the shoulder. "I know you can, son. Just do me one more favor. Try not to talk about Tory. You know how the grapevine works. Certainly Benjy has told his father," Jace frowned upon hearing this, "and Fred's a talker, so by now people will know. But don't feed into it. And don't mention the Belt Wall. There's a time and place, I'll see to it."

Jace donned an oilcloth poncho and wide-brimmed straw hat. She noticed his tall leather boots extending up to his knees, glanced down at her own shoes, the ones the AIs were so proud of, now muddy and already falling apart. *I need a pair of those.*

Jace walked over to the donkey and said, "Hey Precious, ready for an adventure?" The donkey turned its head away, disinterested.

Jace carefully fit a bit into the donkey's mouth and a bridle over its head and ears, strapped a collar harness over its shoulders, another leather band around its belly, and a third strap around and under its tail. Chain traces connected the harness to a swinging crossbar hitched to the front of the wheelbarrow, and long rein-ropes ran along the sides of the animal, through eye hooks, all the way back to the poles in the rear.

"Heya!" Jace called out, lifting the wheelbarrow off its legs, which let slack into the reins. The donkey began to walk, pulling the cart forward. Jace followed behind, guided the wheelbarrow by its handles, and the reins in turn led the donkey. The whole contraption looked overloaded and seemed certain to tip, but somehow didn't, and in fact once it got going, Jace was able to steer it nimbly.

At the main gate Jace turned back, waved his hat, and soon was gone around the bend.

"He's gonna tell everyone," Sara said.

Tec smiled. But his eyes were clouded with concern.

The following morning, Sara came in before dawn and woke up Tory to accompany her on her daily chores. "Dad says this will be good therapy," she whispered as Tory dressed in the dark. "Get those lazy bones moving."

The day started in the kitchen, scooping excess ash from the main hearth into a can and then restarting the fire and piling on wood. At the outhouse, Sara did her business and then dumped the can of ashes into the pit. "Helps keep down the smell," she explained.

Next they stopped at the barn, so Sara could milk the dairy cow, whom she called Daisy, then led the animal out into the meadow so it could spend the day grazing. At the chicken coop, she collected a handful of eggs that had been laid overnight. By this point the sky was brightening in the east.

Back in the kitchen, Sara lifted the trap door, descended into the cellar and popped back up a moment later with a terracotta jug. She carefully poured the milk from the pail into the jug using a funnel. The eggs went into the front pockets of her dress, and she climbed back down the ladder to store both on the cold slate floor of the cellar. Sara counted the milk jugs on her fingers and called up to Tory, "When we get to five we can make cheese!"

The wash table in the kitchen had two inset tubs for cleaning dishes, and on the floor next to it were four empty water pails. Sara took them two at a time out to the hand pump and filled them. Even though Tory's right arm was in a sling, she helped lug a pail back, and was straining from the effort by the time she set it down in the kitchen.

Sara filled a kettle, set it on a stand in the fire and began preparing breakfast—which consisted of a fried egg, some bread and butter, and slices of smoked cheese. When the kettle whistled, she brewed mugs of herbal tea, the loose tea leaves scooped into special little silver balls punched with holes that were dunked in the boiling water. She put a spoonful of honey in each cup. "From our bees," she said. "You'll meet them later."

Tec magically appeared just in time for breakfast with a wicker basket stuffed with grass and containing three red-speckled fish, their bellies sliced open and guts removed. "Mayfly hatch," he said cryptically, by way of explanation.

He promptly fried them with butter and a sprinkle of salt in a skillet pan with the skin and head still on. Tory had no idea how to eat the fish, and so Sara showed her how to flake the meat off and cautioned her not to eat any of the transparent bones. "Nothing like fresh trout," Tec grunted with his mouth full.

He pushed his chair back and stood up. "The red oak that fell in the storm last moon, up on the ridge? I'm going to start splitting it for firewood. Sara, I believe today will be nice and sunny, a perfect day for laundry." Sara let out a dramatic sigh. "Tory, please make yourself at home. You are welcome to any book in our library."

"She is helping me do chores, Dad!"

"Fair enough," Tec said.

Upstairs, while Sara collected dirty clothes from the children's bedrooms, Tory gathered the bedding, washcloths and the few items she'd worn so far and deposited them in a large wicker basket. Then she tentatively entered Tec's room. She found his sweat-stained shirts and underclothes inside a tall standing wardrobe, heaped in a pile at the bottom. As she stripped the linen sheets from his bed, she glanced at the leather bound book on his beside table, and froze upon seeing the gold letters embossed on the cover: *The Testament of Cornplanter.*

She glanced over her shoulder to check where Sara was, then curiosity compelled her to lift the front cover. The first page had an illustration of a square knot, and up in the corner of the page, a handwritten signature in a loopy writing style she'd never seen before. She deciphered the words *Lara Anders.* Turning the page, she read the heading of the first chapter, *The False Paths of the Ancients*—then heard Sara out in the hall, quickly closed the book and resumed tugging the sheets free with her one available arm.

Sara hauled the laundry basket downstairs and stopped at the pantry closet to retrieve a block of soap wrapped in paper, and held it up to Tory's nose. "Rosemary and rose petals!" she said, laughing as if that were funny, then added matter-of-factly, "Aunt Saki makes the best soap. Everyone visits her table at Market."

Sara assembled the laundry station atop the heavy wooden table under the eaves, which straddled a brick-lined ditch that carried water away from the foundation of the house. A utility shed held two wide wash tubs, a wood-framed sheet of corrugated metal, a basket of clothes pins, and a strange device consisting of two rollers and a crank handle, which Sara clamped between the two tubs on the table top, connecting them together. Nearby, two T-shaped poles about five meters apart were connected by a pair of ropes on pulleys. Tory, looking to make herself useful, helped by pumping water into a pail with her good arm. Sara carried it over to the tubs, while Tory filled up the next.

Cleaning the clothes involved getting an item wet in one tub, scouring it with the bar of soap against the metal board, then wringing it through the rollers to the other side, which had clear water to rinse, and finally running it through the wringer once more to squeeze out as much water as possible.

Sara struggled on her tip toes to get the wet clothes hung up on the line to dry, so Tory made a quick decision, shed her arm sling and helped pin them up. She felt a jolt of pain around the wound itself, her right arm seeming twice as heavy as her left, but at same time, it felt good to have free range of motion.

Tory and Sara methodically worked through the pile, one item at a time, and by the point everything was hung up to dry—the clothes on one line, the bedsheets on the other—the sun shone high in the sky and Tory was sweating heavily.

Sara pointed over to a pair of chairs in the shade of a stately maple tree at the rear corner of the yard, near the gate that led out to the workshop. "I'll meet you there!" she said, scampering away, the back door of the house banging shut behind her.

Tory sank deep into the seat, leaned against the slanted chair back, and propped her aching forearms on the wide arm rests. A breeze rustled the leaves and fluffed up the sheets on the line, and some birds dashed across her view. Pickles wandered over and laid down on the ground beside her chair. She draped her arm down cautiously, not wanting to disturb the dog, and rubbed the soft fur of its back.

Soon Sara returned with two bottles, cool from the cellar, water beading on the dark glass.

"Try some of this," she said.

"What is it?"

"You'll have to try it to find out," Sara cooed.

Tory took a swig and an explosion of flavors hit her tongue, swallowed and felt a cool refreshing wave come over her.

"Dad's famous root beer! It's a secret family recipe!" Sara cried, then leaned close and whispered, "It's got sarsaparilla root, birch bark, ginger, spearmint, rhubarb and anise. Dad brews up a big vat of it. Sometimes he'll even take it to Market," she bragged.

As they were discussing him, Tec appeared at the far end of the meadow, coming out of the forest pushing a small one-wheeled cart stacked high with split wood. He called out a greeting and the dog jumped up and trotted over to him.

He brought the wheelbarrow into the enclosed yard and parked it near the existing woodpile. Tory watched as he methodically stacked the split wood into a new vertical row, parallel to the existing firewood, first building square cribs at either end to stabilize the woodpile. He had stripped down to an undershirt, the sun hit him fully and sweat glistened on his arms, the thin cloth clung to his shoulders and back.

Once finished, he approached them and said heartily, "A good morning's work!" Then to Tory, "I see you're out of the sling! Shoulder feeling OK?"

"Yes," she said. "A little stiff."

"May I?" he asked, knelt beside her, shifted aside her necklace and pushed back her dress a little to examine the wound. This close she could smell the dirt and sweat and heat radiating from his body. "It's healing really well. Much better than I expected."

He stood up, squinted into the clear blue sky overhead. Sunlight washed across his face, sweat trickled down his neck. "The clothes are clean, but what about us?"

Sara jumped up out of her chair. "Can we take baths outside? Not in the kitchen?"

"Outside," Tec agreed. "Be a shame not to take advantage of this weather." To Tory he said, "Don't worry, I'll set up the tub on the other side of the clothesline, so the sheets can give some privacy."

Sara ran inside again to get some towels and bath soap and as many empty buckets she could find. Tec retrieved a narrow copper tub with tall sides from the utility shed and strained with the effort of carrying it across the yard. He stationed the tub on the brick patio near one of the drainage ditches, and called out to Tory, who was still relaxing in the chair beneath the tree, "Can you see anything?"

She found all this concern about modesty amusing but went along with it. "You are hidden," she replied.

Tec built a fire in a ring of stones not far from the chairs, set up a tripod with a chain that dangled from the apex, and used a hook to attach a large fire-blackened kettle so it hung suspended just above the flames. Then they set up a relay with the buckets—Tory working the pump handle, Sara transporting the full bucket over to her father, who was tall enough to lean over the fire, fill the cauldron and clamp a lid over top.

After what seemed like a very long time, in which they loitered around the fire circle and watched the flames licking against the pot, not saying much, steam at last began to sneak out from a crack beneath the lid. Now they repeated the relay in reverse to fill up the copper tub with hot water, and added a splash of cold so it wasn't scalding.

Sara was the first to bathe, and while she did, Tory and Tec replenished the water in the kettle over the fire. Then they sat in the chairs under the maple tree, listening as the girl splashed and sang to herself. Sara had only finished half her bottle of root beer and Tec took a drink from it, let out a contented sigh.

Tory took a chance and broke the comfortable silence. "I have a question," she said. "There's a sign in the house, by your desk, the False and Simple Paths. What is that?"

Tec nodded. "That's been in my family since my grandparents time, back when the "Native Revival" swept through here. The reason my name is *Tecumseh*, and my sister's is Saki, whose full name is *Sacagawea*."

He chuckled, but seeing the blank look on her face he added, "They were legendary Native heroes."

He continued, "There was a great chief, a holy man, from among the Seneca people, he came through town on a pilgrimage, and his teachings affected a lot of people, including my grandparents. His name was Cornplanter." He looked over to gauge her reaction.

"John Cornplanter?"

"No, this was many many years ago. *Cornplanter* is the traditional name that the chiefs of the Seneca take when elected. The John Cornplanter you are looking for is the current chief."

"Oh, like the Caesars of Rome," Tory said.

"Well, I wouldn't have made that comparison," he laughed, "But yes. One of Cornplanter's main teachings was the Basic Rule—"

"*If you don't want it done to you, don't do it to others,*" Tory recited.

"You are a quick study," he smiled. "He also described the False Paths of the Ancients. The dangers and temptations of Progress. The things that brought down the United States of America long ago. And provided the Simple Path, a template to avoid repeating them."

From the tub came the sound of splashing and Sara soon emerged with a towel wrapped around her, seeming even skinnier when wet, her hair plastered against her head. "Now you," she pointed at Tory.

Sara pulled out the stopper in the tub and was delighted to watch the sudsy water drain into the gutter. As Tec refilled the tub with fresh hot water, Sara opened a paper packet and dumped the contents in, which turned the water milky.

"Lavender and mineral salts," Sara whispered. "This was Mom's favorite."

Then Sara retreated back to the house to get dressed. Tec returned to refilling the warming kettle over the fire for a third time, in preparation for his own bath. Tory undressed and dipped a cautious toe in—a shock that she quickly adjusted to. Gripping the sides, she lowered herself in, letting the heat rush over her. She had to bend her legs to fit, her kneecaps poked above the water, which reached up to her collarbones—just at the level of the ugly bruise and stitched-up scar.

She gazed up at the sky where a few puffy white clouds drifted past. Each breath brought the pleasant aroma of lavender, the constant strain of gravity released for the moment. She felt her mind go blank.

Tec made a polite cough from behind the clothesline. "You OK over there?" he asked. She realized she must have dozed off—the water had grown lukewarm, the skin on her fingertips now all wrinkly.

"Just getting out," she said, sloshing around.

It was tricky to get the towel wrapped around her body—her right arm and shoulder rebelled at the little movements required—and so without another word she scampered into the house before the towel fell completely.

Up in her bedroom, while she dried herself more thoroughly and dressed, she realized she could see over the clothesline. She stood by the window, off to the side, as Tec undressed. She knew she should look away, but didn't.

Later, Tory sat downstairs and pretended to read a book as she observed Tec and Sara in the kitchen. The idea of a "parent" was completely alien to her, having been raised in a pod of children of the same age cohort, taught by their ever-present mentors and rotating adult instructors.

Tec patiently explained how to do some new technique and let Sara try it for herself. Somehow he didn't lose his temper when Sara let her work space become too crowded, bumped an egg that rolled off the edge and cracked on the floor—or left the metal ladle in the bubbling pot too long, so it burned his fingertips when he grabbed it—accidents that even Tory could see coming.

The meal consisted of broth made from leftover chicken bones, *Amish* egg noodles, ginger carrots that had been preserved in a jar, chopped green onions, and soft boiled eggs, sliced neatly in two and laid open on top of the noodles, their yolks bright orange and gelled. Actually, a similar format to the ramen typically served at cafeterias in Nubai. *But with real ingredients.*

Tory devoured two full bowls.

After cleaning up, Tec built a small fire in the living room and they pulled up chairs. Sara hopped into Tory's lap with a book. "Can you read this to me?" she asked.

Good question. Nobody read in Nubai, not really—most communication was done through a rapid sequence of glifs, emojis, vids—and if there was a requirement to read text of any length, that's what a mentor was there for, to summarize.

The slim book was called *The Song of Hiawatha.* Tory cleared her throat and started reading slowly, getting tripped up on the names which Sara helped pronounce. Tec sat nearby with a book of his own, glasses perched halfway down the bridge of his nose. From time to time he peeked over at them.

"Read the part about *Skywoman,*" Sara said with a yawn. "My favorite part."

Sara turned to a well-creased page, and Tory read:

Downward through the evening twilight,
In the days that are forgotten,
In the unremembered ages,
From the full moon fell Nokomis,

Fell the beautiful Nokomis,
She a wife, but not a mother.
   She was sporting with her women,
Swinging in a swing of grape-vines,
When her rival the rejected,
Full of jealousy and hatred,
Cut the leafy swing asunder,
Cut in twain the twisted grape-vines,
And Nokomis fell affrighted
Downward through the evening twilight,
On the Muskoday, the meadow,
On the prairie full of blossoms,
"See a star falls!" said the people;
"From the sky a star is falling!"

Tory shot a glance over at Tec, afraid the passage about a woman falling from the sky might trigger something. But he was deep into his own book. And then she realized that Sara had fallen fast asleep, curled up against her chest.

"Tec," she said softly.

He came over, gently extracted Sara and carried her up the stairs. Tory, not knowing what else to do, followed them up, and looked in as he tucked Sara into her bed, gave her a little ragged stuffed bear to cuddle, and kissed her on the forehead.

She was embarrassed when he saw her standing there in the hall, and stammered. "I'm pretty tired too. I think I will just go into my room for the night." It sounded strange to say it aloud. *My room.*

"Goodnight," he said. "I'm going to read for a while longer."

He descended the stairs, but at the landing, paused and looked back up. For a moment their eyes met.

In her room, she changed into a nightdress, climbed into bed and a wave of exhaustion washed over her. But try as she might, she couldn't fall asleep. Her mind raced.

5

Over the following days, Tory was folded into their routine. Each day presented a different set of tasks and chores that both Tec and Sara seemed to naturally intuit based on a combination of factors—the weather, the cycle of the season, and above all, necessity. Nothing was written down, no checklist or notifications, just some long-established pattern that Tec himself learned as a child.

One glorious morning Sara and Tory loaded up the small wheelbarrow with various tools from the utility shed—watering cans, a hoe, a pair of clippers, trowels, a hand saw, thick leather work gloves and padded cushions to kneel on.

They pushed the cart out to the garden, where they were greeted by the dog, who sat in the open door of a little wooden house, posed like the sphinx with its paws stretched out in front. "This is Pickle's summer home," Sara said. "He keeps away the rabbits and deer. Don't you, Pickles?" She bent down and rubbed under its chin, and the dog licked her face in return.

She walked up and down the narrow rows of the garden, pointing out the various plants growing—tomatoes, carrots, cucumbers, sugar beets, turnips, rhubarb, spinach, lettuce, squash, beans, peas, watermelons, pumpkins—and at the rear of the garden, several rows of corn. There was also an entire section devoted to the various herbs Tec grew for his medicines, but Sara said those were off-limits—some if handled wrong were poisonous.

They weeded and watered and dug and clipped and adjusted. Sara pinched at the snap peas, found them firm and plump, and picked enough to fill her apron pockets. That night they ate the peas with egg noodles, some crumbled hard cheese, and the last of the cured bacon— which greatly concerned Sara. "Not to worry," Tec said. "We'll be able to collect our share from the Pig Club at next Market."

On another day, during a bright sunny afternoon, while serving Tory some tea and honey cakes beneath the maple tree, Sara stood up, an idea striking her. From the utility shed she brought out an odd white costume for herself, and Tory's patched-up jumpsuit. Sara smiled at the expression on Tory's face. "Waste not, want not!"

They both changed in the shadow of the shed, then donned wide-brimmed straw hats, over top of which Sara draped a linen veil—thin enough to see through—which she cinched around their neck with a bandana. Tory felt like she was back in the spacesuit.

Sara scooped a piece of coal from the smoldering kitchen fire into a strange little can, stuffed a fistful of lavender over top, and clamped the lid shut. Again they took the small wheelbarrow—loaded with a knife-like tool, an oilcloth tarp, a paint brush and the smoke can—but this time, continued past the garden and wheeled through the orchard.

At the far side, where the apple trees gave way to the forest proper, stood a wooden trough, propped up on legs. On one end were a set of holes through which bees entered and exited. Sara removed the cover, revealing a series of twenty wooden slats pressed tightly together like floorboards. She moved down the row, squeezing a small billows on the side of the can, causing smoke to puff out. "This will keep the bees calm," she said.

Sara removed a dividing board located near the middle, which freed up space for the slats to slide free. The first section she lifted for inspection had a small honeycomb dangling from the wooden bar, covered with bees busily working. As she approached the end, the more developed the honeycombs became, forming a perfect trapezoid-shape to fit the interior cavity of the trough. Occasionally she used the knife to crack the wax in order to lift up the section of comb.

"Here's the queen!" Sara called out, holding up the swarming honeycomb on the second-to-last bar. Tory's skin crawled seeing the insects. The queen bee crawled about lazily, easily identified by her bloated orange belly.

"And here are some drones!" Sara said. "Their only purpose is to mate with the queen so she can lay eggs. Once winter comes, the worker bees drive all the drones away to die." She frowned. "Poor drones."

On the last bar, the honeycomb was completely sealed up with wax on both sides and there weren't as many bees. "This one's ready! Use the brush to move the bees off," she said. "But gently!"

Once Tory had swept the bees clear, Sara carried the honeycomb over to the cart and quickly covered it up with the tarp. "So the bees don't notice we're stealing their honey!" she laughed.

She adjusted the divider board, added some more bars, giving the hive more room to expand. Then they brought their bounty back to the workshop, where the honeycomb was cut up and hung suspended in a fine linen straining bag. Golden honey slowly dripped down into a bowl placed below.

As she watched Sara work, one task after another all day long, it was impossible for Tory not to think of her own childhood. Her memories of pod were fuzzy at best, but she vividly remembered the last day—Selection Day—when results for Cohort 636, her cohort, were announced.

Three podmates of hers were awarded the status of Citizen, which allowed them to continue on with higher education, virtually guaranteed a managerial role with one of the Corps, plus above-ground housing with a view outside the Dome, with the potential of entering the Founders' Club in the future, if merited. Citizens were given access to nearly all the genetic enhancements, upgrades, and CRISPR mods that they could afford. Most importantly, their cell lines would be entered into the gene pool, potentially selected by lottery to gestate a new cohort.

Her other six podmates were designated Essentials, meaning after a few years of vocational training based on their aptitudes, they would enter the workforce as everyday laborers. Essentials lived underground and were provided access to a limited set of enhancements, some genetic, some merely cosmetic. Of course, everyone—both Citizens and Essentials—began the long process of de-gendering shortly after exiting pod.

By the time the Selection called out Taurii's name, she felt confident of having achieved Citizen status—she'd outperformed the three children in her pod who already had been designated Citizens. All her instructors—and her mentor too—predicted a bright future at Gamma Corp working on the Starship project.

So when the AI judge pronounced *Variant*, there was an audible gasp throughout the egg-shaped auditorium where the ceremony was held.

She was immediately taken away without any further explanation and shipped to the most dangerous work assignment of all—Water Reclamation—the reservoirs, tunnels, pipes, pumps and filters that supplied water to the million residents of Nubai. The work was physically grueling, and exposed workers not only to raw city sewage, but also the bacteria and organisms that lived in the fresh water that had been hauled back from Earth—carrying exotic diseases to which there was no longer immunity. Reclamation workers who became ill were quarantined, and many simply vanished. Taurii, still a child, was given tasks no one else wanted, because she could squeeze into small spaces and didn't know any better.

Plus Taurii wasn't allowed to go through de-gendering—no explanation provided—so puberty progressed with all the bewildering side effects that entailed. She had no one to guide her, not even her own AI mentor, who she could tell found the various side effects of being female distasteful. She was placed on fertility control in order to suppress her monthly cycle, so as not to distress the others in her crowded dormitory.

Taurii worked six long years in Reclamation with no understanding of why and no hope of ever escaping it.

And then one day Wen Prime showed up to recruit her.

While Tory accompanied Sara just about everywhere doing chores around the house, Tec tackled more physical tasks. He chopped and stacked firewood, repaired sections of the fence that extended beyond the meadow into the forest, mowed grass with a scythe and raked it into hay, then hauled the haypile back on a tarp to store in the barn. Each morning before dawn he would be out fishing on the Stoney Creek, and in the afternoons he'd take his rifle and go for a walk in the hills. One time he came back with a rabbit, another time with foraged mushrooms.

What all his activities had in common: they were solitary. Except on rainy days, when Sara would join him in the workshop so she could learn the craft of medicine. At those times Tory was left alone. She curled up by the fireplace, or on the bench under the covered front porch, reading the book she chose from the library—an adventure tale called *The Old Man and the Sea*. Most of the time she just listened to the rain fall, the sound of the wind whooshing through the trees.

One morning at breakfast, instead of arriving with a basket of fish, Tec brought a handful of daisies—bright yellow buttons circled with white petals—that he put in a jar of water and placed in the center of the dining table. Sara's eyes lit up when she saw them. Tec watched expectantly to see if she would make the connection, and was pleased when she shouted, "Strawberries!"

Tory had no idea what had just happened, but apparently some kind of expedition was in order. Tec gathered wicker baskets, and as Sara was practically dragging Tory out the back door, she turned to Tec and declared, "We have this covered, Dad!"

So Tec stayed behind and washed the dishes.

Sara led the way along a narrow path through the forest. The tree canopy blotted out the sky and cast the forest floor in deep shadow, here and there a glimmer of sun winked through. As they walked, dense ferns clutched at their feet, staining the skin around their ankles green. The fresh smell of crushed ferns was overpowering.

They came across an octagonal structure at the edge of the hill. The little building had wooden columns painted white, a steep shingled roof, and a swinging bench suspended from chains. The trees had been cleared to open up a striking view of the Stoney Creek below and the valley beyond to the west.

"Dad built this gazebo for Mom, back when they were dating," Sara said, giving Tory a knowing look. Then a frown clouded the girl's face, and she continued down the path.

They reached a clearing in the forest, the sun lighting everything dazzling green. Sara pointed to the leafy plants that blanketed the ground here, and it took Tory a moment to see the flash of ruby red, but once she did, she looked around and saw it everywhere.

Sara flung her arms wide and shouted at the top of her lungs, "Strawberries!"

They picked four baskets full to brimming in no time. When they returned to the workshop, a bunch of freshly cut rhubarb stalks were on the table, the pails were full of water, and a fire was burning in the hearth.

"Thanks Dad!" Sara shouted out the door. She turned to Tory, put her hands on her hips and said, "Are you ready to make some jam?"

Sara filled a small pot and a large kettle with water and swiveled them over the flames. From the shelves she took out six empty glass jars and arranged them on the right side of the work table. Then from a box she took out six jar lids and purposely placed them on the left.

"These glass jars are made way up in Glass Town," she said importantly, as if she were a pod instructor about to give a lesson. She handed one to Tory and said, "If you look closely you can see the words 'Glass Town' on the bottom. And look at the pretty fruit image pressed into the glass, the threads at the neck of the jar—those are in the mold that the glassblowers use—" and she twisted her fists in front of her mouth to pantomime someone blowing into a long pipe.

"Dad says Glass Town is so far away—clear on the other side of the Treaty Hunting Grounds—that they need the *Amish* to bring their jars here for them, as part of the East Caravan."

Next she picked up one of the jar lids on the left. She tapped and it came apart into two sections, a band with threads like a screw, and a disc, glazed white on one side with a thin rubber strip around the edge. "These lids are made in Steel Town, and they come in on the West Barges. Dad says they use rollers on hot metal to flatten it like dough. After it's a thin sheet they press it into this band shape, or cut out this disk like a cookie cutter."

She handed Tory a lid. "If you look closely, you will see the rubber ring. That comes from big wheels called *tires* that they dig up in the ground, chop up, and melt down into rubber. Once upon a time all the ancients drove *auto-mobiles* with rubber tires. Everyone racing around trying to get somewhere, I suppose," she said, shaking her head.

The girl continued, "Now here's the most amazing part. Take that jar made far away to the east in Glass Town, and that lid made all the way to the west in Steel Town—and screw them together. They fit perfectly!" Sara cried out with joy.

While the sliced rhubarb was boiling, they dunked the strawberries to wash off dirt, sliced away the leafy top, and mashed the berries in a bowl. Sara drained the water from the smaller pot, added the strawberries to the rhubarb, as well as the bowl full of the honey from their earlier beekeeping expedition, and placed it back over the fire to bring it to a furious boil.

Sara constantly stirred the liquid with a long handled wooden spoon, and called out, "I need the jar of apple pectin!"

Tory scanned the shelves, trying to make sense of the handwritten labels, and finally located a small container filled with a thick pinkish liquid. Without thinking, she gripped the jar in her left hand, twisted with her right—and an electric bolt of pain shot down her arm. Somehow she didn't drop the glass. But to her surprise there was a *pop* and the lid opened. She balled her right hand into a fist—there was pain, but there was strength returning too.

Sara added the pectin into the boiling jam, which thickened it, stirred for a little longer, and then put on mitts to carry the pot over to the work table. The large kettle of water was in a full boil now, and one by one she heated the glass jars by dipping them into the water with tongs, then scooped the jam into the warmed-up jars. They each took turns scraping the pot and licking the spoon clean. It may have been the best thing Tory had ever tasted.

Sara carefully laid the lids on top with the rubber seal touching the glass rim, then gently twisted the bands on. "Righy-tighty," she mumbled to herself. "But not too tight!"

The filled jars went into a metal holding rack and were fully submerged in the kettle of boiling water. Sara flipped a little hourglass.

"When all the sand goes from the top to the bottom, the jam will be done!" Sara said.

After the time had passed, Sara let the jars cool on the work table. The jam inside glowed red in the sunlight. She confirmed a vacuum seal had been created by testing each lid, trying to lift it off with her fingers, and couldn't. Finally, she wiped the jars clean and screwed the band tight.

"I think we should take these to next Market," Sara clapped. She gave Tory a big hug. "I can't wait for everyone in town to meet you!"

Tory lost track of the number of days since she had landed—not surprising, as there were no clocks or calendars to be found anywhere in the house. She asked Tec about this, and he gestured to the needlepoint sign listing the False and Simple Paths.

"The ancients were obsessed with measuring everything. They called it *data*. But we have plenty of ways to observe time—the seasons, the moon, the sun's path across the sky. Calendars, clocks—these create the illusion you can control time. And Pride is what led to the Fall."

Tory was regaining full strength in her arm and shoulder. She could now pump water with her right arm and carry two full pails back, one in each hand. She was able to push the small wheelbarrow, could dig and hoe in the garden. But she still was challenged by things that required fine motor skills. Just dressing in the morning was agony.

Tec noticed Tory wince while passing a plate at breakfast, which gave him an idea. He fetched his fishing pole and led Tory out to a recently mowed section of the meadow. Winged grasshoppers fluttered out of the way as they walked through the shorn grass. Sara, who had no interest in fishing, went to play fetch with Pickles.

"I'm going to teach you how to cast," Tec said. "It will work the scar tissue in your shoulder in just the right way. And you'll learn a practical skill while doing so! Let me demonstrate..."

He lifted the rod like he was carrying a lantern, tilted it back slightly, paused as the fishing line flew backwards, and then flicked the pole forward, causing the line to whip around and shoot ahead. The sun glinted off the line, illuminating its figure-eight path.

"The action is all in the wrist, the pole will do all the work for you," Tec said. "But trust me, you will feel this in your shoulder."

He handed her the pole. She was surprised at how light it was, perfectly balanced. Her first attempts were clumsy, she used her full arm as if she were trying to throw the line out, and not only did her shoulder scream in pain, but the line flopped forward limply.

Tec stood beside her, put his arm around her back and gently gripped her forearm, lifted it up into the casting position.

"Keep your wrist loose. It's just little motions like this—"

Tory felt his body pressed up against her, his breath against her ear. She closed her eyes and pictured the line curving in a wide arc, back and forth …

Then Tec abruptly stepped back. He cleared his throat, and said "I think you're getting the feel of it. Just practice it for a while."

By the time he called a break her shoulder was on fire, but it felt good, her muscles knitting themselves back together.

"You're a natural," Tec said.

That night, as she was getting ready for bed, there was a tentative knock at her door.

"Come in."

She didn't expect it would be Sara, who bounded into the room full of excitement, even though it was well past her bedtime.

"The aurora is here!" she said with joy.

She grabbed Tory's hand and led her out of the room. Tec was seated in his easy chair by the fire, immersed in a book, and looked up in surprise as they clomped down the stairs.

"The aurora, Dad!"

Tec seemed a little puzzled. "But it hasn't even been a full moon since—"

But already they were out the back door.

They pulled chairs out through the back gate to the edge of the meadow, where they had an unobstructed view of the sky. The shimmering green aurora was so intense that the stars had retreated from view, the trees appeared fluorescent. Fireflies pulsed on and off, excited by the aerial display.

"Isn't it beautiful?" Sara said.

Tory nodded, distracted, thinking about the Defense Network orbiting above. Tonight would be a randomized electro-magnetic pulse, unlike the one on the night when she arrived, which was purposely triggered in advance of the tanker's refill, as a precaution.

It was a marvel of Martian technology that the Defense Network had remained in operation, essentially maintenance-free, for over eight centuries. The satellites were like kites, with cables stretching higher in orbit, into the magnetic belts, where sails floated in the solar wind. The sails collected charged ions, and then fired a directed pulse down at Earth, each blast so powerful it created an aurora in the atmosphere and disrupted electronics in a thousand kilometer circle. There were enough satellites to cover the surface area of the planet in a grid. When the Defense Network was first deployed, in a matter of days power across the whole planet went out. And never came back.

"They say when you wish upon an aurora, that your dreams can come true," Sara said. "When the last aurora came, I wished as hard as I could. That was the night you arrived…"

The girl's warm little hand reached out and held Tory's.

"I think my wish came true."

6

The next morning when they sat down for breakfast, Pickles started barking outside and wouldn't stop. The dog ran around the house to the front bank and began a warbly howl. Sara looked at Tec with wide eyes and raced out the door. Between the dog's yelps, Tory could now hear another sound—the distant ringing of bells.

Both she and Tec hurried out to the front porch. It was noticeably more humid this morning, and a haze lay across the river valley as the first rays of sun broke over the ridgetop.

"Pickles, come now!" Tec said sternly. The dog bounded up on the porch and sat beside Tec, who knelt on one knee and ran a calming hand down its back.

The bells were much easier to hear now that the dog had quieted, echoing across the steep hills of the valley. The ringing was not coming from one source, but rather a number of bells ringing, at different pitches and rates, at different distances. As they stood listening, another high-pitched clang began not far downstream, just around the river bend.

At first, Sara was nowhere to be found. Then she appeared down on the landing at the bottom of the stairs. She grabbed the rope dangling from the bell clapper and started banging with all her might.

"The bells announce the East Caravan has arrived," Tec explained. "Market will start the day after tomorrow."

The ringing went on and on, extended further up Stoney Creek valley until it seemed impossible that anyone couldn't know. Sara bounded up the stairs two at a time, out of breath and practically hopping with excitement. "It's time to go to Market!" she sang.

Tec smiled, but once again his eyes betrayed him. "Come on, let's start making a list."

At his desk, Tec shuffled through the clutter until he located a pencil and a blank sheet of paper that he clipped to a portable writing board. He drew a vertical line down the middle. On top of the left column he wrote *Buy*, and on the right, *Sell*. He counted out the stack of colored bills and wrote *58d* at the bottom of the page, which he then circled.

"Our current income."

Tec and Sara methodically went room by room through the house, discussing and in some cases debating what was needed. Sara climbed down in the cellar and called up the status of various items. The list of items on the *Buy* side increased in length, but Tec was able to add one entry on the right, *Root Beer*.

While they were occupied, Tory examined the bills on Tec's desk. They came in two colors, green and orange, both printed with an etched image of a crested duck in the middle. *Mergansers*, Jace called them. At the top of the green bills the words *One Dial* were printed in fancy script, and on the orange, *Half Dial*. To the left and right of the duck were the words *Flood* and *Town*. The bottom of the note had a line with *Tec Anders* scrawled across it. As she flipped through the pile, the bills all seemed to bear Tec's signature, but the further down she went, some of bills had different people's signatures attached.

She was so engrossed she didn't notice Sara beside her. "I like the picture they used this year," the girl said. "But it's kind of boring. I'm hoping next year it can be a bear or a mountain lion."

Next they marched out to the workshop, and here the *Sell* side of the ledger began to fill up. Glass jars and clay crocks filled with teas, powders, potions, and salves were packed into wooden carrying crates, and Tec made note of each. At his workbench he slid colorful lures into paper envelopes labeled *Sulfur Dun, Adams, Blue Wing Olive, Green Drake, Elk Hair Caddis, Pheasant Tail Nymph, Hopper.*

"Plus the strawberry jam!" Sara pleaded.

Tec nodded absently while he scribbled *Pig Club Dues, 4d* to remind himself.

Just then there was a commotion out in the yard, Pickles barking again, the chickens scattering, as a horse trotted in through the main gate with a woman rider, pulling a one-wheeled cart behind it. She reined in the horse and climbed down from the saddle, unfastened a lead rope that was cinched around the horse's neck, and tied it to a post by the barn doors.

Sara sprinted from the workshop, shouting at the top of her lungs, "Auuuunt Saaaaakiiii!" She dived into the woman's arms and practically knocked the straw hat off her head.

Tec came up into the yard with Tory following a few steps behind. Saki disentangled from the clinging girl and adjusted herself to greet them. She was dressed in an embroidered white shirt and blue jeans with a shiny belt buckle, high boots, and her hair braided in pigtails. She had similar features as Tec, but her eyes had a twinkle, her smile a mischievous curve, that were just like Sara's.

"Hiya big brother," Saki said, hugging him.

"Hi Saki. I trust all is well with the family?"

"The boys are ... well, boys," she laughed. "And you know how things go at the Forge. Zeb will be working sunup to sun down now the Caravan's arrived—shoeing, repair-work, plus readying the regular iron goods for sale..."

She peeked her head around Tec to see Tory. "So this must be the one everyone's talking about—"

"Saki—"

But Saki ignored him and approached Tory. "I feel like I know you already! I'm Tec's sister Sacagawea, but everyone just calls me Saki."

"Hello. My name is Tory."

Saki spread her arms and said, "C'mere" as she embraced Tory, who stood stiffly, not knowing how to react. After a big squeeze, Saki stepped back, looked her up and down, and said, "I just love that dress on you!"

She turned to Tec, "I see why you're keeping her hidden."

Tec ignored her provocation and asked, "What brings you all the way out here today? Shouldn't you be getting ready for Market?"

"Well, now that you ask," she said coyly. "It's about Jace. He arrived in town last night along with the East Caravan—"

"Please tell me *with* the donkey."

"Yes, Precious is fine. Jace asked me to give you this," she handed a stack of dials to Tec, who stared at them in his palm as if bird had suddenly landed there. "Should be eight dials and twenty halves in total."

"Why isn't he here, giving them to me himself?"

"He was planning to come out today with the cart, to help bring your goods to Market ... but that sweet little Precious, she seemed so tired from all that traveling, and it was so humid ... so I told Jace, I'd just ride out with Old Jack and lend a hand."

Tec stared at his sister for a while, then asked, "What's Jace gotten himself into?"

"Well *apparently* ... while he was staying at the Portage Inn, the East Caravan arrived, and ... he met a girl."

"*A girl?!*" Tec shook his head. " I knew that place was trouble—"

"She is a musician in a traveling band—"

"Oh, this just gets better."

"—and the band is in town along with the Caravan, playing at the Dance Hall, starting tonight. He asked if he could go. So I said yes."

Tec stared at her.

"He's a teenager, Tec. How do you expect him to meet a girl way out here in the country?" She glanced at Tory out of the corner of her eye. "Not everyone's that lucky."

Tec was speechless. Then after waging some internal struggle, he managed, "Thank you, Saki. I appreciate all your sisterly help and advice."

He exhaled, almost a sigh, and added, "We can fix up Jace's room for you. Tory is staying in ... the other bedroom"

"Oh, is she?" Saki said with a wink. "No, as much as I'd love to stay the night, I'm needed back—as you say, it's busy busy busy getting ready for Market."

She looked over at Sara who had been following the conversation breathlessly. "And you, little girl. I'm taking you back with me!" Sara's eyes lit up. "I need your help setting up our table tomorrow, and Grandma could use a hand with her bouquets. Plus your little cousins are dying to see you."

As she continued speaking to Sara, she looked pointedly over at Tec. "Your dad and Tory can meet us in town tomorrow. We'll set up a tent in the back for all you kids to camp out!"

Tec was about to speak, but Saki cut him off. "All of this is on orders of Grandma! So we best obey." And that was that.

They unhooked the cart to give the horse a break and wheeled it over to the workshop, where they all pitched in loading the cart, taking care to pack all the containers with straw and arrange them tightly so nothing would jostle around. Then they brought the wheelbarrow back to the main yard. Tec climbed down into the cellar to hand the cases of root beer up to Tory, and Saki went to pack a bag for Sara.

"Don't forget my teddy bear!" Sara shouted up the stairs.

Once they finished, Saki revealed that she brought sandwiches in the saddlebags, and so they retired to the shade of the maple tree for a picnic. Sara got cups from the kitchen, Tec took a bottle from the cart. As he poured root beer for everyone, Saki made a *tsk-tsk* sound, shook her head and said, "Pouring away your profits."

Sara laughed as if it were the best joke she had ever heard.

The sandwiches were sliced roast beef, mayonnaise mixed with horseradish, and watercress on thick slices of bread that had been baked that morning, wrapped in cloth napkins that they draped over their knees. Tec and Tory sat in the chairs, Saki and Sara cross-legged on the ground.

"So Tory, I hear you are on a mission to meet John Cornplanter of the Senecas," Saki casually asked after she finished chewing.

Tory flashed a wary look over at Tec, who was engrossed in his sandwich.

"Long journey," Saki observed.

Sara spoke up with her mouth still full, "She is bringing him a secret code!"

"Oh, how exciting!" Saki said.

"Only a Scientist can solve the puzzle," Sara said.

"That's interesting." Saki's eyes narrowed and she turned to her brother. "Where do you propose finding a *Scientist*, Tec?"

Tec continued eating his sandwich without reply.

But before Tory could check herself, words leapt out of her mouth, "Why do you both say *scientist* that way? Like there's a sour smell."

"She really is from the Belt Wall," Saki said.

Tec took his time, finished the last of his sandwich, washed it down with a gulp of root beer. "I'll tell you why," he said, wiping his hands clean on the napkin. "In ancient times, a *Scientist* was a person who ran experiments, one after another, until at last they uncovered some narrow insight of how nature works. Mind you, never the whole, always falling well short of a full explanation. They then pointed to their discovery with pride, as if they themselves were the inventors of it. They put their discoveries to new uses, things the Creator never intended. When things didn't work the way they expected, instead of admitting their failures, they tried to use Science to solve the very problems it had caused!"

"And they built terrible weapons," Saki said.

"Yes, exactly," Tec said. "So the *Scientists* of today look to revive that cult. They have powerful practical knowledge, and their tricks and shortcuts can make work seem more *efficient*. Very seductive. But soon you realize you are running around twice as fast, getting half as much done."

"Sounds like you've had personal experience," Tory said.

"Our family's craft is healing," Tec said. "Of course I've encountered Scientists before—medicine is among their most powerful sorceries. We used to have a Scientist in town, he snuck around, following my rounds, offering the promise of *drugs* that could work far better than my remedies. But then when Lara became ill …" His voice faltered.

"The Scientist knew all about how cancer worked," Saki said. "Just not how to cure it."

Our scientists do, Tory thought.

"Where I'm from, science is considered to be truth," she said in a matter-of-fact way.

"And yet you live in tunnels underground," Tec said sharply.

Saki stood up and brushed off the seat of her pants. "My, look how far the sun has traveled! It's time we get back to town."

Tec excused himself, marched over to the barn and busied himself reattaching the cart to Old Jack. Sara looked a little bewildered by the conversation, so Saki put a hand on her shoulder and said, "Why don't you take the lead line up front and I'll steer from the back. You know the path into town?"

"Of course!" Sara declared, then added, "I think so."

"Well, you tell me which way you're planning to go, and I'll tell you if it's right."

Saki gave Tory another hug and whispered, "Pay no mind to all that. Tec's like an old dog who likes to lie in the sun. You disturb him from his nap, and he'll growl at you."

Then they all said their farewells. "Until tomorrow," Sara reminded everyone. The girl led the horse out the main gate, and Saki followed behind, steering the cart handles. Sara talked nonstop, shouted questions back to Saki, who gamely replied to each of them. Soon they rounded the bend, and shortly after that, their voices faded into the background noise of the forest.

Tory and Tec stood side by side in the hot sun in silence. The chickens were curled up in balls in the shadow of the barn. Pickles was lying in the shade nearby, tongue out, too hot to bother with the birds.

"My shoulder is healed," she said at last, quickly adding, "Thanks to you."

She paused. "But now it's time I continue on."

Tec nodded, looked down at his feet, scuffed his boot in the dirt.

"I have an idea," he said. "Let's go fishing."

The late afternoon sun was sweltering hot, and wearing woolen tights, leather waders, long shirt and vest only made it worse. They waddled down the front steps, loaded down with fishing gear. Across the valley to the west, tall clouds were visible, billowing up like pillars into the sky with frosty white pinnacles.

"Keep your pole up, so you don't jam the tip," Tec chided, unconsciously slipping into the tone he used with his children.

At the base of the stairs, a little cut in the embankment provided a way down to the gravel bar where the boys had landed the canoe that first night. From the left, the river made a sweeping curve, spilling in from the south through a long section of shallow riffles, then widening out in front of the Anders' property to form a pool where the surface was smooth and the current ran steady. Further to the right, at the base of the pool, the banks of the river pinched together creating a narrow, deeper channel that raced around a bend to the north, out of sight.

Directly across from them, the ground was relatively flat and marshy where a hillside creek trickled into the river. A blackbird flew past, flashing a red and yellow patch on its wings, glided across the water into the tall reeds and cattails on the other bank. Tec spent some time looking at the river, and judged, "I think an Adams will be good for you, sits up nice and easy to see. Good for this time of day."

He reached into one of her vest pockets, took out a slim box with a sliding lid, fingered through until he located the fly he wanted. He held it up closely so she could see it. "The Adams is a basic pattern. You can see the hen feathers sticking straight up as the wings, the pheasant tippits jutting out back here along the shaft of the hook, they make the tail, and this spiky stuff around the body we call *hackle* comes from rooster feathers. When this lands on the water, it looks just like an insect to the fish and he's fooled."

He dipped the fly into a tiny jar containing a clear gel, and then fluffed up the fibers, careful not to hook himself. "My own concoction, beeswax and kerosene. Keeps the fly afloat."

Tec put on his reading glasses to see the miniature eyelet on the hook, threaded the line through and tied the knot with authority, relaxed and in his element, not stiff and formal the way he could be around her. He pulled the knot tight and bit off the excess leader with his teeth.

"You can fish this pool here and I'll work up into that riffle at the head-end of the hole," he said. "Cast upstream, try to get close to that channel near the opposite bank. Watch the fly drift down past you, following it with the tip of your pole, and just as the line starts to drag in the water, lift your pole up and cast upstream again. Just as we practiced. If one hits, you'll know it. Raise your rod straight up which will set the hook, and let the pole do the rest of the work. Slowly bring him in with the reel, or pull in line with your left hand, whichever feels more natural. When he gets close, guide him into your net."

Lastly, to keep mosquitoes away, Tec smeared lavender oil on her forearms and the back of her neck, working in a no-nonsense way—but still, it felt strange to feel his rough hands on her skin.

He walked upstream along the bank to the section where the riffles began and without hesitation waded out into the middle of the current. Within a few moments he was casting into the sparkling river, his line tracing long glistening arcs in the afternoon sun.

Tory took a few tentative splashing steps into the water, felt the cold pressure of the river pressing against her boots. She tried to remember the steps for casting the line—which she had become quite good at practicing in the meadow—but here, confronted by the river running past, her mind had gone blank. She flicked the line back and forth like a metronome, with none of the fluidity that Tec demonstrated.

Just as she readied to cast forward, the pole jerked in her hand— during her back-cast, the hook caught in the bushes behind her, back near the beached canoes. She had to lay the pole on the ground, walk over to untangle the line. Her next cast fluffed up and went nowhere, the fly dropping only a couple meters in front of her. She tried to use a little more muscle on the following cast, and the line slapped hard on the water, causing a splash.

Finally she got into a rhythm, the loop of the line unrolled and the fly landed with a flick onto the surface of the water. She followed as it drifted downstream, a tiny speck bobbing along with the current. She made a few more casts in a similar manner, gaining confidence.

Watching the path of the fly as it traveled down the river, she saw the deeper channel that Tec described, flowing along the opposite bank, and that her throws were falling just short of it. She stripped more line from the reel, took aim and made what felt like a perfect cast … but the fly soared well over her target and into the marsh-reeds beyond. She yanked backwards, to no avail. The line was snagged.

She waded across the river. The current pressed against her calves, then rose to her knees and thighs as she entered the channel, the push of the water increasing, threatening to topple her as her boot soles slid across the pebbled riverbed. She clutched a handful of tall reeds to pull herself onto the marshy opposite bank.

She found the fly tangled around a cattail, and as she tried to snap the stalk in two, the blackbird from earlier became agitated, shrieked *terr-eeeeee* and swooped down at her head. She ducked, finally managed to get the fly loose, and quickly stumbled along the bank before the bird could make another sortie, sweating with effort, fuming inside at how difficult this was proving to be.

Upstream, she watched as Tec easily guided a flapping trout into his net.

"Any luck?" he called back, then saw the expression on her face.

"Let's move further up," he shouted over the rush of the water. "There's a nice hole around the corner."

They walked along the river bank, a sheer rock cliff jutting above them. Ahead, a long section of calm water opened up, over a hundred meters in length. A crude staircase of stepping-stones wound down from the heights, and a rope swing dangled from the limb of a leaning beech tree. Giant hemlock pines cast dappled shadows across the slow moving surface.

The hole was alive with insects rising up from the river, flashes of sun catching their fluttering wings as they swirled around. Tec snatched one in mid-flight and showed it to her, partially crushed on his open palm. "Green Drake hatch," he said, with excitement in his voice. As soon as he said it, there was a splash as a trout broke the surface, feeding.

He took a fly from the wooden case and laid it next to the insect in his hand. "The olive colored body is from turkey feathers, and the prickly wings are from elk hair. This one is meant to be a cripple—a Green Drake that's struggling to emerge."

She didn't see any resemblance at all and told him so.

"You're not seeing this the way the fish does, floating above, silhouetted against the sky. Trust me, this will do the trick."

He nodded his approval as she tied the Green Drake onto her leader using a clumsy version of the fisherman's knot. She waded into the lower end of the pool and Tec went to fish at the upper end.

Here the water was shallow, only coming up to Tory's lower calf, with a gentle current. Standing in the middle of the stream, she could easily cast with no obstructions ahead or behind. High above her, at the top of the rocky outcropping, the white pillars of the gazebo poked up. From the forest came the lilting trill of a songbird, but otherwise the air was oppressively still.

Every few moments the silence was broken by a sudden splash and *plonk* as a trout jumped. Always too far away. So she waded over and tried to cast in the same place—but without luck. Tec was experiencing the same thing up at his end, insects swarming, fish jumping, but nothing biting—which made her feel a little better.

A shadow fell over the valley as one of the towering clouds blocked out the sun, a corona of sunlight radiating from behind the cloud top. There was a rumble of thunder in the distance but Tec didn't seem to be concerned, or even notice. He was focused on switching out his fly.

Tory sighed, considered sloshing back over to the bank and sitting there until he was done. *There must be an easier way to get fish …*

As her thoughts wandered, distracted, she performed another cast. The Green Drake landed along the edge of the deep pool and the shallows, where there was a subtle eddy. A pale flash darted upward, water splashed, and her line jolted.

"I got one!" she shouted.

Holding the slender bamboo rod was like touching a live wire—the line tugged, the tip of the pole flexed—and then in an instant the fish jumped in an arc, shaking its head trying to toss the hook free. She could feel every move of the fish, see the yellow blur of its body under the water as it made a dash to escape. And just when she thought it had run out of energy, it would stage another fierce struggle, its body slapping against the surface.

Tec shouted advice, "Keep the tip up!"

She lunged with the net and lifted the trout, hanging curved and eel-like in the mesh, water dripping down onto the black surface of the river.

As Tec approached, there was a bright flash, followed a moment later by a crack of thunder that boomed down the valley. The sky had turned an ominous color. Tec reached into the net, pinched the fish by its jaw, causing its body to go stiff, and twisted the barbed hook loose from its upper lip.

"A rainbow trout. Beautiful fish."

He handed it to her. She felt its weight, smelled the slime that coated its rough scales, saw the bright pink stripe along its side, the spackle of brown and red spots, its eyes yellow and jelly-like, its mouth opening and closing, gasping for water.

She flipped the fish back into the river and in a blink, it swam away.

"I'm not hungry," she said.

Tec's initial shock gave way to a smile. He opened the lid of his own basket, revealing it was empty too. "Me neither."

Just then the surface of the water became pocked as the first globs of rain began to fall. "C'mon," Tec said, and offered his hand to help her up the embankment.

They hurried up the stone stairs as fast as they could and made it to the gazebo just as the rain began to fall in earnest, thunder booming overhead. Tec propped the poles against the railing, took off his water-logged boots and waders and fishing vest, and Tory did the same.

With nothing else to do but wait it out, they sat side by side in their woolen tights on the swinging bench. Rain thrummed on the roof, a brilliant streak of lightning hit the hilltop directly across the valley, thunder roared. A cold damp wind gusted down the valley, causing her to shiver.

And then he was next to her, his arms around her, and they were kissing.

7

Tory woke disoriented. It took her a moment to realize she was in Tec's bedroom. She rolled over to discover he had already gotten out of bed. She stretched out fully, feeling the soft feather mattress and cool linen sheets against her skin. The previous night came rushing back.

On Mars, trysts were frequent, casual, and typically involved a careful calibration of chemicals by each person's mentor, sequenced just right to achieve a shared state of euphoria. Many were attracted to her raw expression of gender, some out of curiosity, or a fetish, some even from revulsion. Most encounters were brief. Only Wen Prime kept a sustained interest in her.

After Wen Prime first made contact, she continued to live in the dormitory, work her same job in Reclamation. But now she was on the lookout for a signal—the number of her cohort, 636—which would appear at seemingly random times, in random places. She would respond by committing some minor violation of protocol, a subtle act of non-compliance, get caught and taken away. But instead of a detention cell, she was led to a private, well-appointed apartment where Wen Prime would secretly meet her.

Here Wen Prime taught her the art of infiltration, going with the flow of events, listening, letting your mark do the talking, responding only when necessary and always in agreement, always flattering their ego. Her record of disobedience got her noticed by the underground resistance factions among the Essentials, who saw her as a kindred spirit—and being a Variant—someone with nothing to lose.

Wen Prime explained that the Variant classification, difficult as it had been for Taurii to accept, was actually a sign that she was special, destined to perform a vital service to Nubai. The AIs may have been afraid of her, but Wen Prime wasn't—and saw her potential.

After the monotony of the dorm, the grueling work, this arrangement seemed like heaven to Taurii. Eventually, their meetings became intimate. Wen Prime had access to drugs and subroutines unlike anything she had experienced before...

Now, she idly touched her lips, scratched from Tec's beard. *Last night was completely different.*

She sat up in bed and looked around. Outside, the river valley was filled with milky fog. The house was quiet. She saw the *Testament of Cornplanter* on the bedside table and flipped it open at random. In the chapter "Technology and Tools" she read: *Tools must be affordable, accessible, understood and repaired by nearly anyone—designed to work at the local scale of a family, homestead or town—and above all, compatible with the universal human need for creativity.*

She heard the back door open and shut, and boots across the floor. "Tory, are you awake?" Tec called up the stairs.

"Yes, just getting dressed," she called back, putting the book down.

"OK, I'll make some breakfast."

They ate without saying anything to each other. Tec avoided eye contact throughout, though at one point he reached over to place his hand on her forearm, which he immediately realized was awkward and withdrew.

"Tec—"

"I know," he said quickly. "I know."

He looked out the front window. "Once the sun burns this fog off, we'll take the canoe into town. Don't worry about packing—we'll get you outfitted for your journey at Market tomorrow." He pushed his chair back and stood. "Now if you'll excuse me, I've got a few things to get ready."

Tec put hay in the feeding cribs for Daisy, filled the trough with water, brought up the rabbit he'd shot, which had been curing in the root cellar, and hung it on a hook in the barn low enough that Pickles would be able to reach it. He assembled a waxed-leather travel bag full of clothes, brought out a box containing the fishing gear and two slender rod cases. "There's a nice fishing hole beneath the bridge in town by the Fair Grounds. It always helps sell my fly-tying with an audience watching," he winked.

He didn't offer an explanation for why he was bringing his long rifle and kit. And in the front garden, he stopped to pick a big bouquet of wildflowers—again, with no explanation.

Out front, Tec whistled and called, "Pickles!" The dog came running around the side of the house, tail wagging. "You're in charge now."

All Tory brought was a borrowed dress and straw hat, the all-but-shredded soft shoes, her necklace and the satchel bag containing the message. She remembered the strips of jerky were still inside and asked Tec if it was all right to give to the dog.

"You'll have a friend for life," Tec said.

Pickles eagerly took the treasure up on the front porch, laid down and started gnawing away.

Tory helped Tec carry everything down the stairs to the landing. The fog was now completely gone, the sky above shone brilliantly blue. The river was running high from the rain, muddy brown and churning, spilling into into the marsh on the other side, the gravel bar underwater but the grass embankment high enough to be clear.

Tec flipped over one of the canoes—not the battered one the boys took from Ninety-Three—but a graceful canoe made of lacquered black cherry, a little over three meters in length. Two matching paddles were kept underneath.

Tec stowed the travel bag, the fishing gear and his rifle under the center yoke, then carefully slid the canoe over the embankment into the lapping water. He knelt on one knee gripping the gunwale tightly in one hand and his paddle in the other. Tec sensed Tory hesitate at the sight of the canoe bobbing up and down in the rushing river, and said, "Step into the bow—the front—put your foot down on the centerline, keep your balance low, and sit. Just don't make any big moves."

She stepped aboard, the canoe wobbling, and sat down as quickly as she could, almost dropping the paddle in the process. After she was settled, Tec allowed himself one last glance up at the house on the hill.

Then he jumped into the stern and they were off.

Tory's initial excitement of getting underway immediately was replaced by concern, as the swirling water rushed past on all sides. Ahead, the tree limb that jutted out over the river—the one that she had admired from the front porch for its scenic qualities—was now steadily coming toward her, at head level.

She shouted, "Tec! I don't know what to do!"

He called back over the rush of the water, "Cup your left hand into a 'C' and put it over the butt end of the grip, and grab the shaft midway with your other hand. Yes! Now reach out, put the blade in the water in front of you and pull back. That's it! You're canoeing!"

She made a few strokes, but all that did was accelerate them on a collision course with the looming branch. She tried to sweep the paddle in an arc, hoping to push the front of the canoe away, but Tec's voice boomed out from the stern, "Don't worry, I'm steering from back here!" And just like that, the bow of the canoe neatly swung to the left and they easily coasted past the limb.

Tec was not phased in the least by the rushing river current, and deftly maneuvered around swirling pools and submerged rocks. Tory became accustomed to the even rhythm of the paddle stroke, and began to enjoy herself.

The late morning sun lit up the banks of the river, bulging with vegetation—tall elderberry bushes, reed-grass, cattails, thistles, creeping vines, and wildflowers. Here and there, giant silver maples and majestic willow trees anchored the river banks. Tec called out the names of the birds that happened to criss-cross in front of them—*cardinals, blue-jays, orioles, red-winged blackbirds*—of which she was already well-acquainted—a *red-tailed hawk* spiraling overhead, and a *great blue heron* that stood one-legged on a stump, staring at them as they floated past.

Every so often they would pass a grassy bank with some boats tied up, or wooden docks, and in one place, a boat-house. Each location sported a bell on a pole near the river bank. Higher up on the hill, glimpses of houses could be seen among the trees. Tec shouted "Halloooo!" as they went by, and usually people would come out to an overlook, wave back, and exchange greetings, "Beautiful day!" and "See you at Market!"

They entered into a canyon-like valley and she caught her first glimpse of the town, a red-brick tower topped with a spire, poking above the trees. Ahead, the river curved widely off to the right and entered a stretch of whitewater, where jagged boulders that had tumbled down from the mountainside gnashed the frothing water. She became concerned again.

But well in advance of the rapids, Tec steered the canoe to the left and entered a wide, shallow canal that bisected the river bend, like the stem in the letter "D". On the grassy bottomland between the canal and the river, dozens of colorful canoes lay hull-up, tied to stakes in the ground. Further down, where the canal rejoined the river past the rapids, a deep pool was formed by a canal lock. Long flat-bottomed boats were docked near a stone bridge that crossed the river.

As they pulled the canoe into an empty patch of ground, a voice called out to them. It was Sara, who sprinted across the bridge pushing a small wheelbarrow. She weaved in and out among the beached hulls. Upon arriving, she ran immediately to Tory and delivered the same full-body tackle she'd given Saki the day before, as if they had been apart for months.

She gave her father a more formal little hug and said, "I told everyone you'd wait 'til the fog lifted to come."

"You know me too well," Tec smiled.

"Tory, what did you two do yesterday after we left?" Sara asked.

"We went fishing," Tec said, before Tory could reply. "Now let's unload the canoe."

When Tec handed Sara the freshly-picked bouquet of wildflowers, the girl's demeanor instantly changed and became somber. "Do you want me to go get Jace?" she asked. "He's been hanging around the Caravan campground."

Tec flipped the canoe over and tied it to a stake. "No, I'm afraid that would be a lost cause." He stood up, stretched his back from sitting so long, then took his daughter's hand. "C'mon honey, let's go."

Instead of crossing the stone bridge into town, as Tory expected, they took a wooden footbridge over the canal toward the forest. Even more puzzling, they left the wheelbarrow behind, parked next to the canoe.

"Aren't you afraid someone will steal your things?" Tory asked.

Tec gave that perplexed look of his. "I'd be more concerned with a family of raccoons coming by." Sara chuckled, picturing that.

They walked along a narrow path cut into the near-vertical hillside on the left bank, the river rushing past them on the right, dense forest rising up and up, trees somehow clinging to the steep slope.

As the path curved, another stone bridge across the Stoney Creek became visible. At the near end of the bridge, a small hut perched on the hillside. An old man with a grizzled white beard was drowsing on a bench beside the hut, a book open on his stomach, a fishing rod propped against a branch of a nearby tree. He startled awake as Tec called out to him.

"Why if it isn't Tec Anders," he said, blinking.

"Hiya, Jonas. All's well?"

"Can't complain," the old man replied. "And hello Miss Sara!" Sara gave him a little wave in return. "You've shot up like a beanstalk!"

Tec introduced Tory as a "visitor from Ferry" and Jonas winked, "A pleasure to meet you, ma'am."

Tec removed an envelope from his shirt pocket for the old man. Inside were a miscellaneous set of fishing flies. He pointed to the Green Drake and launched into the story of how Tory landed a big rainbow the previous night using that pattern. When he spread his hands to show how big the fish was, it had grown to twice the size.

They talked fishing for a while, then Tec asked, "How's the missus?"

"You can ask her yourself," the old man chuckled and walked over to the little hut. A brass bell was mounted next to the doorway and he rang it three times.

It was then that Tory noticed the "hut" was actually a kind of rail car, mounted on top of an iron frame and wheels. Looking up, she could see another rail car perched at the very top of the hill, and a parallel set of tracks in between.

Three bells rang in response up on the heights. "Sara, can you do me a favor?" Jonas asked as the three of them entered the rail car, "There is a wheel crank in there that opens the holding tank. You've got a bit more energy than I do," he grinned.

Sara eagerly spun the wheel by its handle, and a torrent of water gushed out from an exhaust pipe at the front of the rail car. Nothing happened for a few moments, and then the wheels began creaking and the rail car slowly began to climb the hill. Jonas waved to them.

As the car gradually gained elevation, a panoramic view of the valley opened up. Tory realized she was looking at the same view as in the painting that hung by the Anders' dining table. Tec took it upon himself to point out the landmarks as they went.

The main feature of the valley were the three rivers in the shape of a "Y" lying on its side. One branch, the Stoney Creek, was directly below them at the base of the mountain-wall. The other branch, called the "Little" Conemaugh, emerged from a deep notch on the far side of the valley to the east. These two joined together at a sharp point to form the Conemaugh which continued up the valley to the northwest.

Much of the triangle of ground between the rivers was taken up by a grassy park punctuated by shade trees called the "Fair Grounds", now dotted with the tents and carts and cook-fires of people in town for Market. Upstream along the Little Conemaugh, in a strip of ground between the hills and the river, the campground of the East Caravan was marked by tents, covered wagons and fluttering pennants on poles.

"The East Caravan has been in existence for hundreds of winters—in fact you could say it was the reason for this town. When our brethren the Amish of Lancaster first began to resettle these highlands, they encountered pioneers from Steel Town here. Treaties were signed between the two people, establishing Flood Town, and the East Caravan and West Barges have arrived here ever since."

Three stone bridges crossed the rivers—the one near the canal docks, the second below them at the bottom of the Incline, and third much wider bridge over the Little Conemaugh at the point. On the opposite side, situated along the right bank of the Conemaugh, clustered a set of buildings and water wheels and fenced-in lots where the main products of Flood Town were produced—a grist mill, a saw mill, a paper mill, stock yards and a tannery.

They were about half-way up the hill when the other rail car passed, descending on the other track, empty of passengers. "The people of Steel Town knew how to build these inclined planes," Tec observed. "At Portage, there are a whole series of them that bring the Conestoga wagons of the East Caravan up over the Allegheny Front."

He pointed to the red steepled tower at the center of town, situated at the base of another hill. "The only thing the settlers found standing was the Bell Tower, built of steel and brick. It once was part of a great cathedral church. Everything else had long since been swept away."

"Is that why it's called Flood Town?" Tory asked.

"You are right in that this valley experiences big floods all the time, it acts like a natural funnel for all the snowmelt and spring rains. It's why all the houses you see in town are up on the hill slope behind the Bell Tower, far above the highest water mark. But that's not why it's called Flood Town."

"Oh, I know this story," Sara whispered to Tory.

"Back in ancient times, Steel Town was a great city of industry. The richest men in the world lived there, chief among them a man named Carnegie. These men owned the railroads that ran through this valley, owned the factories, even claimed ownership of the coal beneath the ground and the timber of the forests! Up on a branch of the Little Conemaugh," he pointed to the east, "they built an earth dam, created a lake that only members of their "Bosses Club" could fish in. And then one night during a big rain storm, the dam broke, and sent a wall of water down the valley. It crashed into this very hill here, and destroyed the entire town below. Thousands of people died. And none of the 'Bosses' were ever punished ..."

The rail car finally reached the top and came to a squeaky halt. An old woman named Marya was waiting to greet them as they exited. Tec made introductions again, and fished from his pocket a thumb-sized jar of cream for her. "Just a pea-sized drop rubbed into your knuckles will help with the arthritis..."

As they continued with small talk, Sara wandered over to a scenic pond nearby where a group of ducks were paddling. Beside the pond stood a small cottage with a thatched roof and whitewashed walls, not much different than the one at Ninety-Three. The lower end of the pond cascaded in a waterfall over a stone wall, forming a creek that then tumbled over the mountainside. But Tory's eyes were attracted to a feature of the holding dam—a sluice gate that could be raised or lowered with a hand crank, allowing water to flow into a brick-lined channel that angled down toward the rail cars, into an underground cistern.

In a flash, from all her years working in Reclamation, she under-stood how the inclined railway worked. Water from the pond was used to fill the tanks on the rail car. The two rail cars were connected by a giant pulley—when the car at the top was filled with water, the one on the bottom was emptied, and the difference in weight caused the full car to descend and the empty car to ascend. The descending rail car would need to hold more than enough water to offset the weight of passengers—that's why they rang the bell, to signify how many people were aboard.

No power needed beyond water and gravity. *Pretty clever.*

But then a different thought crossed her mind. The Incline was yet another instance of something easily observable from space that the AIs had neglected to tell her about. *Why?*

They waved goodbye to Marya and headed along a trail that followed the crest of the ridge, passed a grassy dome which Tec described as an ancient Native burial mound, already a thousand winters old when the first American settlers arrived. Beyond the mound, the flat top of the mountain opened into a beautiful glade, scattered with maple and oak trees and a few tall hemlock pines, where a flock of wooly white sheep grazed on the grass among rows and rows of evenly placed stones.

Tec walked with purpose over to a newer stone, not yet weathered like the others, the rectangle of grass in front a slightly different shade of green. On the stone was inscribed *Lara Anders, Beloved Wife and Mother.*

Sara knelt and placed the flowers down. Father and daughter both stood quietly, heads bowed, holding hands, Tec whispering something inaudible. Birdsong trilled back and forth in the trees, a breeze moved through the branches and the leaves murmured.

Tory wasn't sure what to do, so she drifted a distance away, but watched Tec's face closely. She knew him well enough by now to see that even though his expression was calm, just by the way his jaw was set, his thoughts were churning.

On their way back, Tec gestured at the graves that filled the entire hilltop as far as they could see. "All those people who died in the big Flood are buried here," he said. "But the ones that died from the Blackout …" he shook his head. "There weren't enough people left to bury them all."

As they approached the Incline, they heard five bells ringing from the base of the hill. "People are coming up!" Sara said.

"Hurry ahead, Sara. Let Marya know we're right behind."

Sara sprinted off, and as soon as she was out of earshot, Tec said to Tory, "When we get into town, before we go to Saki's house, we need to stop and see the Constable."

Tory froze. She wasn't familiar with the term *Constable*, but just by how Tec said it, she was certain of its meaning. *Police.*

Seeing her reaction, Tec quickly moved to reassure her, "No, it's not what you think. We need to register you as a resident of Flood Town, and the Constable is the person who does it."

"Tec, I've been trying to tell you. I like this place, I am thankful for what you've done. But I've got to continue on, to deliver the message. I've already lost so much time–!"

"That's what you think of it as, lost time?"

"No, I didn't mean—"

"The journey ahead is across lands governed by ironclad Treaties, which have brought peace for countless winters. The Seneca particularly—they don't abide by Treaty-breakers. You will be turned back—or worse—unless you have a valid Writ to be crossing into other's lands. Being a resident of Flood Town can provide that."

Tec pleaded, "You have to trust me on this."

She searched his face, and decided that she did.

They entered Flood Town along the main thoroughfare, Market Street, paved with cobblestones and wide enough for two carts to pass each other. To the left, down the slope toward the Fair Grounds, a covered pavilion stretched the entire length of the street. Stalls lined the arcade all the way down to the end, tables and carts shoulder-to-shoulder, some in the process of being set up, others already covered with tarps, ready to be unwrapped the next day at Market.

Hundreds of people of all ages could be seen throughout the town, in and out of the campsites on the Fair Grounds, strolling up and down Market Street, greeting acquaintances and striking up conversations, children running around playing games, seniors sitting on benches, taking in the crowd.

As Tec slowly pushed the wheelbarrow up the street, people took notice of Tory and stared. She was no stranger to being gawked at, but here she found it impossible to read their expressions. *So much easier with circlets broadcasting everyone's emotions.*

Tec knew most of the people they passed, offered greetings as they went, but she could tell he wasn't used to this kind of attention, and wanted to get away from it as fast as possible. Sara on the other hand loved it, held Tory's hand proudly, and waved to people as if she were marching in a parade.

The right side of Market Street was lined by a row of specialty craft stores—farm tools, a bakery, saddles and horse tack, cookware, jewelry, pottery, eyeglasses, a hatmaker, a tailor, a bookstore—culminating at the far end in a brick building that housed a brewery. Younger adults spilled out into the street from the adjacent beer garden, mugs in hand, swaying to music being played by a band. As they passed the window of the cobbler's shop, Tory spied a pair of high leather boots that she immediately coveted. Sara tugged her hand, as their destination was across the street, next to the Bell Tower—Town Hall.

Town Hall was a two-story square brick building with cutouts at each corner, so that it resembled a thick cross. The entry portico was flanked by massive wooden columns that looked to be hewn from whole trees. Four sections of gabled roof met in the middle, topped with a decorative cupola dome and a copper wind vane in the shape of an angel.

Tec parked the cart and asked Sara to wait outside as he and Tory entered. The first story of Town Hall was a single large chamber, the floor tiled in a colorful mosaic pattern, the ten-meter high ceiling supported by two massive girders that also appeared to be whole tree trunks. The interior space was so big, it had two fireplaces, on opposite sides.

All four walls as well as the cutout corners had tall arched windows that were opened to catch the pleasant cross-breeze. Decorative vases bursting with white, pink and red roses were set on the floor in the spaces between the windows and in the corners. Above one fireplace hung a landscape painting that was a much larger version of the one in the Anders' house, and above the other hung the depiction of a circular field and white stone wall that Tory immediately recognized as the Wall of Names at Ninety-Three.

People wandered in from outside and milled about, simply admiring the craftsmanship, the flowers, the paintings. A group of men congregated, all dressed the same in blue shirts and suspenders, straw hats, each sporting curious beards with their upper lips shaven. A tall broad-shouldered man with a brushy mustache was in their midst, explaining how the bricks used in Town Hall had been recovered from an ancient cathedral that once stood on this spot. The man caught a glimpse of Tec approaching in a beeline.

"Tec, my friend, it's good to see you!" and they shook hands vigorously. "I was just giving some of our brothers from the East a little tour."

"I apologize for interrupting," Tec said, and the visitors shook their head, offered their thanks and moved on.

"Tory, I'd like to introduce you to Gerry Braun, our elected town Constable. Everyone calls him 'Bull'. Bull, this is Tory, who comes from—"

"—the Belt Wall. Yes, we all know, Tec. Worst-kept secret in town! But where are my manners?" Bull took off his hat with a flourish and made a small bow. "It's a pleasure to meet you Tory, and on behalf of my fellow residents, I want to bid you a warm welcome to Flood Town—"

"About that," Tec said. "That's why we are here. Tory would like to declare herself as a resident."

"Really?" Bull rocked back on his heels and crossed his arms, his brow furrowing. "That's ... unexpected."

He took a moment to reappraise Tory. "Are you serious about this?"

"Yes," she answered without hesitation.

"She's been here for a moon, and I'm prepared to vouch for her," Tec said.

Bull nodded, "Yes, I know how it works, Tec. It's just ... we've never even seen anyone from the Belt Wall before, let alone had them become a resident..."

Tec and Bull stared at each other for an uncomfortable length of time.

Finally Bull gave Tory a weak smile. "Again, I must apologize for my un-Christian like behavior. Of course you're welcome to join our community."

He clapped his hands together. "Let's do it now, it won't take but a moment. If you could just meet me at the desk over there, I've got to get some things out of the vault."

Bull went down a set of rear stairs. Tec and Tory waited in chairs at an a oaken table that looked like it had been carved from a single block of wood, with floral bouquets in cut glass jars placed at either end. Bull returned with a thick leather-bound book and a stack of colored bills, a jar of ink and a feathered quill. He sat down in the chair with a heavy sigh, placed the book down with a thud, took out a pair of glasses from his pocket.

"Knowing our friend Tec, I expect he's told you almost nothing about being a resident of Flood Town, and even what little he's revealed has left you confused and with questions." Tory found herself nodding. "Not to worry, my dear! I will be your guide, like a shining lantern on a foggy night."

Tec rolled his eyes.

Bull flipped forward through pages and pages of handwritten entries until he came to the most recent, and dipped the pen in the ink. "OK, let's get you entered into the Registry," he said.

He wrote *Tory* in cursive then paused, looked up over his glasses. "Your last name?"

She blinked, the question stumping her. She stammered, "I … don't have one. My full name is Taurii … Six-Three-Six."

Tec scowled, affronted by the idea of using numbers as a name, while Bull leaned back in his chair thoughtfully. "Well, now's your chance to pick one," he said, taking out a handkerchief and cleaning his glasses.

Tory looked around, her mind completely blank. She looked at Tec who was no help at all, staring right back at her. She glanced over his head, at the lintel beam above the front entrance, into which were carved the words FLOOD TOWN.

"How about *Flood*?" she asked.

"I like it! A solid choice. *Tory Flood*," he said as he wrote on the page. "No one'll have any doubt of where you are from!"

He captured her gender as *Female*, her status as *Unmarried*, her age as *Adult*. For place of birth, he looked up and raised an eyebrow. "You can write *Belt Wall*," she said. "I've got nothing to hide."

"Children?" She shook her head no.

"What's your craft?"

"In the Belt Wall, I worked in the water system—"

"Absolutely perfect!" Bull exclaimed, smacking his hand against the desk. "You'll never have an idle day here, Tory! In fact, I can think of one project that's been talked about for many winters, constructing a water pump on the Stoney Creek—"

"Can you please keep going?" Tec interjected.

Bull shook his head in amazement. "And here I thought adding someone from the Belt Wall into the Registry was going to be the strangest thing that happened today ... But Tec Anders in a hurry? That's one for the ages!"

Tec made a wry face. "Don't worry, my friend," Bull said. "We're almost finished. Tory, I just need you to sign your name here next to your entry..."

Bull reversed the book so it faced Tory, slid the pen and jar of ink across the desk to her. She awkwardly gripped the pen, never having written anything by hand before. Slowly she scratched out her name in shaky block letters. Both Tec and Bull exchanged glances at the way she spelled *TAURII*.

Next, Bull placed two stacks of bills in front of her, green and orange. "Your Allotment is fifteen dials and thirty half-dials. Please sign them all at the bottom—yes, on that line—and while you do, I'll tell you a little bit about how things work here in Flood Town."

Bull cleared his throat. "The main events here in town. Market, as you can see for yourself. Usually there's one every other moon, from spring until after harvest. Alternates from the East Caravan to the West Barges, each bring different kinds of goods. When you hear the bells ringing like mad, it means Market will be in two days.

"Also important is Atonement Day, which happens at the final Market before winter, when all debts are settled, and everyone is given their new Allotment for the next year."

"The boundaries of town," Bull continued. "To the west, the Treaty House at Salt ... to the east, the Incline at Portage, and to the south, the Wall of Names at Ninety-Three. Pretty much anywhere in between, you're in Flood Town. Go too far to the south and you'll cross into the Mountaineers' land—best avoided. And over that first ridge to the north is the start of the Treaty Hunting Grounds—only those with a Hunting Permit are allowed to enter. Same with traveling west to Steel Town or east to Lancaster—if you want to go, before you do, you've got to get a Writ of Passage from the Town Council."

Tory had finally finished signing the dials and moved to the stack of half-dials, stopping first to shake out a cramp in her hand.

"About your Allotment," Bull said. "Dials are meant to pay for goods and services other residents supply. Of course, you're free to barter direct, no one's stopping you—but if someone offers you a fair price, you've got to accept payment in dials. Any disputes, the Town Council will sort out, and their judgment is final. And don't squirrel away your dials, because they expire at Atonement! We have a big bonfire and burn them all, and then hand out a new batch—"

"That reminds me," Tec spoke up. "Sara wanted me to ask, can next year's animal be something more exciting than a duck? She suggested a mountain lion."

"Please let Sara know that I will pass that along. I'm certain the Town Council will take it under advisement," Bull said, his eyes twinkling.

"If you ever run out of dials, don't worry," Bull added. "There is plenty of employment here in town. The pay is one dial per day. There are longhouses for travelers and short term stays, and the townhouses are kept for people who work in town year round—at the mills, the public works, or the workshops on Market Street. And of course, our old folk, if they wish, always have a place here in town, so they can see all their friends—and gossip!" He laughed heartily.

"If you are planning to start your own homestead, let us know. The Town Council will grant you a vacant parcel—there are some good hollows down near Tec's for example. We'll organize a house-raising for you, get you started with a dairy cow, some chickens, help you plant a kitchen garden, everything you need to get going—"

"We don't have to go into all that," Tec said. "She's going to be staying at our farm for now."

Again Bull raised his eyebrows, but said nothing.

Tory finished signing the bills and Bull said, "Go ahead, put them in your bag. They're yours!" He stood up and reached across the table to shake her hand. "All right, Miss Tory Flood. You are hereby an official resident of Flood Town!"

As Tec and Tory were turning to leave, Bull said, "There is one more thing I've got to ask you, now that you are a resident."

He came around the desk, and Tory suddenly realized how he had subtly placed his body between them and the exit. He adjusted his posture, straightening to his full height, and in a serious voice asked, "Tory Flood, do you want to press charges against Jace Anders?"

Tec exploded in surprise, "*What?!*"

"Correct me if I'm wrong, but I heard that young Jace shot Tory with his rifle up at Ninety-Three."

The color drained out of Tec's face.

Then he felt Tory's hand squeeze his. "Jace and I have put that behind us," she said. "No need to arrest him."

Tec exhaled deeply. Bull's serious demeanor gave way to a broad smile. "That's a good thing," he said. "I don't know what I would have done if you said yes. We don't even have a jail!"

Sara was laying on her back in the grass beside the front stairs, arms crossed behind her head, staring up at the sky. She saw them exit, and muttered to herself, "At last."

Without even realizing it, Tec and Tory were still holding hands.

"Wait!" Sara exclaimed, jumping up. "Did you two … *get married?!*"

Six cobbled streets extended from Market Street and ran in parallel up the hillside, named after what was located at each intersection—Brewery at the north, then Book, Bell, Bakery, Bridle, and finally Ice Street on the south, which led up the hill to caves that had been packed with blocks of river ice in the winter to keep food cold year-round.

A dormitory-style longhouse was situated at the foot of each street, behind the workshops. The rest of the way up, the streets were lined with single houses, of similar style as the Anders' house—a porch out front, a mansard roof with windows on the second floor—but these homes were narrower, built in red brick, with the kitchen extending from the rear of the house. Each property ran street-to-street, was enclosed by a stone wall, with a tall shade tree in the back yard and a narrow side yard running along the length of the house. The dwellings were staggered so that a house fronting on one street was adjacent to the rear of the house the next street over.

Saki's was the last place on the left on Bell Street. Past her house, a set of stairs led up to a public park—a level strip of ground cut into the face of the hill at the same elevation, so that each street had access. People were beginning to congregate, and smoke started to rise from fire pits.

When they entered the house, all the activity was out in the kitchen, where Saki and an old woman were busy cooking. Tec took one peek in and promptly announced, "I'm going to take a nap," and tramped up the stairs.

The old woman saw Tory and waved her in, "Tory, my dear! So nice to finally meet you! I'm Alice, Tecumseh's mother. Now, grab an apron!"

Sara had beat her to it, already tying the apron string around her waist and crying out, *"Pierogis!"*

The kitchen worktable was completely filled with bowls, trays, scattered flour. Two little children were up on stools. One boy spooned mashed potatoes and shredded cheese from a bowl and handed it to Alice, while the other boy provided Tory dollops of a pungent sausage and sauerkraut combination. Tory watched Alice work and quickly caught on. The lump of filling went into the center of a disc of dough which was then folded in half, and the edges pinched together. Sara's job was to further crimp the edges together with a fork then hand them to Saki, who tossed them into a kettle of boiling water. When the dumplings floated to the surface it meant they were cooked, and Saki fished them out with a big slotted spoon. Sara then sorted them onto wooden trays, easily able to tell potato and sausage apart by the color of the filling inside.

There was very little talking beyond simple instructions, though Alice sang songs throughout. Once the last batch was in the pot, the old woman moved over to the cutting block and rapidly chopped big stalks of leek onions, until there was a mountain piled up, which she scooped into a big bowl. Strangely, Tory realized tears were streaming from her eyes. *But I don't feel sad at all ...*

Sara noticed and laughed, "The onions!" She led Tory over to the sink, where she dampened a towel with cold water for Tory's eyes. "Look at how they have a water pump *inside*," Sara whispered with a mixture of awe and jealousy.

When they finished, they had six heaping trays of pierogis. Everyone hung their aprons on hooks and took turns washing their hands. Alice came over and gave Tory a warm hug. "You are a natural!" she declared.

The front door opened and in came Saki's husband Zeb, who had just finished working at the Forge. He was short and square-bodied, with red hair and a beard worn in the same style as the visitors at Town Hall, with the upper lip shaved. His sleeveless shirt revealed heavily muscled arms, covered with soot and reeking of sweat, cradling two enormous jugs filled with beer.

"Heya, Tory!" he shouted, as if they'd known each other for ages. "Hope you are thirsty!"

Tec came downstairs rubbing sleep from his eyes. Zeb put down the beer, the two men shook hands, and then Zeb took a little packet from his shirt pocket. Tec tapped the contents out into the palm of his hand—iron fishing hooks, with very tiny eyelets and sharp barbs at the end.

"What craftsmanship!" Tec exclaimed. "Thank you!"

Zeb beamed with a smile, white teeth shining in his smudged face.

"I'm going to run over to the Bathhouse," Zeb said, leaning in to gave Saki a kiss, leaving a streak of dirt against her cheek. "I'll meet you up there."

By the time they came out of the house, the sun had dipped behind the Incline, but a sliver of light still struck the high hills to the north across the Conemaugh, illuminating the tops in a golden glow. Saki led the way bearing a giant cast iron skillet with a wooden handle almost a meter long, followed by Tory and Sara each carrying three stacked trays of pierogies. One little boy had a crock of sour cream, the other a crock of butter, while Alice brought the bowl of diced leeks, and a giant jar of applesauce. Tec brought up the rear, lugging the jugs of beer. A cheer went up from the neighbors as the procession entered the park.

At the fire pit, chunks of meat and whole chickens were being roasted on spits. Saki raked some coals to the side, placed the skillet on top, added a slab of butter, and began to fry the pierogies with the chopped leeks. An incredible mix of smells rose from the fire.

Then Tory spotted Jace climbing the street with a teenaged girl. They held hands, though as they drew near the park, he let go and put his hands in his pockets. The girl was very pretty, her hair in long box-braids held back with a colorful orange bandana. She wore a simple sleeveless dress that showed off her youthful figure, open-toed leather sandals, and stacked hoop bracelets of gold around her wrists and ankles. A guitar was slung over her back.

Jace approached Tec, who along with Alice and the other neighbors were arranging a picnic table of food—carved-up meat, piles of steaming pierogis, stacks of clean plates and eating utensils. A line was beginning to form.

"Dad, I want you to meet someone," Jace said. "This ... is Jasmyn."

Everyone stopped what they were doing for a moment to look.

"Pleased to meet you, sir," the girl said and made a little curtsy.

Tec looked at Jace and then at the girl, then back at Jace. The stern look on his face melted and he broke into a big smile. "Nice to meet you too! And perfect timing—we are just about to eat!"

Jace spied Tory nearby and brought Jasmyn over. "Jasmyn, I want you to meet Tory. She is ... staying with our family."

"I've heard so much about you!" Jasmyne said, flashing a dazzling smile. "A fellow traveler."

"And where are you from?" Tory asked. From her appearance and breezy manner it was easy to see she wasn't from here.

"Oh, I'm from the South, way down the Ohio River in a land called *Can-tuck-kee*. But my family works on the river boats, so I've been traveling all my life. This is my first time as far east as Flood Town."

Sara, who had been running around with other children up on the forested hillside, zoomed past and shouted, "*Jace and Jasmyn, sitting in a tree, k-i-s-s-i-n-g!*"

"Shut up Sara!" Jace shot daggers after her, and Jasmyn blushed a little.

"Jasmyn, will you play us something?" Saki called over.

"Certainly!" She found an empty chair near the fire, strummed her guitar a few times to tune it up. She cleared her throat, and said in a loud and clear voice. "Where I'm from, this music is called 'The Blues'."

She launched into an upbeat melody that got people tapping their toes, and belted out lyrics in a surprisingly deep, gravelly voice:

I'm selling my pork chops,

But I'm givin' my gravy away!

Tec frowned at the lyrics, but Saki nudged him with her elbow, and he sighed in resignation.

Just then Zeb arrived all cleaned up, almost unrecognizable. The beer was uncorked and poured into empty canning jars and passed around to all the adults. Tec put his fingers into his mouth and let out a shrill whistle. The various conversations died down and people turned as Tec raised his glass.

"Friends, family, neighbors! Please join me in welcoming our newest town resident, Tory Flood!"

Everyone shouted "*Prost!*" and gulped their beer.

Tory took a sip of the dark amber liquid, and then another.

People came up to her in waves, introduced themselves, shook her hand, explained where they lived and what their crafts were, and how they were related to so-and-so, wished her well and how happy they were. It quickly became a blur.

Someone handed her a full plate of food and she found a bare spot to sit in the grass at the edge of the park. Each mouthful was a burst of flavors, washed down with beer. From this vantage, she could see down into the enclosed yards and houses, past the stately Bell Tower, to the small fires flickering throughout the Fair Grounds.

Sara suddenly plopped down beside her, sweat glistening from her forehead. The first stars were beginning to appear in the dark blue sky overhead, and she pointed to a cluster above the northwest horizon. "Look you can see the Big Dipper," she said. "It looks like a big pierogi skillet with the long handle. And if you trace a line from the bottom two stars over to the right, you can find the North Star."

Tory mentally pictured Earth rotating at a tilt on its axis and realized the "North Star" would consistently be apparent at the center of rotation above the northern pole. *Makes sense.*

"Oh and look!" Sara exclaimed. "That red star that's not twinkling. That's not a star—that's actually the planet Mars!"

Then another girl about Sara's age raced over, tapped Sara on the shoulder and cried out, "Tag, you're it!" Sara immediately sprung to her feet and chased off in pursuit.

For the moment, Tory was by herself. Tec was over in a circle of men, regaling them with fishing tales. Jasmyn played an intricate romantic ballad, and Jace sat nearby, wearing the same expression as when Pickles first saw the strips of jerky come out of her satchel bag. Tory looked down the long river valley bathed in moonlight, looked up at the distant red dot of Mars.

One thought kept entering her mind, as much as she tried to push it away.

What if I just stayed here?

8

With everyone in town for Market, the sleeping arrangements at the house were all jumbled. Tory was put in the twin boys' room. Their bed frames were too short for her, so both mattresses were laid onto the floor, but still her ankles dangled over the edge uncomfortably. Her head ached and the room felt spinny from the beer she drank. At one point the two mattresses slid apart and toppled her onto the hard wooden floor. Eventually she fell into a fitful sleep, and was jarred awake by Saki in the dim twilight before dawn.

"Let's go take a bath before it gets too crowded," Saki whispered.

All the other bedroom doors on the second floor were open. Tec, who had slept in Zeb's room, was already up and gone, as was Alice, whose room was across the hall. The door to Saki's room was open a crack and Zeb could be seen still fast asleep in her bed.

They crept down the front stairs to find Jace sprawled on a bedroll in the entry room. No sign of Jasmyn, for which Saki was relieved. The tent in the backyard near Saki's work shed, where the children were sleeping, was quiet too. Saki grabbed a basket full of towels and soap on the way out.

They climbed the stairs to the park. The full moon was setting over the Incline and the grass glistened with dew in the silvery light. The ashes were cold, the plates and cups all cleaned up, as if no one had been there. Tory realized she didn't remember leaving or how she got back to Saki's house.

Down in the valley, wisps of fog rose from the three rivers. From this elevation she could see clear past the Fair Grounds to the bridge across the Stoney Creek. Below the bridge a few tiny figures were out in the river fishing, one of whom she figured had to be Tec.

At the end of the park, they crossed a footbridge over a cascading stream and came to the Bathhouse, a one-story brick building with an arched roof and chimneys belching steam. Alongside, wood-fired furnaces with iron doors were set into the hillside. Running water was diverted to fill tanks above the furnaces, and pipes led from there into the Bathhouse. An incredible quantity of firewood was stacked nearby in a covered shed.

An older man who was stoking the fires took a break to lean on his long iron poker and waved to them, saying, "Bright and early as always!" Saki wished him a happy Market Day in return.

But instead of entering the Bathhouse, they continued along the trail a bit further, rounding the front of the hill to the public outhouses, which were neatly tucked out of sight. Directly below, Tory noticed a curious set of terraced ponds which occupied the bottomland between the base of the hill and the well-traveled road that led east along the Little Conemaugh. The first pond was still, and stank, even from this height. But in the other ponds things were moving, enormous carp fish, rising every now and then to take a gulp of air at the surface. *Is this their... sewage system?*

Further up the valley, beyond the ponds, she could smell more than see a row of pig-pens. Her stomach began to turn and she rushed into the outhouse, which only made everything worse.

After a while she exited and Saki was there waiting for her.

"A good sweat will help," she said, patting Tory's arm.

The Bathhouse was divided in half, with separate entries for men and women. The interior was like entering a cave. Dim predawn light filtered in through small circular windows set into the vaulted ceilings, and a few flickering wall sconces illuminated the center hallway. The air was very humid and tasted of minerals. There was no sign of anyone else.

The first room past the entry hall was a changing area with a vent in the ceiling that let some fresh air from outside spill in. Saki undressed without any of the modesty Tory had come to expect, as if the rules were different in here. Despite all of Tory's training to bulk up, Saki was curvy and shapely in ways that made Tory feel lanky in comparison. *Most Martians would look like skeletons here.*

Saki came close to examine Tory's shoulder scar and the yellowish bruise that still bloomed around it. "You are lucky Jace is such a terrible shot," she grinned.

In the next room, Saki provided a bar of her homemade soap and they showered. Once they rinsed off, they walked past a large steaming pool and entered the door to the sauna. They sat on wooden benches in the near-dark, a heavy layer of steam obscuring the skylight above. It was too hot to talk, almost too hot to breathe. Sweat dripped from every pore on Tory's body.

Just when it became unbearable, Saki tapped her on the shoulder. The air which had been hot and sultry when they entered, now felt cool as they exited the sauna and slipped into the hot pool. They sat on under-water benches, leaned back and listened to the drip of condensation from the tiled vault overhead. Some kind of mineral salt was dissolved in the water and it felt amazing, the warmth seeping into the marrow of Tory's bones.

"About Tec—" Saki said, breaking the silence, her voice reverberating off the tiles.

"Since Lara passed ... he's been out there working the farm by himself with the kids. We're here in town ... and with the twins, we just don't get out to see them as much as we should. I think's he's about driven Jace crazy."

Saki glided across the pool to sit next to Tory. "So when I first heard about you ... arriving ... I thought, this is just what Tec needs. A woman in his life, to wake him back up!"

Saki looked up at the vaulted ceiling. "But seeing him yesterday ... I know Tec is up to some scheme. He's an open book to me. Having you register as a town resident—I don't know what it's all about, but that's Tec's idea for sure..."

Then she locked eyes with Tory. "You may have everyone else fooled, including Tec. But not me."

Tory became conscious of how Saki had backed her into a corner of the pool. "I know you haven't changed your plans to go find a Scientist, and John Cornplanter," Saki said. "My ask is, leave Tec out of it."

She drifted back across the pool. "You seem like a good person, Tory. I really like you. Please just let him down easy."

"I don't want to hurt Tec!" Tory exclaimed. "I actually think I—"

Just then there were voices in the hall, and two other women entered and climbed into the hot pool. Seeing Saki they immediately started talking to her about Market Day, what they had on their shopping lists, rumors of what goods had arrived from the East, what was in season from the Kitchen Garden. Occasionally they cast sideways glances over at Tory in the corner, who had slunk down as far as she could without going under.

When Saki and Tory rinsed off again in the shower room there were other women in there as well, and the changing room was filling up with people too, so that it was difficult to get dressed without jostling into a stranger's body.

Outside, even though the sun hadn't crested the east ridge, it seemed bright as midday after emerging from the darkness. A line had formed waiting to go into the women's side, but not on the men's, who apparently did not wake early to bathe. Saki gave a flutter-wave to some acquaintances, and didn't bring up the conversation from the hot pool again.

From this vantage high on the hillside, they could see down and into the Kitchen Garden, like looking into an open box. The garden was easily a hundred meters long and half that as wide, enclosed by tall brick walls over four meters high, and burgeoning with green vegetation. At the northern end, an ornate glass greenhouse stood with window frames painted brilliant white. Gardeners pushed the familiar one-wheeled carts along neat gravel paths, stopped to pick ripe produce. A cat on was out on the prowl.

"Let's pay a quick visit to Ma," Saki decided.

They found Alice by the south-facing wall, busy picking runner beans from a willow frame covered in vines. She put down her basket, wiped her hands on her apron.

"Well look at these pretty young flowers in bloom!" Alice said. "And smelling so pretty."

"Hi Ma," Saki said. "We managed to beat the crowds to the Bathhouse."

Tory said hello as well, suddenly concerned about what she may have said—or did—after too many beers last night. But Alice offered nothing but a sweet smile on her face.

The morning quiet was suddenly split by a booming bell-clap from the Tower. Startled doves flew from their perch atop the wall and circled, as the cat watched them stoically from below.

"It's one bell to Service," Saki said. "I better go back and made sure the kids are up and dressed." Before Tory could say anything, she added. "You can stay here, Tory. I'm sure Ma can spare a few moments to give you a tour."

"Of course, would be my pleasure," Alice said. "But Saki, before you go..."

She walked to a fruit tree that had been pinned and pruned so it grew flat across the brick wall, and returned with her apron pocket full of ripe cherries. "For the children," she said as she placed them in Saki's basket.

"We'll meet you at Service!" Saki said as she turned toward the gate. "If you're there first, save us a bench."

Once Saki had left, Alice took out a cherry from her pocket for Tory. The fruit was a burst of tangy flesh and squirt of sweet juice in Tory's mouth, with a surprising hard seed in the middle that she bit into, and grimaced. Unsure what to do next, she spit it out.

Alice laughed seeing the mix of expressions that crossed Tory's face. She waddled over and emptied her basket full of green beans into a container on a nearby wheelbarrow. "Let's take a little stroll, dear."

As they walked, the old woman offered her hand for Tory to hold. Alice's palms were calloused and leathery, her nails split and embedded with dirt, the skin on the back of her hands and forearms criss-crossed with red scratches. She wasn't very tall, with her spine hunched over, only coming up to Tory's chest. As they walked around the gravel path, Alice pointed out the vegetables being loaded onto the push carts—lettuce, squash, broccoli, cabbage, cucumber, onions. "A little too early for the tomatoes," she remarked.

"You know, walled gardens like this came from a curious group of people who lived in ancient England, known as 'Victorians' after their Queen," Alice said. "Their *kitchen gardens* kept the manor house and its guests entertained with fresh produce throughout the year. The Lords and Ladies of the manor were people of leisure—frivolous people, really—but the gardeners they employed were truly masters of their craft."

They passed top-rack beehives of which Tory was now familiar. Alice paused, noticing something, frowned, and called across the yard. "I'm afraid these bees may be ready to swarm!"

A man stood and waved back. "I'll get the smoker!"

Alice continued on. "Where was I? Oh, yes. The Lords fancied themselves *scientists*—and got their gardeners to conduct *experiments*, cross-breeding to produce new varieties, more resistant to pests, hardier, growing faster, larger, more colorful, sweeter. They began using chemicals as fertilizer and poisons to kill insects, all under the banner of *Progress*. The *data* from their experiments helped inform the theories of one particular English scientist—a man named Darwin, who went on to develop one of the most powerful scientific theories, called *Evolution*. Have you heard of it?"

Tory nodded, holding in a laugh. *Evolution was taught at the youngest pod levels!* Also she saw where Tec got his curious manner of speaking when worked up.

"Darwin claimed that all of Nature was little more than a random process—something the Victorians believed they could *improve upon*. Now, mind you—the people who introduced these ideas were God-fearing—really just wanting the perfect rose or heaviest gooseberry—but their descendants began to combine these ideas with machines and ... well, that led them on the path to ruin."

"The False Paths," Tory said. "I saw them on the wall at Tec's house."

She chuckled. "So strange to hear the farmhouse described as Tecumseh's! You know, I grew up there as well. My grandmother stitched that sign!"

"I had no idea," Tory said, and Alice patted her hand as if to say, *not to worry.*

They had reached the glass house. The sun peeked above the east ridge and lit up a strip of crimson bricks along the top of the west and north walls. Alice opened the creaky door and crossed through a potting area to the central room. "And now we come to the most controversial part of our garden—the Melon Room."

Exposed hot water pipes made the glass-enclosed room uncomfortably warm. On both sides of the center aisle, vines climbed from raised planting beds and wrapped around wooden trellises, and in among the broad leaves, striped green watermelons hung suspended in nets that prevented them from falling.

"I can't tell you how many debates we've had over the years about these watermelons." Alice said. "In order to grow in the mountains, we have to keep them under glass, to protect from the elements. To germinate the seeds, the pots must be placed directly on top of the hot water pipes, and to get the water down here, we are reliant on the Bathhouse up the hill. Once sprouted, the shoots are planted in loam dug from the banks of the fish-ponds, transported here, and layered on top of special metal grates for plenty of drainage. We have to use a brush to hand-pollinate the flowers! As the vines grow, trellises are needed to support them, and then, when the melons get large enough, we have to suspend them in hammocks else they will break off from their own weight. Just the right amount of watering is needed—too much and they will split open."

She shook her head sadly. "All that, over four moons of daily tending, just to get a watermelon."

"Not a Simple Path," Tory observed.

"Exactly, my dear! Unlike Nature, which follows its course without any need of human help—here, if any part of this *system* fails—the watermelons will perish. So the question we ask, are we much different than the Victorians?"

Alice smiled, "But then you eat a slice of cool sweet watermelon on a hot day at the end of summer … well, you decide it was worth it."

Outside, the Bell Tower stuck twice.

"We best hurry along," Alice said.

The last room in the glass house was filled with flowers, a dazzling burst of color and smells. Alice hung up her apron and washed her hands in a bucket. By the exit door were two ornamental vases arranged with bouquets of flowers—a burst of white-and-yellow daisies, red poppies, golden brown-eyed susans and blue cornflowers. Alice asked if Tory could help by carrying one.

"It's beautiful," Tory said, and Alice gave her a little squeeze of thanks.

They carried the flowers out through the archway of the garden and walked down past the Brewery to the northern end of the Market. Crowds were beginning to gather on the grass slope below, not far from the red and yellow pennants of the East Caravan campground, where rows of benches were arranged in a wide arc. Cook fires were lit near the Dance Hall and fragrant smoke billowed into the sky.

Alice displayed the vases in alcoves on the brick columns at the end of the Market arcade, where an old standing fountain trickled. Everyone knew Alice and stopped to greet her, and welcomed Tory as well. Some people she vaguely remembered from the night before, but was hopeless with their names, though it didn't seem to bother them in the least.

Then the Bell Tower struck three and the townsfolk began to walk down and assemble on the Fair Grounds. She felt a little tap from behind and turned to see Sara's beaming smile, with Saki and Zeb and the boys in tow, Jace and Tec coming from further back. Tec's eyes met hers from a distance and he smiled.

Sara handed Tory her satchel bag with the dials inside. "You're going to need this!"

Books had been laid out on top of the benches, with the word *Ausbund* embossed on the leather-bound covers in a flowing gold script. At the bottom of the cover in smaller font was printed *Flood Town Press*. Many of the people in the audience were from the East Caravan, the men all dressed like the visitors she'd seen at Town Hall, in blue shirts, suspenders, straw hats, and beards shaved on the upper lip. The women wore starched white linen caps on their heads and long dresses.

Tec's family occupied one whole bench, with Tory at the end and Sara pressed close beside her. Everything settled down as people got into place. It was quiet for a long period, until a man stepped forward and announced, "Song 47". There was a rustling of pages as people opened their books to the hymn. Sara handed Tory a book opened to the correct page. The left hand side was printed in thick squiggly calligraphy that Tory, try as she might, could not make any sense of. The right column, however, was printed in clear English.

The congregation began to sing in a slow, measured chant, and it was impossible to tell what words they sang, or even what language it was in—definitely not English. Occasionally between stanzas a person would sing a brief higher pitched solo, almost as if in a plaintive cry.

As they sang, Tory read the lyrics to "Song 47" in English:

> *The winter cold, raw and unpleasant,*
> *Has turned itself, comes to an end,*
> *This brings man joy.*
> *The lark soars about, its song rings out*
> *With echoes of joy loudly, everywhere,*
> *Graciously does the sun shine.*
> *To us breaks forth the summer*

With pleasantness so sweet,
That all the fruits of the earth revive,
That man may partake of them.
Plants, leaves, and grass, in right proportion,
The trees show forth their blossoms,
The vines produce buds so beautiful,
Their fruit to yield.
The fields grow forth anew,
Showing us that summer is here.

After what seemed like a very long time, the song reached a conclusion. Then they started into a second song without announcing it, and nearly everyone sang along, without the hymnal, already familiar with the tune. Tory glanced at Sara with a questioning look, and Sara leaned over and whispered, "This is the *Lob Leid*. Song 131."

After that song finished, everyone grew quiet, and a man from the crowd came forward and read aloud a passage about how the Son of their God, Jesus, was tempted by His mortal enemy, Satan—first to turn stones to bread, to overcome His hunger, then from the top of a tall building, to jump and be saved by angels, and finally atop the summit of a mountain, to take dominion over everything He could see. Each time Jesus rejected Satan's offers.

The man spent a few minutes reflecting upon the passage and what it meant to them in their daily lives and as a community, and how Jesus had died to save them all. Then they sang another plaintive tune, and as the notes droned on, Tory hungrily smelled the cook fires. The sun had climbed high above the ridge and it was hot on the benches. *How long does this go on?* she wondered.

She glanced down the bench to see Tec singing devoutly along with everyone else. Religion of any kind was a foreign concept to Tory—little more than a curious historical fact, used in pod lessons to show how primitive humans had once been, like believing the Earth was flat and sat at the center of the universe. There was simply no equivalent on Mars.

The song ended, and as if by a silent signal, people stood up and began to disperse. A moment later, the Bell Tower burst into protracted ringing that echoed back and forth in the deep bowl of the valley. When the bell tones had finally faded, Bull Braun appeared at the top of the slope, standing by the fountain near the floral arrangements.

His voice boomed out, "Market is … OPEN!"

There was no rush to the stands and stores, and in fact most people carried their bench from the service over to tables in the Fair Grounds so they could eat first. Some of the congregation stayed behind and made their way down to the river, where the man who gave the sermon waded out and dipped a woman in a long white dress under the water. She staggered to shore and everyone clapped. Next a man also clad in a white gown was dunked.

The source of the sweet-smelling smoke was the stand operated by the Pig Club, which offered roast pork sandwiches with greens and sharp cheese on what looked to be whole loaves of bread, with a giant dollop of *German* potato salad on the side—easily enough for two or more people—all for the price of one half-dial. Tec bought two, and also remembered to pay his membership dues. "I'll take a quarter-portion today and the rest can be kept in storage," Tec said, and a person scribbled a ticket to that effect for him to take up to the Ice Cave.

Jace helped Tec carry the trays of food over to a table and Zeb cut the sandwiches with his pocket-knife. A band began to play on an outdoor grandstand next to the Dance Hall. Jasmyn was out in front, strumming her guitar and singing, and behind her was a rag-tag group of musicians on a drum kit, an upright bass, a muted trumpet, plus a strange keyboard instrument with a fan that billowed in and out, which Sara informed her was called an *accordion*. They played a mix of lively tunes, some *Blues* like Jasmyn had sung the night before, but also some folk music called *Polkas* that prompted many people to get up and dance.

Once they finished, Alice said she'd take the boys with her over to the garden stands, and Zeb excused himself to head back to the Forge. Tec mentioned that he and Tory were going up to Market Street, so he could help her purchase the things she needed.

"Wait! I can't allow this to continue!" Saki cried, putting her hands on her hips dramatically.

She addressed Tory, "There's simply no way I'm allowing Tec to pick out clothes for you. I'm coming along!"

Everyone but Tec laughed. Saki asked Tec's children if they would mind the stand—Sara nodded, excited, but Jace let out a groan.

Up on Market Street, the first store they entered sold leather goods. "Remember, we need practical outdoor gear," Tec said. "Nothing fancy or frilly."

They exited the store with a plain waxed leather traveling bag, exactly the same as Tec's—but also with a belt that sported a flashy silver buckle like Saki's, and soft buckskin leggings in a pale palomino color, with a decorative beaded-tassel fringe.

Next door at the tailor, woolen flannel shirts were made to order. While examining the rolls of fabric, Tec pointed to somber green and browns, but instead, with Saki's encouragement, Tory picked a bold plaid in orange and sky blue. As they took her measurements, the tailor mentioned, "We can have your order ready in a few days." Tec asked if it could be tomorrow, which surprised the tailor. "What's the rush?"

But her daughter called out from the back, "I can get it done, Mom!" Apparently, the orange-and-blue pattern was an original design of the girl's, and she was thrilled Tory was the first person to have chosen it.

Saki and Tory also picked out some underwear tops and bottoms, at which point Tec pretended to notice someone in the street and stepped outside. At the hat shop, Tory bought a wide straw hat with a leather cord and slider so it could attach under her chin if windy. At the cobbler, the soft boots Tory had seen in the window fit perfectly and she was able to walk out of the store in them. She smiled to herself, thinking of all the trouble the AIs put into those shoes, now left behind in the store for scrap.

They passed the bookshop, which had placard out front that read *Flood Town Press—Our Summer Catalog is Here.* Saki parted with them, having some of her own errands to run, and to check in on the twins.

"Tec Anders, my best customer!" the woman behind the counter exclaimed as they entered the shadowy store.

"We have three new books in our summer catalog," she announced. "For children, *The Wind in the Willows,* it's got a toad that drives a motor car. Sara will love it! Also a book of beautiful verse from the poet Emily Dickinson. And then the one we've worked on for some time and are very proud of—a history of the First American Revolution, called *1776.* In fact, it's by the same author as one of our very first prints here at Flood Town Press. Here, let me find a copy..."

The woman opened a door to the rear workshop, cluttered with trays of metal type, jars of black ink, brayers, screens, leather aprons, and at the center of it all, the printing press with its long handle and screw. Half-printed sheets were hanging in rafters to dry, and at another table were thread, glue, leather, and cardboard to bind a book together. She returned with a slim volume, slightly dusty, and handed it to Tory. Embossed on the cover was title *The Johnstown Flood.*

"It's yours. Required reading for any resident," she winked.

"Now Tec, as you know, the Courier departs for Steel Town tomorrow…" She went over to a list on the counter, dipped a pen in ink, ready to write. "What titles do you want to request from the Library?"

"You know, I've fallen behind on my reading," Tec said sheepishly, "I don't have any requests."

"Well, that's a first. I'm afraid the Librarian will think you have passed and send condolences!"

As they were exiting the bookstore, Tec remembered one last thing. "Sara wanted me to pass along a message. She likes the ducks on this year's dials, but would you consider a bear or a mountain lion for next year's?"

"Duly noted!"

By the time they were done outfitting Tory, she'd spent nearly all of her allotted dials—but even so, she realized people must have been giving her a discount by the way Tec and Saki exchanged glances any time a price was quoted.

Tec had some more business to conduct and took the small cart with him. A few of the things he needed could only be purchased from the East Caravan—glass jars in particular—but also wheat, which was delivered to the Grist Mill across the river to be ground into flour that townsfolk could purchase.

Tory stayed at the Anders stall along with Sara, relieving Jace, who immediately dashed toward the Dance Hall. A passing customer examined the jars of jam, and Sara said, "The two of us made that from a secret patch of wild strawberries up on the mountain!" The result was a sale, with a few cakes of Saki's soap thrown in as well.

The sun seemed to have raced across the sky and Market began to wind down. People began to close stalls, break down campsites, pack up carts and retrieve horses and donkeys from the stables. Canoes paddled away on the rivers.

Tec and Saki returned with the cart full of goods and the two boys hanging off the sides. Their stand had sold out of the jam and root beer, nearly all of the soap, most of Tec's remedies and a handful of his fishing flies. Tec counted up the dials they had earned. Even though they had spent quite a bit, they were leaving with a full cart and only a few less dials than they had come with. He split the proceeds evenly with Saki.

Just then Bull Braun appeared, walking up the center aisle of the Market. "Very sorry to interrupt you folks," he said, removing his hat. "But the Town Council wondered if they might have a word with you, Tory." The way he said it didn't sound like she had a choice.

"I'm coming too," Tec declared.

Bull led them across Market Street and into the beer garden behind the Brewery, to a corner table near the outside wall of the Kitchen Garden, where a rose-covered trellis glowed in the late sun. At the table were four old women playing cards, with glasses of beer in front of them and a small wick burning fragrant oil to keep biting insects away.

"Ladies, this is Tory Flood, our newest resident. Tory, allow me to introduce to you the Town Council," Bull said, and went around the table. Hetti was sitting up straight and proper, wearing owl-like glasses and a prim expression on her face, a shawl over her shoulders despite the warm weather. Ronni was across the table from her, with curly snow-white hair in an unkempt mop and glasses with matching white frames. In between the two sat Verna, slouched back in her chair, wearing a shapeless dress—almost a nightgown—in a bold floral print, gold bracelets on her wrist, smoking a thin cigar.

"... and I believe you are already acquainted with Alice," Bull said. Alice turned in her chair and looked up at Tory. She was smiling but had that same concerned look often seen in Tec's eyes.

Hetti sensed Tory's confusion and tried to be helpful. "Our tradition says the only requirement to stand for Town Council is that you are a grandmother."

"—and are still alive," Verna added.

Bull took the opportunity to excuse himself and headed directly over to the counter to get a beer.

"She's very tall and exotic, isn't she?" Ronni observed.

"Never thought I'd meet someone from the Belt Wall," Hetti said.

Verna interrupted them and said, "We've heard a lot of rumors. We're hoping you can help clear things up."

Tory retold her story, tactfully leaving out the part where Alice's grandson shot her. The old women listened politely. When Tory handed over the coded message, Hetti puzzled over it, turned it this way and that. "I can't make any sense of it!"

"I'm pretty sure whatever this means, it's a trick," Ronni declared after her examination. "Probably sent from Mars," she added.

Verna leaned forward and re-lit her cigar on the wick flame, took a few puffs. "So the message is for John Cornplanter of the Seneca? Interesting choice."

Hettie said, "Our Courier departs for Steel City tomorrow, and he has Free Passage. By treaty, he could carry the message all the way to the Seneca at Buckaloons—

Tory shook her head. "I've got to deliver the message myself."

"But why?" Ronni asked sharply.

"Because I said I would."

After a pause, begrudging nods around the table.

"So how do you propose getting there?" Ronni asked.

Tec interjected before Tory could answer—not that she had a good one. "Grant her a Writ of Passage. She can take a direct route and travel through the Treaty Hunting Grounds."

Ronnie said, "A-ha! Now we know why you were in such a hurry for her to be a resident."

"She has met all our requirements," Tec asserted. "And tell me, has there ever been a case where a resident was denied a Writ of Passage? This is a town—not a prison."

Verna smiled coyly at Tec, just a few ragged teeth left, her laugh a rasp. She glanced at Alice over her bifocals. "Always said your boy was too clever by half." Alice's jaw tightened.

"But how will she know the way through that wilderness?" Hetti asked. "There are no trails."

"I will travel with her. I know that country as well as anyone from back when I carried a Hunting Permit."

"But Tec, you are raising two children—on your own. You are the town healer. You have responsibilities here!" Hetti said.

"And where do you think he learned his craft?" Alice spoke for the first time. "I'm perfectly able to fill in for Tec. The Kitchen Garden is well looked-after, and these next moons are times of luxury, nothing to do but water and watch things grow. So I'll spend the summer out at the homestead, making medicine. It will be good for the little boys. And Sara can assist me."

Tec gave his mother a look of pure gratitude, then added, "Jace has shown he can make my rounds."

"I've heard about enough," Verna said, waving her cigar. "Set aside for the moment the notion of us permitting you to cross over the Treaty Hunting Grounds. The Wardens will see right through it. And please don't tell me you know how to evade the Wardens!"

Verna leaned forward, her elbows on the table, her forearms crossed in front of her, her bracelets clinking together. "I have a much bigger concern. Imagine what the Chief of Steel Town will think when he learns we bypassed him with this important message and went direct to the Seneca? No, Tec—your plan is reckless and will come crashing down on all of us."

Verna leaned back in her chair and took a deep draw on her cigar. "I have a different proposal. We *will* grant you a Writ of Passage—but only to Steel Town. The Chief employs a Scientist—ask *him* to decipher your message.   And if you can convince the Chief to grant you further passage to the Seneca—well then, you will have accomplished your objective. And broken no Treaties along the way."

Verna jabbed her cigar at them. "But think long and hard before you do anything that could anger the Seneca, OK?" She looked around the table. "I put it to the Council. Any objections?"

Nods from the other three.

She waved to Bull over at the bar. "Bull, a moment?" she called out. "Can you draw up a Writ for Tory and Tec for travel to Steel Town? And I'll send word ahead with our Courier so they know to expect them."

She turned back to Tec and Tory. "You can travel with our Agent who departs in a couple days for Salt. Give you time to get your family's affairs in order." Verna dismissed them with a flick of her hand. "Now go. I was in the middle of bidding five hearts to close out this rubber."

When they had left the beer garden and were a good distance away from anyone else, Tory spun around and confronted Tec angrily. "Why did you do that? I can take care of myself—I don't need your help!"

Tec put his hands out, palms up. "I have no doubt of that, Tory! I'm confident you're going to accomplish your mission, come hell or high water."

He paused. "It's not that."

He gently grasped her hands. "I want to come with you. I … don't want to lose you."

She pulled him close and whispered in his ear, "I don't want to lose you either."

Then she backed away a little and said, "From what everyone has said, there's a long and challenging journey ahead. We need to be focused, working together. And above all, trust each other."

She looked in his eyes, searching. "Do you trust me?"

Tec met her stare. "Yes."

PART TWO

———

REUNITE

9

Two days later the Anders family gathered at the docks to bid Tec and Tory farewell. The gray and gloomy morning matched the long expressions on faces.

Tec had been late in breaking the news to everyone. All were too tired after Market to broach the subject, and Tec was occupied the entire next day, holding his customary health clinic at Town Hall, examining the ailments and dispensing remedies and treatments for a long parade of townsfolk. Alice was tight-lipped, not giving any indication of the Town Council's decision.

Tory took long walks through town to stay out of the way. She crossed the bridge over the Little Conemaugh to see the various mills in action, read a few pages of her new book in the park, picked up her tailored shirts, which fit perfectly. She purchased a few more items Tec said they'd need: oilcloth tarps, ponchos, some rope, canteens, cast iron cooking pans. Even though she had only been in Flood Town a few days, the shape and contour of the surrounding hills had already grown familiar.

At the family dinner, Jace tried—unsuccessfully—to hide his reaction when hearing Tec and Tory would be away. Earlier he'd learned that Jasmyn would be staying in Flood Town until the West Barges arrived, which was at least another moon from now. There was little need for traveling musicians further east among the Amish in Lancaster. Jace could hardly believe his good fortune, not to have Tec's watchful eye over his every move.

Saki's initial frown of displeasure quickly gave way to resignation, knowing there was no way to talk her brother out of it. As Zeb listened to his mother-in-law explain how she would be taking the children out to the farm for the summer, like Jace, he had trouble concealing a smile—for the first time in years, he and Saki would have the house to themselves.

Sara pleaded to come along and pouted in anger when Tec gave her a flat "No," and sulked the whole evening—but this morning, as the fact they were actually departing sunk in, she began to sob uncontrollably.

When Tory heard they would be accompanied by an Agent, her blood ran cold. *Was that their word for Operative, the secret police?* But the Agent, whose name was Leo Brechtel, seemed harmless and looked as if he could be Tec's father, sporting a long white mustache and goatee, and tired bags under his eyes. He wore matching shirt, trousers and boots made from tanned buckskin, and greeted the small assemblage with a tip of his enormous floppy hat, the brim as wide as his shoulders. It was clear from his manner that he was ready to depart.

Hugs and kisses were exchanged. Zeb shyly offered a parting gift that he had made for Tory—a gleaming knife in a leather sheath. Tory felt the balanced weight, ran a finger along the sharp blade. "It's steel."

Alice took Tory by the hands and said, "When you're done, come back home."

Their gear was loaded into the hull of the canoe and lashed down under a tarp, while Leo paddled a solo kayak. Zeb and Jace cranked up the sluice gate of the canal and the pool slowly lowered, giving the strange impression that the family was ascending above them. When the pool level matched that of the river, the main gates were opened. As the boats entered the Stoney Creek, Sara sprinted ahead, across the bridge at the docks and through the Fair Grounds to the stone bridge at the Incline, running to the middle so that she could wave goodbye as they passed underneath.

At the confluence of the Conemaugh, Tory glanced back to see the small figure on the bridge, still waving.

Immediately downstream from the town, the stink was palpable as they passed the leather Tannery. The river curved west and on both sides the forested hills rose up and up. Eons ago, the river cleaved through this mountain ridge and over time cut a canyon over five hundred meters deep. This was but a wrinkle compared to the great *Valles Marineris* on Mars—but still, passing silently beneath the cliff-walls, she was impressed.

The river was murky green, the bottom not visible, the surface calm, the current steady. Leo was a man of few words, only speaking to point out some tricky section that lay ahead. The day became warm and muggy and they smeared Tec's lavender oil over any exposed skin to ward off clouds of insects. Tec brought the fishing poles and gear along and as they floated past some promising holes he was itching to make some casts, but they only stopped once, for a quick lunch, before continuing on.

The skies remained overcast with no sun, no way to tell if they were making progress, no map to reference or measure their speed, just the steady cadence of paddle strokes and the endless series of ridge tops above them. By the end of the day, as the gloom deepened, they came to a horseshoe loop in the river encircled by high hills where a set of houses stood above the floodline. Tory wasn't sure if this was the homestead of a family named Blair, or a village of the same name, and was too tired to care.

A barbeque had been prepared in anticipation of the Agent arriving from Flood Town. Everyone dined on picnic tables by lantern light.

Fireflies flickered across the bottomlands, and the trill of frogs was deafening. Tory's arms felt so leaden from all the canoeing that she could barely lift her fork to her mouth. Tents were pitched on high ground and Tory fell asleep the moment she laid down on the bedroll, totally exhausted.

She was awakened by the patter of raindrops on the tent canvas. If possible the weather was even gloomier this morning, fog hanging above the river channel and a damp chill in the air. They donned ponchos, ate a cold breakfast of leftovers, expressed thanks and made payment for the hospitality they had been shown, one dial per person, then shoved off and continued downstream.

A cold wind gusted up the valley from the west, and the pale green underside of the leaves fluttered in the breeze. The rain was sporadic at first but soon became steady and increased in intensity until it was a full downpour. Their ponchos were oilcloth, which provided some protection at first, but every paddle stroke, every crease in the fabric, was exploited by rivulets of water, until the ponchos were of no use anymore and they were soaked.

This continued all day, and Tory felt certain they would have to stop, construct a shelter, a fire to dry out—but Leo continued to paddle onward methodically, unphased by the weather, his ridiculous hat now showing its worth, acting as an umbrella. But after a time, he was completely drenched too.

As if urging himself on, Leo said, "Got to stay ahead of any high water."

The river followed a meandering path, winding snakelike through the mountains, in some places nearly looping back upon itself, ten kilometers traveled by river to advance one kilometer westward by land. Daylight began to fade like a curtain being drawn down, and still they pressed on.

Finally, in the very last moments of twilight before everything plunged into inky blackness, they rounded a bend and a stone bridge lit with lanterns appeared. A wooden walkway crossed the marshy lowland and terminated at the base of a bluff, atop which sat a stately house with lights gleaming in all the windows. Tory had never seen anything so welcome in her life.

The Inn was called "Salt Treaty House". On the front porch, there were two main doors, and Leo was deliberate in entering through the one on the right, which had a little sign above the lintel that read *Flood*. The other door read *Steel*.

Inside the main parlor, the innkeeper and her two grown daughters, both in their twenties, were waiting to greet them. There didn't appear to be any other guests, or perhaps they had already turned in for the night. Chairs were arranged in front of a roaring fire in the center hearth, crocks of steaming chicken noodle soup were promptly brought out from the kitchen, and no concern was given that the travelers' wet clothes dripped puddles onto the polished wooden floors.

The women doted on Leo as if he were a favorite uncle, hung on Tec's every word as he described their miserable journey—but all three shot cold looks over at Tory. After eating, Leo downed a single dram of whiskey, then stood stiffly and bid all a good night. In the rear of the parlor were a twin pair of staircases and he slowly ascended the one on the right to the room reserved for him.

The two daughters supplied Tec and Tory with umbrellas and then, carrying their own plus hooded lanterns, led them out a side door, through a small walled garden and out the gate on the other side, where a cobbled trail led up into a dark forest of hemlock pines. A series of tiny log cabins were arranged along the path, Tec getting the first and Tory the second, well out of sight from the Inn. The young women left the lanterns behind, wished them a good night, and headed back in the dark, giggling as they went.

The log cabin was a single room with a bed, table and two chairs, and something Tory hadn't seen before, a cast iron stove with a pipe chimney, standing on legs in the corner. A pile of dry firewood and some kindling had been provided in a basket alongside. As she knelt and opened the front grate of the stove to get a fire going, there was a soft knock at the door and Tec entered.

"You read my mind," he said.

Even with a fire , the cold damp of the cabin remained, and to her surprise, she was shivering. From somewhere, Tec produced a small flask and sat down at the table. "This will work much faster." He took a nip and offered it to her. "I know you had a bad time with whiskey on your way to Ninety-Three. But just take little sips."

The liquid felt like fire in her throat going down and she grimaced, but then a warm glow began to spread outward from her chest. She took another drink, then asked, "What was that all about? The way they were looking at me."

He chuckled. "Oh, I figure it has something to do with the innkeeper being a widow, and both her daughters at marrying age, and I'm ... well, in their eyes, I'm an eligible bachelor ..."

He took another sip. "And here you are."

The two sat in silence for a while, the fire popping in the stove, rain drumming on the roof shingles, the flask of whiskey sitting untouched on the table between them. Finally Tec yawned and stood up, stretching his arms dramatically. "Well, I think I'm going to turn in for the night."

He opened the door and was headed out into the rain when Tory called out to him. He turned to find her standing near the bed, unbuttoning her shirt.

"Don't go," she said.

The following day saw little improvement in the gloomy weather, with on-and-off periods of cold rain. Heavy drips from the hemlock boughs plucked against the roof of the log cabin like falling pebbles.

Leo departed early in the day to visit family and acquaintances at the nearby Salt Wells, so named because of their high-saline water, which was pumped up to the surface and then boiled down in vats to produce a residue of pure salt crystals. Leo asked if they wanted to accompany him, and while the thought of seeing the operation interested her, going back out in the weather did not.

Tec decided to try his luck on the small feeder streams in the valley, swollen but still fishable. He asked if Tory would like to join him and got a similar response.

So Tory stayed curled up in bed for most of the day, reading her book and dozing off from time to time, only getting up to add more wood to the stove, and peek out the front door at the skies. Once she ventured to the Inn to get a pot of tea and some freshly baked biscuits, with butter and strawberry jam. She gasped when seeing the jar—it was the very same batch she and Sara had made and sold at Market! This helped break the ice with the innkeeper's younger daughter, who proceeded to take Tory's arm and lead her on an impromptu walk through the village.

It was a brief tour. The village of Salt was not much to speak of, consisting of the Inn, a boathouse and stables, a stone warehouse filled with kegs of salt, and a few homes. The village was located a short distance downstream from where the smaller Loyalhanna Creek flowed into the Conemaugh. For some reason Tory couldn't quite understand, from this point onward the river changed names and was called the

Kiski. With all the rain, the river had turned muddy brown and risen considerably.

Tec returned happy from his expedition with a bunch of trout, including one monster whose head and tail draped out over the edge of the wicker fishing basket. Tec donated the catch to the kitchen, and upon returning to the cabin and finding her still in bed, promptly crawled in with her.

Later in the afternoon there was commotion at the Inn, as the Agent from Steel Town arrived from the west, traveling on foot across the bridge, with five other companions. Confusion broke out as the Agent was not the older man the innkeeper was expecting, who had been coming here for many winters, but instead a young woman. The most striking thing about her was the Native-style haircut she sported, shaved close on the sides with a topknot dyed bright red. Her ears were pierced in multiple locations with silver hoops, and she wore thick boxy glasses. But once she removed her traveling cloak, her outfit underneath was identical to Leo's, head-to-toe buckskin.

She introduced herself as Katya Red Clay. Even with the requisite signed and wax-sealed letters from the Chief of Steel Town that established her as the town's Agent, the innkeeper remained skeptical, and a crowd of villagers gathered on the porch of the Inn. But when Katya passed through the left entrance, under the *Steel* sign, almost as if by habit, there were nods all around.

The five travelers were a mix of people—a married couple with a boy about Sara's age headed to Flood Town, dressed head to toe in black clothing, the man and boy both wearing black *fedora* hats with curly ringlets hanging down by their ears, the man with a long beard, the woman with a scarf tied over her hair. There were also two Amish craftsmen who were journeying onward to Lancaster. They all traveled under Writs of Passage like Tec and Tory, and were shown to the other log cabins behind the Inn.

By evening, the skies finally cleared and a beautiful golden light washed across the valley, lighting up the receding clouds in shades of orange, purple and pink. Leo returned with an entourage of salt miners, and the Inn quickly became a bustling place.

A bell rang summoning everyone to dinner. In the dining room, a long table had been placed in the exact center, the other tables pushed back against the walls to provide a buffer of space. The center table was covered with a crisp tablecloth, set with glass candlesticks, silver cutlery and fine plates. There were only two chairs at the table at opposite ends, facing each other.

The room grew quiet as the two Agents descended the staircases, Leo on the right and Katya on the left, mirroring each other at an even, deliberate pace. Each wore a belt of *wampum* around their waist, decorated with intricate beaded patterns. As they sat down at the table, the bell chimed again.

Large *steins* of beer were brought to them, baskets of fresh bread and butter, and then platters of food. One featured the giant trout Tec had caught earlier, split and deboned and steaming, another held a roasted beef brisket stewed with carrots, potatoes and green peas. A bowl of salt was placed in the middle of the table, and each took a pinch and sprinkled it over their meat and fish. Katya and Leo raised their mugs and the assembly all cheered "*Prost!*"

The room burst into loud conversation as the rest of the guests were served. It was so crowded, additional picnic tables had to be set up on the front porch. Tec and Tory had a seat by a window that looked down toward the surging river. That attracted Tec's attention, while Tory stole glances over at the center table. She was not the only one, as nearly everyone else was curious what the two Agents were discussing.

Katya spoke easily, gesturing freely with her hands, while Leo listened, methodically chewing his meal. Katya became even more animated in the story she was telling, her eyes twinkling behind the frames of her glasses. Her enthusiasm was infectious, bringing Leo out of his shell and getting a few chuckles even from him. As the innkeeper's daughters came out to serve the table, Katya peppered them with questions—and compliments that made them blush. From time to time, she glanced over at Tory, and one time when their eyes met, Katya winked.

After dinner had been cleared away, the villagers and travelers excused themselves to the parlor where a fire was roaring, or drifted out to the front porch to take in the sunset, happy to see clear skies after all the rain. The two Agents were left alone in the dining room to conduct business, but the doors remained open so it was easy to see their discussion. People did their best not to stare.

Each of the Agents produced long handwritten lists on sheafs of paper which they placed at their elbow to reference as they bartered. At first it seemed there was a lot of agreement, heads nodding, check marks being tallied. But at some point they reached an impasse, and here Leo became taciturn once again, crossing his arms over his chest, and for the first time Katya's beaming smile vanished into a hard straight line. They sat and stared at each other across the table for what seemed like a long time.

Then Katya produced a long pipe hanging from her belt and suggested they step outside for a smoke. They exited the side door into the falling dusk, two shadows wandering through the walled garden together, with the occasional spark of embers from the pipe.

Soon they returned, Katya's hand on Leo's elbow, both laughing. At the table they sat and briefly spoke a few words, then stood again, made a point of walking around the table, to meet halfway and shake hands. Everyone clapped and cheered as the two emerged into the parlor, their business completed for another cycle. The West Barges would travel up river once again.

The innkeeper's daughters brought around trays of beer, and once again mugs were raised and the salute *"Prost!"* rang out. Katya made her way over to Tec and Tory. "Looks like we're going to be spending some time together!" she smiled.

Then, seeing the blank look on Tory's face, continued, "I'm going to escort you the rest of the way back to Steel Town. End of the line for old Leo, though I've left him with a nice set of traveling companions."

"You came over land?" Tec asked.

Katya nodded. "Because of the rain. If it were just me and my kayak? Hey, no problem. But we've got some... um... novice canoeists along as you've noticed. We'd still be a week away! What a miserable trek though." She took a gulp of beer and wiped the foam from her lip with the back of her hand. "Headed downstream, that's different story, we can ride the flood crest and be in Steel Town in a couple days. If you're up to it, of course."

"We're up to it," Tec said.

"I'm sure you are!" Katya once again winked at Tory.

"Probably worth going to bed early tonight," she said, patting Tec on the arm. "Lots of river ahead. So I'll see you both bright and early, OK?"

Katya raised her mug and clinked it against theirs. "Cheers!"

Then she excused herself and headed in the direction of the innkeeper's older daughter, who was across the room mingling with the guests.

As night fell and the party continued, kerosene lanterns were lit out on the front porch. Someone brought out a fiddle and another person played percussion with a pair of spoons. Songs were sung loudly, more beer was poured. Tory tugged Tec by the hand and, thinking no one noticed, the two snuck away together into the darkness.

The journey downriver from Salt was harrowing, the Kiski River at flood stage, twisting and thrashing like a giant snake. In the bow of the canoe, Tory's job was to always be on the lookout for logs and stumps, as well as the tell-tale crest waves of submerged boulders. Tec handled the canoe competently as always, but was nothing compared to Katya, who'd been provided a beaten-up kayak from the boathouse at Salt, yet still danced like a water bug across the raging river, turning on a dime, dashing forward to scout ahead.

Unlike Leo, Katya was a talker. Whenever there was a straight stretch she paced herself alongside the canoe and chatted.

"I'm sure you're asking how someone as youthful and attractive as me—at least, compared to dear old Leo—ended up as an Agent of Steel Town? Well, my mom is from Steel Town, and my dad is Seneca. Every summer we trekked north up the Allegheny to camp with my father's people at Chautauqua. I can see every bend in that river when I close my eyes. I know the Seneca well and their ways, was raised in the Native Revival Church, with *Creator Sets Free* and the *Good Story.*" Seeing Tory's confused look, she clarified, "Jesus and the Gospels."

Not much better.

Katya continued, "I know the Chief took a chance picking me as his Agent—but I think he likes my bargaining style, how I handle the river trade. And I'm pretty good dealing with the Pirates, too." She flashed a big smile. "Yeah, there are Pirates."

"Anyways, the Agent who usually handles trade with Flood Town, the arthritis in his hip got too bad this winter, so the Chief expanded my territory. My first trip to Salt," she laughed, "You witnessed a little piece of history!"

Also unlike Leo, she stopped and let Tec do some fishing along the way. While Tec was out casting, Katya started up a small cook-fire. As she prepared lunch, she turned to Tory and casually said, "So, about John Cornplanter…"

Tory stared back at her.

"Hey, if you're going to deliver a secret message to anyone, I'd say he's a good choice."

"Why do you say that?"

"There have been lots of wise men—and women—who have held the name Cornplanter down through the ages. Of course, the wise Preacher who spoke of the Simple Path so many winters ago. But I never met any of those ancestors. John Cornplanter, I've met. He's a man of peace. He knows when to push, when to compromise, and when to be quiet. Honestly, I learned a lot of my trading style from him. And he's not jealous of the power of the Seneca Nation—if anything, he wants to share its peace and prosperity. He talks a lot about a broader union of peoples, beyond just trade …"

Katya looked Tory in the eyes. "But he's no fool. Neither is my boss, the Chief of Steel Town. So if this message from the Belt Wall is some kind of trick, trust me, they will see through it."

By that evening they reached Free Port, a village located at the junction of the Kiski and the much larger Allegheny, marking the northern extent of Steel Town. They slept in a dormitory-style longhouse with a bunch of other boatsmen who worked on the river. Tory's cot was between Tec on one side and Katya on the other, who snored when she lay on her back.

Tory couldn't sleep. For the thousandth time, she turned over in her mind the brief message fragment the AIs had provided her in advance.

LZ: SE 25km, T-8h.

"*LZ*" stood for the landing zone. Presumably a drone shuttle would be sent to extract her after her mission was complete. "*SE 25km*" was southeast 25 kilos ... *from where?* And "*T-8h*," that signified eight hours *before.* So there had to be additional information in the encoded message she carried, a date and time and location, something that would snap it all together to make sense.

Did I already miss the window? Her gut said no—given the distances involved, the AIs had to assume it would take time for her to locate John Cornplanter.

And what about Katya? Their little chat was clearly meant to put Tory on notice. And as for who's being fooled ....

Maybe it's me.

The next morning brought bright and clear summer weather, and the remaining journey down the Allegheny was scenic, but uneventful. Coming out of the highlands, the surrounding hills weren't nearly as imposing and canyon-like, and the river flowed broad and wide. On the river banks were docks, houses, small farms. As they passed long flat-bottomed barges being poled up and downstream. Katya made a point to wave hello to each one, and all hollered back.

In the distance, Tory saw a great bridge straddling the river, columns of smoke rising above the hills, the forest canopy punctuated here and there with church steeples. *Steel Town.*

Despite the cheerful sun, the pastoral landscape, she couldn't shake a sense of dread about what lay ahead.

No turning back now.

10

During her training, in between endless op sims, the AIs provided Taurii with a curated playlist of old Earth vids from before the Severance, stuff that had been purged for hundreds of years, with obscure titles like *Gone With The Wind*, *1917*, *Schindler's List*, *Apocalypse Now*. All were stories about human conflict, suffering and war, presented to her by the AIs with a not-so-subtle undertone of, "See why we had to start over?"

But they also wanted Taurii to be prepared, as a biological female, for the inter-relationship of the sexes among humans, and so made her watch an epic saga called *Friends*. She suspected this was an inside joke among the AIs. But she had nothing but time to kill, holed up in a luxury suite in the Founder's Club, forbidden to leave except for off-hour meals, gym and pool time. Beyond the characters and storyline and jokes, little of which she understood, she was fascinated with the glimpses of a pre-Severance American city it provided—the taxicabs, the apartment buildings, the skyscrapers.

Steel Town must have once had been a great city—maybe only a fraction of the size of *Manhattan*—but still, the ruins were evident everywhere. Skyscrapers built in concrete and glass had long since collapsed into heaps, like the burial mound atop the Flood Town Incline, but ten times the size. Brick buildings decomposed from the roofs downward and jutted up here and there like worn red molars. An enormous triangular building constructed entirely of steel was cracked and twisted down to earth, like a giant bent knee, its rusted trellises covered in wild grapevines. There was one structure among the ruins that remained intact, a square granite tower which rose above the trees—similar to the Bell Tower in Flood Town, but bone-colored instead of brick red.

On the left bank, they passed a series of covered arcades identical to the Market in Flood Town. Here they navigated around crumbling stone piers where bridges had once spanned. Now only one remained—a steel suspension bridge with two stately arched towers. As they passed beneath, Tory paid special attention to the curved cables, formed of linked eye-bars, bolted together like a gear-chain—the most advanced engineering she had seen so far. The bridge had been refurbished with new steel and gleamed with yellow paint.

"Clemente Bridge," Katya said. "Isn't she beautiful?"

Tec was skeptical. "What do you need a bridge that size for?"

Downriver, two colossal structures dominated the right bank, built-up earthen embankments encircling bowl-shaped interiors—one smaller and wedge-shaped, the other a long rectangle, both open on the side facing the riverfront. Katya made a point of paddling past so they could see the people working inside, dressed in the recognizable Amish style. Terraced gardens climbed the interior side-slopes, and rows of corn grew in the fields in the center.

"Sporting games were once played here," Katya said. "Those terraces were completely filled with spectators, I'm told."

Tory recalled the roar of the crowds at Founders' Arena on Nubai, one of her favorite places, where she could easily blend into the mass of people, lose herself in the football matches, the Olympic events, thrilling tests of who could push genetic enhancement the furthest.

Tec expressed disbelief, "All the people of the Ten Towns could fit inside."

The Allegheny joined another river of equal size called the *Mon*. Again, out of some tradition Tory didn't understand, the combined river was given a new name, the *Ohio*. At the traingle formed by the two rivers, trees had been cleared for an open grassy park. Boats were out everywhere—barges, small sailboats, canoes and kayaks.

Just then a loud whistle blew, and from further down the Ohio, a column of white smoke approached. A long flat-bottomed boat rounded the bend, with a raised deck, two smoke-stacks standing like columns, and a large cylindrical paddle-wheel churning. The craft made steady progress upriver against the current. As it steamed past, it created a huge wake that threatened to capsize the canoe. The steamboat turned into the channel of the Mon River, and after the waves subsided, Katya followed behind.

The color of the river changed from the muddy brown of the Allegheny to a murky emerald at the mouth of the Mon. Another steel bridge spanned the Mon, of a different design than the Clemente bridge, featuring a matched pair of curved trusses that looked like a pointy figure 8 on its side, with ornate portals like bookends on either end.

"We believe the Smithfield Bridge is one the oldest of all the bridges," Katya said. "And it's survived the longest."

The steamboat docked just downriver from the bridge on the south bank, the bow section folding down, creating a ramp to the shore. Here the hillside thrust up like a wall, and just like in Flood Town, an incline railroad climbed the steep slope. In fact, everything about the landscape of Steel Town—the confluence of rivers, the encircling hills—reminded her of Flood Town, just magnified in scale.

They tied up at docks along the north bank, across the bridge from the steamboat. Katya spied a couple of children skipping rocks nearby and called out, "Can you please run up, see if the Chief is in and let him know we're coming?" The children eagerly dashed off, happy to be sent on a mission by an Agent of Steel Town.

A cobbled path led up the hill into the forest, quiet and peaceful, no houses or shops in sight, just birdsong, dappled sunlight through the canopy, and the ruins of the city lurking among the trees. They passed a few people headed in the opposite direction who recognized Katya and said hello.

At the crest of the small hill, the forest opened up into a wide clearing, at the center of which stood a massive castle-like building, five stories tall, constructed from blocks of granite, with square turrets at the corners, arched windows, and a steeply gabled roof. The main feature was the central tower, visible from the river, rising about a hundred meters tall. To the rear, another fortress-type stone building squatted, connected to the main building for some reason by an arched bridge high above the ground.

In the clearing, a number of tarnished bronze statues were arranged to create a garden—a man with thick glasses seated on a rock smoking a cigar, another man crossing his legs as if changing his shoes, a life-like panther cat bearing its fangs, and a few men in jumpsuit-like uniforms swinging clubs. Near the entrance two men were depicted, one with a shaved head and feathered topknot, carrying a pipe like Katya's, kneeling next to a seated man with long hair in a pigtail, buttoned vest and great cloak, both men leaning in close, staring each other eye to eye, their knuckles just grazing.

"The Seneca Chief Guyasuta and George Washington," Katya remarked. Tory had no idea who Guyasuta was, but she recalled the name Washington vaguely from pod lessons, a slave-holder and leader of a rebel faction during the early days of America.

162

Just then the children emerged from the building and sprinted past them, yelling, "He's there! But he said you'd better hurry, he's got to head out on *Official Business*."

Katya laughed, then seeing their puzzled looks, added, "That's the name of his fishing boat."

The entrance at the base of the tower resembled the dimly-lit tunnels of a medieval dungeon, with arched ceilings and massive stone columns. Katya led them up a central stairwell to a grand foyer, where murals were painted in the arches—a stern woman seated on a throne with a sword, entitled *Justice*, shirtless workers wrestling a steel beam, called *Industry*, and a red-coated soldier shaking hands with a frontiers-man dressed head-to-toe in buckskin just like the Agents, with some Native people in feathered headdresses watching solemnly, captioned *Fort Duquesne*.

Their footsteps echoed, there were no people around, the building seemingly deserted. Katya led them down a long corridor lined with windows that overlooked a center courtyard, where a fountain splashed. They entered a large audience room. At the far end, a raised bank of seven leather chairs were arranged behind a curved wooden panel.

Mounted on a shelf behind the chairs were ten identical shiny silver statues, each with a pyramid-like stand crowned by a strange spheroid shape—a laced sports ball of some kind—with the letters *NFL* embossed on the front. Two documents printed on large sheets of paper were framed on either side of the trophy shelf—one was the now-familiar False and Simple Paths, and the other was a text Tory didn't recognize that began "*In Congress, July 4, 1776...*"

More obscure dates.

Katya peeked her head through a side door and whistled loudly. "Heya, Chief! You here?"

"On my way!" a deep booming voice called back.

A moment later a man entered the room, striking in appearance with his clean-shaven head and thick wiry beard, muscles bulging underneath the simple black T-shirt he was wearing, a steel chain around his neck with a cross-shaped pendant, and a pair of reading glasses tucked into his shirt collar.

His broad smile gleamed as he greeted Katya. "I trust your journey was fruitful."

"Very much so," Katya said. "And let me introduce Tec Anders and Tory Flood, from Flood Town. Here are their Writs of Passage…"

He waved the documents aside. "Let's dispense with the pomp and circumstance. Welcome to Steel Town. I'm the Chief here." He made direct eye contact with both of them as he shook their hands, and his grip was like an iron vise.

"The Courier brought this a few days ago," the Chief said. He produced a letter from the rear pocket of his blue jeans, unfolded his reading glasses. As he scanned over the florid cursive handwriting, he chuckled. "That Verna, she certainly has a way with words."

He peered at Tory over the rim of his glasses. "So I guess you're my problem now."

Tec, who had been agitated ever since they had arrived, spoke up. "Seems to me you have bigger problems here than Tory." He pointed over to the framed print of the False and Simple Paths. "We saw the bridge, the steamboat, this palace. Soon you'll be changing the name to Steel *City!*"

The Chief slowly removed his reading glasses and tucked them back into his collar. "Mr. Anders, I don't know you, and you've just set foot in my town." He fixed Tec with a fierce stare, but then relaxed and smiled. "But I appreciate your candor. And your concerns. I'm here to reassure you, there are no closer adherents to the Simple Path than the humble residents of Steel Town."

"How can you say that with steamboats running on the rivers? Next you'll be building a railroad."

"The inclines run on rails. I seem to recall one operating in Flood Town ... and I'd hardly call *steam* an advanced technology."

Tec was caught off guard by that reply, and sputtered "But what about the giant steel bridge? What purpose could it possibly serve other than *industrial?*"

"Civic pride," the Chief responded, but seeing Tec's blank reaction, he changed tack, "It's important to realize Steel Town is not a singular 'town', in fact its an assembly of seven *boroughs*, scattered across the surrounding hills and valleys."

He ticked them off on his fingers, "The Orthodox Jews of Squirrel Hill ... the Catholics of Polish Hill ... the Native Revival out in Liberty ... the Black Baptists—my own people—in Oak Land ... our brethren the Amish over on the North Shore ... plus the shopkeepers and artisans in Shady Side ... and the mill workers atop Mount Washington. About five thousand souls in total. Not to mention all the residents in the countryside villages who come to our Market."

He gestured to the semi-circle of chairs. "The leaders of each borough are represented at this council table. Yes, I've been elected the Chief across all the boroughs, which is a great honor. But we make no decisions here that aren't unanimous."

The Chief continued, "Take this building—this *palace* as you've aptly described it. In ancient times it served as a court of *Law*. Yes, this entire building, all the floors and *courtrooms*, the grand columns and stately arches, the imposing tower—all of this was built for one purpose—to enforce the Law. Most of the time, in favor of the rich men who ran the city, with names like Carnegie and Mellon and Frick—"

"The men behind the Johnstown Flood!" Tory burst out, before she could check herself.

"Very astute, Ms. Flood," the Chief nodded. "Also worth noting, the fortress-like building located directly to the rear of us? That was a prison. They called the bridge from here to there, *The Bridge of Sighs*. Now that tells you something. A society so broken they needed all … *this*."

He gestured around with his arms. "So what's missing from this building now? That's right—people. It's all but empty. We use the prison out back as a stable and a storehouse. We have no *bureaucracy*," the Chief said proudly, then pointed to the sign listing the elements of the Simple Path. "But trust me, we do achieve *consent*."

"Why even keep this building if it serves no purpose?" Tec said, confused.

"This building is constructed entirely of granite blocks and steel. If you've looked around, about the only thing left standing! So I think she's made herself clear on whether she's staying or going," the Chief laughed.

"But in seriousness," he said. "Our ancestors, the people who clung to these river valleys through the darkest ages, they wanted to preserve things—not for usefulness alone, but for their beauty. To remind them-selves what we as a people were capable of. And ultimately, a reminder of how the False Paths led to ruin. Flood Town does the much same thing with the Memorial at Ninety-Three, if I'm not mistaken."

That point struck home with Tec. "The steel bridge?" he asked weakly, the fight going out of him.

"About ten winters ago, the Chief that preceded me and the Council voted on refurbishing the Clemente Bridge. It was in tatters. We were just recovering the Bessemer process for producing steel, and wanted to demonstrate to ourselves we could accomplish what the ancients had done. Volunteers from every borough worked together on it."

The Chief became animated. "Now the Clemente Bridge *does* serve a purpose—it's strong enough to withstand all but a biblical flood, and thus provides a vital connection to the terraced gardens on the North Shore, our main food supply. You may come from Flood Town, but remember we are downstream from you all. We know about floods."

He paused. "But I'd be lying if I didn't say its beautiful to look at."

Katya added, "The Chief's next project is to build a fountain at Point Park, like they had in ancient times."

The Chief nodded. "Katya, I know the discussion between Agents is held in confidence. But would you mind letting our visitors know about the proposal you made to Flood Town?"

"OK. So up until recently, we'd make batches of gunpowder using bat guano from deep caves—but it was hard to find and small quantities at that. Krystol, the scientist, has shown us how to mix manure and urine and straw to produce *saltpeter*—one of the main ingredients for gunpowder—"

That got Tec animated once again. "A scientist making gunpowder! What could possibly go wrong? And it's not surprising to hear his solution involves shit."

The Chief raised a calming hand. "Please continue, Katya. Tell Mr. Anders the rest."

"Sure thing, boss. So what I told Leo, we're offering to share this craft with Flood Town, so that gunpowder could be reliably made locally, and you wouldn't be reliant on the West Barges."

Tec was astonished. "You mean, you're going to give the recipe away? What am I missing here?"

The Chief said, "We all know that gunpowder is a necessity if you are a homesteader, or have a Hunting Permit. But given the … historical precedent … we also think its important that no town or people has this technique all to themselves. I'm offering the same to the other

Towns, and the Seneca too. Well, I'm not bothering to ask our brethren in Lancaster, that will fall on deaf ears!"

"But *why*?" Tec asked.

"We believe the best way to avoid armies is if everyone is armed."

Tory, who had been listening to all this closely, suddenly spoke up. "But what about the Victorians and their kitchen gardens?" They all looked at her as if she were speaking in tongues.

She tried to paraphrase Alice in the glass house, "The Victorian gardeners, their intentions were good, they just wanted to grow the sweetest melon. But future generations had no qualms using their discovery, genetics, for completely different purposes." *If only you could see the Founders—Omega's see-though skin, Delta's tank, Alpha's forked tongue.*

Tec was impatient, "Well this has been very enlightening. But you know why we're here. To see if your *Scientist* can decipher the message Tory is carrying. So can we meet him?"

"I have an idea," the Chief said. "How about you and I head down to the river, and do some fishing. And Katya, you can take Tory over to see Krystol."

"Wait, I'm coming along too—" Tec said, and Tory unconsciously reached out and took Tec's hand, something that didn't escape the notice of the other two.

"Tec, maybe it's for the best," she said.

Tec sighed deeply, then turned to the Chief. "What kind of fishing?"

The Chief's smile beamed. "Catfish, carp, bass. And I heard that some fishermen below the Point spotted a sturgeon as long as a barge! C'mon, let me show you my secret escape route …"

Tec started to follow him, then exclaimed, "Hey, wait! How did you know I like to fish?" He looked suspiciously at Katya and the Chief, as if they had some kind of secret language between them.

The Chief took out the letter from Verna again, donned his reading glasses, and cleared his throat. *"If Tec becomes a pain in the ass, offer to take him fishing. Seems to help him work out most of his problems."*

Tec could not argue with that.

On the way back down the ornate staircase Katya and Tory passed two out-of-breath teenaged boys on their way up, who gasped, "River boat's arrived from Falls-of-the-Ohio!" Outside the afternoon had become hot and steamy, even more pronounced after exiting the cave-like interior of the Courthouse. As they were halfway down the hill, the bells atop the tower began ringing, and within a few moments, accompanying bells rang out across the valley, spreading outward in a slow wave.

A parade of one-wheeled carts crossed the Smithfield Bridge, some pushed by hand, some pulled by horses, laden with cargo from the steamboat, heading toward the storehouse in the old prison. Tory spied goods that weren't offered at the Flood Town Market—dried tobacco, rolls of indigo-dyed denim, sacks of rice, even miniature citrus trees standing in pots.

On the far side of the bridge, a wide cobbled road followed the base of a steep hill called Mount Washington. Upriver about a kilometer away, plumes of dark smoke rose into the sky from a series of mills along the south bank. A third bridge crossed the Mon, a basic design, with bracket-shaped trusses resting atop brick piers. Flat-bottomed barges with pole men at the bow and stern accessed a canal that ran behind the mills, where they unloaded coal, shredded tires, and salvaged scraps of iron and steel. Water-wheels tumbled in the steady current.

In the workshops, rubber was cooked down in vats, sheets of metal were crimped into canning lids, iron and steel were hammered into tools. The largest factory was at the end of the row, its big barn doors open.

"Oh, they are making steel today!" Katya said. "Let's stop and take a look."

Inside was a cavernous space, with high ceilings and a skylight. About twenty men were working, clad in thick leather aprons but no shirts because of the tremendous heat. A water wheel powered billows, which in turn supplied hot air to the blast furnaces, where scrap iron, coal and lime were melted down together. A glowing orange stream of molten iron poured into a crucible suspended by heavy chains, which the workmen emptied into a second furnace, a big metal egg with a cone shaped opening at the top. Large gears cranked the egg upright, more air was pumped in—and suddenly a spectacular multicolored plume of flame and sparks burst out of the top cone.

Some of the millworkers spotted them in the doorway and sauntered over. Katya seemed to know them all. The younger men circled around Tory, wondering how long she would be in town, would she be going to Market the day after next? Katya tried to shift their attention by asking if they had seen the Scientist around. They thought he might be over at the gunpowder mill.

One of the old-timers said, "Once upon a time, there were six giant blast furnaces over on the north side of the Mon, maybe ten times the size of the one we have here." He pointed to the egg-shaped furnace, "And there were big Bessemers over here on the South Side. You saw how we carried the molten iron from the furnace to the converter in that bucket? Well they would run rail cars across that bridge out there, all day and night. That's why it's called the Hot Metal Bridge."

When the burn-off was finished, the men headed back to work. The egg was tipped once again and liquid steel poured out. Still-glowing ingots were pushed by handcart over to the Forge next door, others were left to cool and be stacked for shipment by barge.

Katya tapped Tory's elbow and they continued onward, crossed a footbridge over the canal, out of sight of the row of mills. At the base of a rock cliff, draped in shadow, a small stone mill and water wheel operated. A pair of teenaged boys wearing neckerchiefs as masks raked a mix of straw, manure and urine under a covered pavillion. Even from a distance the smell was sharp and pungent.

"No fire of any kind from this point on," Katya warned.

She asked the masked teens if Krystol were around, and they pointed toward the mill. As they turned, there was a figure standing in the doorway watching them. He was dressed in drab canvas pants cut off at the knee, exposing his calves and feet in open-toed sandals, and a blousy loose shirt that did little to conceal his bulging belly. His straw hat was similar to those of the Amish, but more angular and not as wide-brimmed. His skin was pale, his face puffy, and as they approached, his thin purple lips curled in a bemused smile.

"Heya, Krystol! Nice day, huh?"

"A little too humid for me," he grumbled. "You know the ancients invented air conditioning for days like this, to make life tolerable."

Katya smiled her winning smile and brushed off the comment. Tory immediately saw the wisdom in not bringing Tec along.

"The Chief said you'd be coming," he said. He eyed Tory closely.

"This is Tory. She is carrying a message—" Katya began.

"Yes, yes, the mysterious message." He sighed deeply. "Well, as you can see, I'm a busy man." He gestured vaguely about. "So let's just step into my office and take a look at it."

Katya took a step forward, but Krystol raised his hand. "Not you. Just her."

"Hey sure. I'll just wait out here and smoke a pipe," she teased. Krystol frowned and huffed and went inside, and Tory followed.

Her nose wrinkled at the smell of charcoal and rotten eggs and ammonia, but Krystol didn't even seem to notice. Skylights coated in dust and grime cast a gloomy light over the factory floor. The men stopped what they were doing and watched her climb a set of rickety stairs to Krystol's workshop. Inside the narrow space, a desk was cluttered with jars, powders, papers, sketches, and books. *There's one thing Tec and the Scientist have in common.*

Krystol plopped down into a wooden chair on wheels, letting out a deep breath as he did so, as if climbing the stairs had been a major effort. He gestured for her to sit on a nearby stool.

"You can dispense with the charade now," he said wearily. "I know you're not from the Belt Wall …"

Tory felt a jolt of adrenaline.

"Too tall and healthy—everyone there is pale and bloated… and you're much too pretty."

A crafty grin spread across his face. He pointed up, toward the skylights, and winked.

"Don't worry, your secret is safe with me."

"I don't know what you're talking about," Tory said.

He snorted. "OK, sure. Have it your way."

He retrieved a corked bottle of wine and a pair of dusty glasses from a nearby shelf, which she declined. He shrugged and gave himself a deep pour.

"I have my own secrets as well. You may wonder how I know about the Belt Wall. Well, I grew up there. I was always curious what was outside. When I graduated from University and decided on Field

Work, the faculty told me it was a dead end, that my studies should be solely focused on Mars. At any moment the signal could arrive, the transport ships could appear! They insisted there was nothing interesting to discover outside the Wall."

"Well, about that they were right," he sighed dramatically. "It wasn't a jungle filled with savages, like the Media portrayed—no, it was much worse. Boring sleepy little farms where nothing ever happens."

"After years of wandering, chased from village to village, town to town, mocked as a 'Scientist', I gave up on Field Work. There are ... ways ... of getting messages in and out of the Belt Wall, and I pleaded to be allowed back in. But they rejected me. Said I'd been exposed for too long, carried unknown diseases, likely compromised."

"Exiled!" he spat, "Luckily, I ended up here in Steel Town, where they at least ... *tolerate* me. In turn, I've helped them with the Bessemer process, gunpowder recipes ... all mere parlor tricks compared to what I carry around up here." He tapped the side of his head.

"Take electricity. Oh, the things I could accomplish with electricity! But the materials needed, the factories, the power sources—to have electricity, you need *scale*. And of course the damned auroras—impossible to predict. The atmosphere becomes so overcharged with ions—well, everything sparks and catches fire and you're back to square one."

"But the biggest obstacle is ... *them*." He waved broadly towards the outside. "Of course you see it now. They have made a religion out of stopping Progress. I can only imagine what this looks like to someone coming from Mars!"

He took a sip of wine. "Tell me, what's it like there?"

"It's beyond your wildest dreams."

His eyes lit up. "How are you getting back? Can you ... *take me with you?*" he whispered, his cheeks flushed red.

"Nothing's happening until this message is decrypted," Tory said, handing him the folded paper from her satchel.

"Yes, yes—of course!" His whole demeanor toward her had shifted.

"You know it is curious," he mumbled, as he unfolded the paper and smoothed it out. "When I left for Field Work, my faculty advisor told me that, in my travels, if I ever encountered a ... *Visitor* ... carrying a coded message, I should do whatever I could to assist them. This was ... over twenty five years ago! I'd all but forgotten until the Chief stopped by..."

Twenty five years! How long had they been planning this mission?

The message was a 10 x 10 block of plus and minus signs:

-	-	-	-	+	+	-	+	-	-
-	+	-	+	+	-	+	+	+	+
+	+	+	-	+	+	+	-	-	+
+	+	+	+	+	+	+	-	+	-
+	-	-	-	+	-	+	+	+	-
+	-	-	-	+	-	+	+	-	-
-	-	-	-	-	+	-	+	-	-
-	+	-	+	+	+	-	+	-	+
-	-	+	+	+	-	+	-	+	+
-	-	-	-	-	+	-	+	-	-

Krystol chuckled to himself, "A-ha! Haven't seen this encoding technique since University! All right, hm. First thing, I will need your name ..."

"Tory Flood."

"No, your real name."

"Taurii."

A flash of annoyance crossed his face. "Your full name."

Tory hesitated before saying, "Taurii 636."

"Yes—that's it!" Krystol exclaimed. "The three digit number is the key. And how strange that my advisor all those years ago knew the *number* would be in your name. *Make sure you ask the Visitor's name...*"

He shook his head in wonderment as he oriented the paper, so that the colored corner of the grid was positioned in the upper left. Then he rotated the paper to the right, counting each turn, "*One ... two ... three ... four ... five ... six.*"

Now the colored corner was in the lower right. He counted down three rows, and then over six columns, and circled the location with a red wax pencil.

"It's really very simple from here. The message is in an old format, from the early days of electric communications called *Morse Code*. Dots and dashes."

His brow furrowed, he pinched the bridge of his nose as he transcribed the code onto a piece of scrap paper. "A little rusty," he muttered.

The output was a jumble of letters that he puzzled over, then drew vertical slashes between the letters to form word breaks. Satisfied, he slid the paper over to Tory, who read:

for | too | for | for | n | sev | nin | sev |
for | w | oct | one | tre | egt | a

"What is this—?"

"The message is compressed," Krystol explained. "This is a location as well as a calendar date and time. *42.44 degrees North latitude, 79.74 degrees West longitude, October 13, 8 a.m.*"

She stared at him blankly. "Do you know where that is? When that is?"

Krystol leaned back in his chair and laughed. "Whoever composed this message was too clever by half! As you may have noticed, there are no calendars, no clocks, no maps with latitude and longitude around here."

"Can you figure it out?" she pressed.

"I was never much for cartography. Perhaps with the right equipment … an astrolabe … maybe. I have no idea where to find one, and even if I did, a little error could easily be off by a day's travel."

"What about Cornplanter's scientist?"

"Old Barnabas! Hahaha! His specialty is in botany. No, I expect he'll be of even less help."

Then an idea struck him. "But I think I know who could solve this—the Librarian. At the Free Library, in Oak Land. Though … he and I don't exactly see eye to eye. He doesn't approve of the books I check out, believes I'm up to mischief," he giggled. "But he's powerless to stop me. It's against his beliefs about the Library, *Free To The People* or some rubbish."

Then, noticing the growing look of impatience on Tory's face, he said, "What I mean is, you will have more luck going there on your own."

She stood up and nodded, took the note and saw herself out.

"Don't be a stranger!" he called after her.

Back outside, Tory blinked at the bright sun and shivered as if to shed the chill from indoors. Katya was waiting for her patiently. "Did he do it?" she asked.

Tory handed her the scrap of paper, and Katya frowned. "But what does this mean? It's gibberish."

"A code within a code." *Exactly the kind of games AIs love to play.* "It's a location and a date. But he can't read it, and neither can I. Apparently the answers may be found at the Library in Oak Land."

"The Library? Sorry Tory, you're on your own there! I'm a gal with many interests, but reading ain't one of 'em."

Together they walked back to town, not noticing Krystol had reappeared, standing in the shadow of the door frame, his eyes narrowed, silently watching them go.

11

Katya put Tory and Tec up at her house in Liberty, the most recently established borough of Steel Town, located to the northeast atop a high plateau. The borough was comprised of log cabin homes, arranged haphazardly among the trees, with no real streets or main thorough-fares. At the center stood an immense cathedral, built of limestone in the medieval gothic style. From a distance, Tory mistook the soaring spire for a rocket on a launchpad.

Katya's cabin appeared abandoned, the forest encroaching right up to the front door. The interior was just as neglected. Katya shrugged, "I'm always traveling."

The neighbors were pleased to meet Tory and Tec, but alarmed to hear that Katya had offered to host visitors at her place. They quickly mobilized into action, bringing a steady procession of food and common household goods to fill empty shelves.

The next morning Katya was gone, on Agent business. She left behind a wad of elk-head dials, a hand drawn map that showed the way to the Strip, where Market was held, as well as to the Library in Oak Land. *Keep quiet until I'm back*, she scribbled.

The fishing expedition with the Chief had worked its medicine on Tec. He whistled as he prepared breakfast, clearly the first meal cooked in the hearth for quite some time. Outside, a bright hot morning greeted them. A strange melody drifted on the air, coming from the direction of

Liberty Cathedral, where a small crowd had assembled outside to listen to the pipe organ, booming from the open doors of the church. It was tempting to stop, but they continued on.

Liberty and Oak Land were connected by a wood-planked path that cut across rolling pastures where dairy cows grazed. Out ahead, the main landmark of Oak Land was impossible to miss, the ruins of a tall tower that pointed up to the sky like a skeletal finger. The iron gate at the entry to the borough was tipped with spikes, artfully entwined with ornate wrought-iron flowers, with the phrase *Here Is Eternal Spring For You, The Very Stars Of Heaven Are New* written in gothic script across the transom. The gate was open, and from this point forward, the streets were cobbled and neatly maintained.

The houses in Oak Land were constructed of red brick in a similar fashion to Flood Town, with mansard roofs, broad porches and balconies, walled-in yards and gardens, but these homes were considerably larger, in some cases three stories tall. Shade trees grew everywhere, keeping the temperature cool even on a scorching day.

A park stretched from the base of the crumbling tower to a deep ravine, where a monumental building stood at the edge of the cliff, a block of gray sandstone, grim and foreboding despite the sunny skies. The building had a pyramid-shaped cupola on the roof and was fronted by two classical porticos. Statues of robed women peered dolefully down at the steady traffic of one-wheeled carts, horses, donkeys and pedestrians moving along the main street. Pedestals of bronze statues were chiseled with the names *Galileo, Michelangelo, Bach, Shakespeare*.

On the nearby lawn, two teenaged girls in colorful headdresses watched over a group of young children playing tag, growling dramatically at each other. Tec asked if this was the way into the Library, and the girls pointed to the far side of the complex.

"We're dinosaurs!" one of the children roared at Tory.

The southwest corner of the building was indented like a squared letter C, with a flagstone plaza between two extended wings, and the words *FREE TO THE PEOPLE* engraved above the main doors. The entry foyer was a dizzying array of columns, arched ceilings and tiled floors, giving the impression of entering a labyrinth. Hanging iron lanterns in the shape of pineapples cast flickering light. No sounds or daylight from outside penetrated.

The first room was a reading area under a high vaulted ceiling. Illumination was provided by lanterns on tripods, suspended over sand-rings as precaution against fire. A few people were at tables, heads down, oblivious. Tec approached the nearest, a young woman about the same age as Jasmyn, wearing a similar box-braid hair style and brightly colored bandana.

"Pardon me. Can you help us find the Librarian?"

She bowed politely and vanished into the gloom. A few moments later, a figure appeared in the shadows. At first it looked as if a child was coming out to greet them, walking with a shuffling side-to-side gait. But when the person stepped into the light, it became apparent this was a middle-aged man of short stature. He was bald on top, with wild curly hair on the sides, and wore thick glasses in goggle-like black frames, the bifocal lenses creating a kind of crazed look in his eyes.

"Tory Flood, if I'm not mistaken?" he said. "And Tecumseh Anders? Katya left me a note to expect you. I'm Niko Brod of Polish Hill, the Librarian here at the Carnegie Library. It's a real pleasure to meet you!"

"Call me Tec."

As they shook hands, Tory could not help noticing Niko's arms and fingers were much shorter. *He must have been born with a genetic anomaly!* On Mars, there were many kinds of body morphism, but they were all done by choice, many for shock value or irony—but there were no accidents. Those were disposed of.

"Tec, I feel like we've already met," Niko said. "With all your book requests over the years—you are without a doubt one of the most learned healers in the Ten Towns. You certainly keep my researchers busy!" He gestured at the young people scattered around the reading room.

"I hope I haven't been too much trouble. You know how it goes, one book mentions another, and soon you are down a rabbit hole."

"Not at all! That's why we are here," Niko grinned. "Now tell me, what is all this about a message from the Belt Wall? Katya's note was cryptic."

Tory handed him the paper, "The scientist Krystol decoded it."

"I know Krystol well," Niko muttered. He stepped into a sphere of lantern light and examined the paper, stroking his chin. "Asha, Levi, could you join us?"

Asha was the young woman who went to fetch Niko, and Levi was a slender young man, wearing ear-ringlets and a *yamaka* cap atop his head, the wisps of a mustache growing on his upper lip. Both were friendly and eager.

"Levi, tell me, what is today's date?" Niko quizzed.

"*29 Tammuz*," Levi responded. "In the year 6652."

"Hebrew calendar," Niko explained. "A continuous record has been kept down through the centuries at the Tree of Life synagogue in Squirrel Hill. Levi, now here is your challenge. The date *October 13* in the ancient American calendar, we need to determine precisely how many days from now it will occur."

"And Asha," Niko turned to the young woman. "The puzzle contains *latitude* and *longitude*—you know what those mean, right? So you'll have to find a map... but see here, this decimal notation. That may be tricky … you'll likely have to use mathematics to pinpoint the exact location."

Both of the researchers hurried back into the book stacks, whispering to each other. Niko said, "While we allow them to work their magic, how about I give you a tour?"

He led them down a long arched corridor lit by flickering wall sconces. "When our ancestors rediscovered this place, it was shut up like a Pharaoh's tomb, with everything preserved. Of course, some parts didn't survive. For example, the Art Museum, a later addition to this main building, was built of concrete and has long since crumbled. So interesting, don't you think, that the ancients became progressively worse at building things…"

They arrived at a small door, which Niko opened with a flourish. Beyond, an astonishing chamber opened up—a great square hall with decorative marble colonnades. Diffuse light cascaded from a full ceiling of skylights high above, dazzling after the gloom of the Library. The chamber was jammed with monuments and statues, as well the entire facades of classical buildings.

"You have heard of Andrew Carnegie, right?" Niko asked. "The Victorian-era industrialist that built the steel industry and became the richest man in the world …"

"Don't forget, he caused the Johnstown Flood, too," Tory said.

"Ah yes, I'm sure there is quite a different memory of him in Flood Town! Here, his name is hard to escape."

"We've noticed," Tec said.

"This museum was Carnegie's proudest creation, and this room, the Hall of Architecture, was the centerpiece. His vision was to assemble the wonders of the world under one roof, and make it available to the citizens of his city."

"Sounds like a guilty conscience," Tec observed.

Niko laughed, "If so, he went to great lengths to soothe it! The pieces you see assembled here are actually plaster casts of the originals..." He walked around, pointing out various pieces. "Here are the *Gates of Paradise* from Florence in ancient Italy ... and that is the facade of a gothic abbey in ancient France," pointing to a single casting that looked as if the entire side of a church had been transported here. An arched entryway was "*The Portal of Spires* from another cathedral in France." A portico with statues of robed women serving as columns, "*The Porch of the Maidens*, from the Acropolis in ancient Greece."

Tory gazed up at a statue of a winged lion with the head of a human female, perched atop a tall column. "*The Sphinx of Delphi*," Niko provided. She pictured Alpha Founder gazing down, able to penetrate her thoughts, even without her circlet and though she was millions of kilometers away.

"Can we move on?" she asked.

The adjacent chamber was called the Hall of Sculpture, a companion gallery in similar style, but smaller, with a raised balcony and statuary in between the columns. "This room is meant to resemble the interior of the *Parthenon* in ancient Greece. Carnegie even got the marble from the same quarries."

Tec pointed up at the ceiling. "The skylights...?"

"Did you see the pyramid on the roof when you arrived? That was built with giant steel girders—of course, produced from Carnegie's steel mills—and serves as a cover over the skylights, which are made of thick plate glass. Somehow they survived intact all this time."

Next they passed through a dark corridor filled with gem stones, sparkling and glittering in the flickering light of a few strategically placed lanterns. Ahead, the sound of children laughing and giggling echoed off the walls.

They entered another enormous sky-lit chamber called Dinosaur Hall, filled with the skeletons of dinosaurs, posed as if in mid-action. Wall murals depicted a scene from prehistoric Earth, a jungle landscape draped in mist and fog, with huge shapes lurking. The children from outside scampered around, the teenage girls doing all they could to corral them. Stern warnings were issued if any tried to get close to the exhibits.

"Sara would love to see this …" Tec said quietly.

Niko stopped at the main attraction—the tail, spine and neck of a giant sauropod, forming an elongated sine-wave which practically filled the entire chamber.

"Carnegie became obsessed with dinosaurs. He assembled a team of scientists to dig for fossils, ship them back here. The bones were so large, rail tracks were laid in the basement to move them around. This dinosaur here—probably the largest creature to ever walk the earth—was given a Roman name in honor of him, *Diplodocus Carnegii*. He was a big believer in Darwin's Theory of Evolution, the survival of the fittest. In his mind, there was no question of who that was."

Alpha Founder and Carnegie sound like kindred spirits.

"It's strange to think of these creatures as survivors," Tec said. "At the height of their dominance, the dinosaurs were wiped out." He snapped his fingers.

"Yes," Niko said solemnly. "We think about it the same way. How very close humankind came to walking in their footsteps"

They exited through a small door in the back and arrived at a series of workshops bustling with activity, one with blocks of stone being carved with hammers and chisels, another where bronze statues were being cast, and finally a print shop with several presses in operation.

"Up until now, all the books printed here have been reproductions, popular books that are distributed across the Ten Towns." Niko picked a freshly-bound book from a stack, "But now we are attempting something different—an original work. Here is an early copy, we haven't released it yet."

The Decline and Fall of the American Empire was embossed in gold, and beneath that in smaller type, *by Nicodemus Brod, Free to the People Press, Steel Town.*

"Catchy title," Tec said.

"An homage to Gibbon, though nowhere near as ambitious! We've been working on it for ten winters, trying to piece together what happened from the materials here at the Library. It wasn't easy— during the final years, there were fewer and fewer books published. People shifted all their reading to their *phones*, and all that information vanished in the Blackout. So we had to make some educated guesses, fill in the blanks."

Tec opened the book to the first chapter and read aloud, *"Chapter One, Never Forget."* He raised his eyebrows, and continued, *"September 11, 2001 dawned with clear blue skies across America, the most powerful nation in the history of the Earth, and as the citizens began their day and went about their business, they had no idea of the attack that was coming, nor that this day would mark the beginning of the end of their Empire."*

"Wow, Niko—that is incredible," Tec said. Niko took a half-bow.

"But what actually happened that day?" Tory asked.

"I'm surprised someone from the Belt Wall doesn't know about September 11!" Niko exclaimed. "Back then, the ancients flew back and forth between cities in *airplanes*. I know, it's hard to fathom why. On that day, a band of Pirates seized four airplanes, and turned them into weapons, like giant arrows. Two struck the *Twin Towers*, the tallest buildings in their greatest city, *Manhattan*, killing thousands. Yes—thousands. As many as all the people who live in Steel Town, if you can believe it."

Niko adjusted his glasses. "They also attacked the main fortress of the American military, called the *Pentagon*—you know of it, right? That location now sits within Belt Wall ... perhaps it still exists?" Niko probed.

Tory recalled the surface scans the AIs had shown her, remembered seeing the outline of a massive five-sided building. "It's nothing but ruins now."

Niko filed the information away somewhere in his head. "The last airplane, called *Flight 93*, targeted their main assembly house, *Congress*. When the passengers on the plane realized what was happening, they rose up and stormed the pilot-house. During the struggle with the Pirates, the airplane crashed into an empty field, south of what's now Flood Town. No one survived."

That's where I landed. The Wall of Names.

Noticing her distant stare, Niko remarked, "I'm guessing they tell a different story about that day inside the Belt Wall?"

"They don't even talk about it ..." she mumbled, letting her thoughts slip out.

"Then please take this copy, it's yours," Niko insisted.

At that moment Asha and Levi came running in, their arms filled with large books. "Niko, we believe we have solved the puzzle!"

"Come, come," he pushed aside the clutter to make space on a work table.

Levi launched into his explanation, "Let's start with what we know. The summer solstice occurred on *8 Tammuz* on the Hebrew calendar... which was three-quarters of a moon ago, twenty-one days to be precise. In the American calendar, the summer solstice happened on *June 21*. He laid down a page containing a grid with numbers in each of the boxes, and counted forward twenty-one squares, turning the page and continuing on a page labeled *July*. Here, you see, today is labeled *July 12*."

"Now, if you continue counting forward ..." he flipped pages to *August, September, October*. "Here is *October 13*, exactly ninety-three days from now by my count. The equivalent of *4 Cheshvan* on the Hebrew calendar. A little more than three moons from now."

So I haven't missed the date.

"Amazing work Levi! And you, Asha—what have you found?"

Asha opened an oversized blue book titled *National Geographic: Atlas of the World*, filled with maps, the ancient political boundaries highlighted in pastels, the areas of water colored bright blue. Almost every bit of land was labeled with the names of towns and cities, page after page.

So many places. So many people!

Asha stopped at a page containing a large rectangular shape at the center and put her finger on a dot labeled *Pittsburgh*. "We are here. This line running north and south is the 80th meridian of longitude. 79 degrees passes near Johnstown—the ancient name of Flood Town. So, the location in the message has to be somewhere in between, a little east of here."

"You mean we passed by it?!" Tec sighed.

"No ... next we have to look at latitude. See the line that forms the north boundary of *Pennsylvania*? It is labeled 42 degrees. And 43 degrees latitude is up here, near *Niagara Falls*. So the location is halfway between the two." She put her finger on the map. "Here."

"But ... that spot is in the middle of Lake Erie!" Tec exclaimed. "How does that make any sense?"

"How far away from shore are the coordinates?" Tory asked.

"The little bars down in the corner are the scale of the map. The closest shore point is southeast about fifteen *miles*, or twenty five *kilometers* ... here. Not far from this little lake, called *Chautauqua*—"

"Chautauqua!" Niko exclaimed. "That is on Seneca lands. The great preacher Cornplanter held his sermons there. It's where the current Seneca chief, John Cornplanter, has his longhouse …"

"Well it makes sense this message is meant for John Cornplanter," Tec said. "Something is going to happen right in his backyard!"

"In ninety-three days," Levi added.

"What does Katya think about all this?" Niko asked.

"We don't know, she's away and didn't tell us when she'd be back," Tec said.

"Ah yes, that woman is always in motion, never sits still … well, if you've got time on your hands, I might have a few book recommendations for you, Tec …"

As the two of them fell into a discussion about novels, Asha came close to Tory and said in a hushed voice, "I like the pattern in your shirt."

"I know the young woman who designed it! I can tell Katya, maybe she can request one for you on her next trip?"

Asha smiled, clearly liking that idea, and excused herself, exiting with Levi. Tory watched them go, then glanced down at the map and the calendar. Here it was, all laid out before her—where she needed to go, when she needed to be there, how she would escape afterwards. *But why did the AIs want other people to know?* Now that the message was decoded, word would certainly get out.

There's something I'm not seeing...

Tory and Tec attended Market the next day. Unsure of how long they would be staying at Katya's, or what might happen next, they purchased enough food to last them a half-moon. They browsed the shop-aisles of the Strip, curious to see what things the steamboat brought. There were barrel casks and one-wheeled carts built in Wheel Town, and from Falls-of-the-Ohio came magnificently crafted horse tack and saddlery, and ground chicory root which could be brewed to make a bitter black tea.

A popular stand sold loose-leaf tobacco and rolled cigars—which Tory found repellent—but Tec seemed to enjoy, claiming there were medicinal benefits when smoked in moderation. When he bought some loose pipe-tobacco for Katya, he got a few cigars for himself as well. Tec also bought himself a new pair of blue jeans with copper rivets at the seams. From one of the vendors, they ate a *bratwurst* sausage on a long bread roll, with pickled cabbage called *sauerkraut*, mustard, and a special tomato sauce famous in Steel Town, *ketchup*.

Days passed as they waited for Katya to return, and Tec came up with activities to keep busy. In the mornings they listened to the organ recital at the Liberty Cathedral. On nice days, the doors were flung open and people gathered on blankets on the lawn. If the weather was too steamy, or it rained, they went inside, sat on a bench, and gazed up at the soaring arches, the glimmering panes of stained glass. Tec folded his hands and whispered to himself in a low voice. She asked what he was doing and he replied, "Praying."

To whom? And for what?

After the music, a preacher from the Native Revival read a passage aloud from what he called *The Good Story*. Tory half-listened out of one ear, daydreaming. But during one sermon, about how *Creator-Sets-Free* went into the wilderness to fast, and was tempted by an evil trickster snake called the *Accuser*—Tory snapped to attention, realizing it was the same story she had heard at the congregation on Market Day in Flood Town. Satan tempting Jesus in the desert—just told with different names.

The next day she paid closer attention to the reading from the *First Nations New Testament*:

When Creator-Sets-Free saw this great crowd, he went back up into the mountainside and sat down to teach the people. His followers came to him there, so he took a deep breath, opened his mouth, and began to share his wisdom with them and teach them how to see the Creator's good road.

Creator's blessing rests on the poor, the ones with broken spirits. The good road from above is theirs to walk.

Creator's blessing rests on the ones who walk a trail of tears, for he will wipe the tears from their eyes and comfort them.

Creator's blessing rests on the ones who hunger and thirst for wrongs to be made right again. They will eat and drink until they are full.

Creator's blessing rests on the ones who are merciful and kind to others. Their kindness will find its way back to them—full circle.

Creator's blessing rests on the pure of heart. They are the ones who will see the Great Spirit.

Creator's blessing rests on the ones who make peace. It will be said of them, 'They are the children of the Great Spirit!'

Creator's blessing rests on the ones who are hunted down and mistreated for doing what is right, for they are walking the good road from above.

Others will lie about you, speak against you, and look down on you with scorn and contempt, all because you walk the road with me. This is a sign that the Creator's blessing is resting on you. So let your hearts be glad and jump for joy, for you will be honored in the spirit-world above. You are like prophets of old, who were treated in the same way by your ancestors.

Tory glanced over at Tec, who listened intently, nodded in agreement. She wished the AIs had bothered to brief her on religion. She'd never heard anything like this before. But from her years in Audit, working undercover among the Essentials, she got the meaning immediately. *These words were meant to start a revolution.*

Each day, they hiked around Steel Town to local landmarks of interest. One day they visited the domed Immaculate Heart of Mary atop Polish Hill, the oldest surviving church. They rode the Mon Incline up the side of Mount Washington, and explored the ice cave tunnel that ran underneath, called the Tubes. They walked the terraces of the Stadium Gardens, on the North Shore across the Clemente Bridge, which were versions of the Kitchen Garden in Flood Town—but on a massive scale. The Conservatory, on the opposite side of the ravine from the Library, was much like the Melon Room, but ten times the size, with citrus trees inside that grew lemons, limes and oranges. *What would Alice think of all this?*

Afterwards they found a secluded place, under the shade of the trees, ate a picnic lunch, and spent time reading, the drone of cicadas marking the slow passage of time. Tec was engrossed in a stack of mystery novels Niko had recommended about a monk named *Cadfael*, who tended a medicinal herb garden in a medieval abbey, but also solved murder mysteries. Tory worked her way through Niko's *Decline and Fall*, which was proving just as challenging as the sermons at Liberty Cathedral.

Like every child in pod, Taurii's primary source of history was watching the epic saga *To Mars*. The series, which ran for over two hundred episodes, started with the earliest humans evolving in Africa and spreading out across planet Earth, recounting the great ages of exploration and conquest, all with a common theme—humans were destined to explore and conquer and push ever outward. The narrative covered the history of spaceflight, the discoveries of computing machines, nuclear power, the lunar landing, the space station, the dawn of artificial intelligence, genetics and the CRISPR revolution, the earliest probes on Mars—and culminated with the establishment of the colony of Nubai and the exodus of the Founders.

Over the centuries, the series had been remade over and over again, with new cast members, with slight variations of plot and theme—so by the time Taurii was in pod, the Earth factions were depicted as cartoonish villains, bent on nothing but savagery and destruction. The Mars colonists were brave, scrappy, and able to overcome impossible odds and treachery to persevere. When the Severance occurred, it was pretty clear that no other option was available to the Martians, that they acted out of concern for Earth, preventing an all-out nuclear war.

About two centuries ago, a companion series was introduced called *Beyond,* set in a not-too-distant future where Martians had successfully established colonies further out in the solar system, on the moons Enceladus, Titan, and Ganymede. In *Beyond,* all efforts were focused on an interstellar spaceship sent to colonize the nearest inhabitable exoplanet, orbiting Proxima Centauri, five light years away, a journey that would take over fifty years, even with the advancement in engines.

Beyond was not passive viewing like *To Mars.* Instead, Citizens each had avatars and immersive roles to play, participating in the plot lines and sweeping narrative arcs—solving problems as they went. In turn, crowdsourced issues discovered inside the interactive story helped inform the current roadmap of the Starship project. It was everyone's obsession, the basis of rank and status among Citizens, and nearly all free time was spent in the game. *To Mars* was considered little more than dusty curriculum for early pod, learned and then quickly forgotten.

Tory still struggled to read printed text, but Niko's writing style in *Decline and Fall* was clear and direct, very visual, so she could easily picture the events as they unfolded. The main protagonists of the book were two warring factions, the Reds and the Blues, each of which controlled various geographies within the United States of America—the

Reds the rural countryside, the Blues the city cores. Despite their simi-
larities, and the incredible prosperity during this period, they argued
over everything. The attack on September 11 came shortly after a bitterly
contested election, and from then on the divisions grew more sharp. A
sequence of weak leaders, whom they called *Presidents*, were confronted
by one crisis after another—regional wars that dragged on for decades,
man-made viruses that caused pandemics, financial crises.

The founding of "Nubai" colony—the central event in *To Mars*—
was considered a distraction during this time, an expensive boondoggle
for the world's richest people. As Tory read about the wealthy tycoon
who spearheaded the exploration of Mars, the development of artificial
intelligence, as well as the neural mesh devices that were precursors of
the circlet—it suddenly struck her: *This was Alpha Founder!*

Each crisis on Earth became more acute and intractable, the cycle
of decline seemingly inescapable, with armed gangs running wild, food
shortages, assassinations, riots and terror attacks, the decay of basic
infrastructure. The public's ire towards the wealthy grew. Nubai offered
an escape hatch, and so the elite began sending their sons and daughters
to space.

One critical early struggle Nubai faced was finding a water
supply. In planning for the colony, scientists assumed frozen water at
the Martian poles would be adequate, but try as they might to purify
it, people grew sick. In desperation, they concluded the only way to
get fresh water was to transport it from Earth, an enormous technical
challenge. The Great Lakes of North America were the most abundant
and accessible sources, and the Blues—who controlled the American
government at the time, and many of whose children were now living
on Mars—readily granted access.

At the same time, reports filtered back to Earth about innovative genetic modifications, attempts to engineer immunity to the effects of Martian water.

Oh Niko, if you could only see where that led …

Levi had drawn out a calendar for Tory to keep track of the countdown to October 13—but even with it, the days began to blur together. A storm front blew in and the weather switched abruptly, from hot and humid to overcast and cool, with days of wind and rain sweeping across the mountains. Then, during a one of the heavy downpours, Katya arrived, as abruptly as she departed. She opened the front door, crossed the room, and collapsed in a heap on a chair by the fire, dripping wet.

"What did you learn at the Library?" she asked, shivering.

Tec quickly detected a fever, and concocted an herbal tea with willow bark, honey, and the exotic lemons from the Conservatory. Tory ran to a neighbor and paid a dial for a chicken, which went directly into the pot to make a hearty soup.

Tec suspected it was just exhaustion and ordered a few days bed rest. Katya didn't resist too much. Once she heard the information contained within the message, she knew a challenging journey lay ahead of them, and she would need to be at full strength. She was curious about Niko's book, and so to help pass the time, Tory pulled a chair alongside her bed to read passages to her. Tec would occasionally stop in the room to listen, watching Tory as she read.

In the narrative, another contested election led to the Reds winning control of the main branches of the American government, which would have swept the Blues from power. But the Blue leaders refused to seat the new delegation, and deployed the military around the

Beltway, a highway that circled the Capitol city, blocking all entry. Soon the ring of tanks were replaced by the construction of a barrier wall.

The Reds responded by assembling the *Third Continental Congress* declaring a new, parallel American government. The Reds' political message was hostile not just to the Blues, but also towards Mars, accusing them of absconding with much of the country's wealth. The Reds demanded reparations for the fresh water being taken. When Nubai refused, the Blues, who were friendly to Mars—in fact many of whom hoped to one day to migrate there—lent their powerful military to protect the water transports.

Both the Reds and Blues possessed nuclear arsenals and in their posturing, threatened to use them, which would have doomed not only each other, but the water supply of Nubai as well. Just as the rhetoric escalated to a fever pitch—suddenly everything went dark—the Blackout.

And that's where the book ended.

The three sat in silence for a long time, listening to the gusty wind blowing through the trees outside, the branches brushing against the side of the cabin. Tec lit up a cigar and passed it to Katya, who took an appreciative puff.

"It's easy to forget sometimes, but they are still up there," Tec pointed to the rafters with the tip of his cigar.

"I wonder why they haven't tried to come back." Katya said. "What could possibly be better on Mars?"

Good question.

Just then they were startled by a knock at the front door. Tec answered to find a young boy, breathing heavily as if he had run the whole way. Katya's name was on the front of the envelope that was handed over.

"It's from the Chief," she said, as she broke the wax seal. "There's a meeting of the Steel Town Council tomorrow." She looked up from the letter, "He wants all three of us there."

The Chief spoke first. "I apologize in advance for all the formality, but we are gathered here today on town business, and this historic place is where we conduct it."

He introduced the others on the podium, three to his left and three to his right, representing six boroughs of Steel Town—plus the Chief himself who served for the seventh, Oak Land. He then went down the line of people seated at the main table facing the Council—Niko the Librarian, Krystol the Scientist, Katya the Agent, Tec Anders and lastly, Tory Flood.

"I believe everyone is up to speed on why we're here," the Chief continued. "Our discussion for today is, what are we going to do about it? My hope and expectation is that once we've reached a collective decision—whatever that may be—that all present will depart this chamber confident they had a chance to speak their mind, that the outcome was the result of an open, free and fair debate."

Nods up and down the podium.

"All right then, without further ado, I'll open up the floor."

Tec looked nauseous while waiting for the first question, which came from Ari, the councilman from Squirrel Hill, who wore a black suit, a tasseled shawl over his shoulders, a heavy white-streaked beard and ear-ringlets, round wire-rimmed spectacles and a yamaka cap atop his head. "My question today is no different than most of the matters we deliberate here. How does this benefit Steel Town?"

The councilman from North Shore, Luk, dressed in the familiar Amish garb and hairstyle, asked, "What happens if we just do nothing?"

Bruno, the councilman from Mount Washington, spoke next. He had a shaved head, long goatee beard, a sleeveless leather vest that showcased his massive arms covered in tattoos, and looked like he had just walked off a shift at the mill. "This location, in the middle of the lake. Is this for real?"

Niko said, "We've triple-checked the coordinates on different maps. Unless the original decipher contained an error—"

Krystol interjected, "There's no error. The fact that the decrypted message contains a location so close to the intended recipient is proof enough of its accuracy." He raised his palms. "Occam's Razor."

Dani, the councilwoman from Liberty, a woman with striking red hair shaved on one side, said plainly, "We must honor our Treaties with the Seneca."

Ari from Squirrel Hill responded, "Lake Erie is not Seneca territory. Yes, it is bound by the Fishing Treaty. But I could argue Lake Town has as much interest as the Seneca in this—"

Krystol sighed audibly.

"Is there something you'd like to say?" the Chief asked.

"Its obvious to me—the message is about Martian water ships."

"What Krystol is saying rings true," Niko chimed in. "It's the one dependency Mars had to Earth—they needed fresh water. Perhaps the message describes the time and place of a future landing ..."

Dani from Liberty asked, "How is it no one has seen these water ships?"

Krystol waved his hand dismissively, "They likely land at night, out in the middle of the lake ..."

"Our synagogue in Lake Town has reported seeing strange light-ning over the lake at night, when there are clear skies," Ari offered.

"Static electricity, from the charged atmosphere," Krystol said. "Let me guess, there are auroras on those nights..."

"Now that you mention it—"

Niko jumped out of his chair, the cushion he was sitting on tumbling to the floor. "The auroras! Ah, I see it now, Krystol. In ancient times, auroras were described as occurring far to the north, near the poles. It was very rare to see auroras this far south, let alone with such frequency as we are used to. But now I'm wondering—perhaps they have to do with the water ships, with what caused the Blackout!"

Well done, Niko.

"The auroras are the product of supercharged ions in the atmo-sphere," Krystol explained, to blank stares. "And yes, a powerful aurora would interfere with the ancients' electrical systems. I thought I told all of you this before ..."

Bruno from Mount Washington leaned forward, squinted and stroked his beard. "I smell a rat. Someone here is holding back." He pointed at Tory. "Tell me, why should we trust her?"

Before Tory could open her mouth, Tec rushed to her defense. "She has nothing to gain from this mission!" he said angrily. "She has risked her life to come here with this message. And I for one believe her!"

Bruno cocked an eyebrow and settled back in his chair.

The councilman from Polish Hill, Boniface, heavyset with a long wild beard and black robes, spoke in a booming voice. "We live in the time described in the Book of Revelation, when the Dragon—who is Satan—has been cast into the *Abyss*, which of course means Mars. Those who did not worship the Beast nor take its mark—our ancestors, the survivors—now live in peace here on Earth for a thousand years, when

Satan will be unbound for a short time. This message is a sign—the thousand years are nearly ended! Mars will return."

An uncomfortable silence followed. Then the councilwoman from Shadyside spoke for the first time. She was a slight woman named Kim, her short hair streaked with gray, wearing a simple silver necklace and matching bracelets. "If I were John Cornplanter, I'd want to know."

The Chief made a steeple of his fingers. "In listening to this discussion, it strikes me that the question before us is actually very simple. So let's cut to the chase. I put it to the Council: Do we send the message to John Cornplanter? Yes or no."

The Chief allowed some time to pass before he looked around the table. One by one, each of the six councilpersons nodded yes.

Then they all looked to the Chief, who spoke in a tone of authority, "First let me say, I share your concerns. For all these years, the Belt Wall has been shut off from the rest of the world, becoming a ghost story to frighten children. And now suddenly there is a message and messenger coming from the Belt Wall itself! And the message is for John Cornplanter, a man I respect, leader of the Seneca, with whom we share our most sacred Treaties. I agree with Boniface—this message is the product of a clever mind, and is meant to sow discord. I'll be damned if I let that happen."

He paused and took a deep breath. "But I agree with Kim. Even with our concerns, we should allow the message to travel onwards. The Basic Rule applies. If it were me, I'd want to know."

Katya stood up. "I'll escort them. I know the Seneca well. They will want this to be done formally, in accordance with the Treaty."

Krystol raised his hand and said, "I think I should accompany them too. I know the scientist who lives among the Seneca, Barnabas. I can lend confidence to the authenticity of the message—in case anyone doubts the translation." He shot a sideways glance at Niko.

Ari asked, "But what about the gunpowder mill, the steelmaking process?"

Bruno from Mount Washington waved his hands. "*Pssh*. Don't yinz worry about that, we got it covered. Krystol has taught us well."

Krystol nodded his thanks at the note of support. The Chief looked around the podium. "Any objections to Krystol accompanying them?"

Tory cast an alarmed, pleading look at Katya, who spoke up, saying, "Um, Chief ... the less people traveling, the better. We'll be crossing some pretty wild territory and don't want to draw attention—"

The Chief interrupted her. "I have full confidence that whatever the challenges, you'll be up to the task, Katya. I'll have the Writs of Passage drawn up. Please pull together the list of what you need for the journey. You can depart the day after next."

"Hey Katya, bring back some of that sweet icewine while you're up there," Bruno said to laughter.

The Chief stood. "I believe that concludes our business here. Thank you all." He looked out the window. "What a beautiful day outside! Would anyone like to join me on my boat for some fishing on the Allegheny?"

Tec practically leapt out of his chair.

12

The party of four travelers took a barge up the Allegheny to Free Port, a journey that took two days upriver versus one in the opposite direction downstream, with a man in the bow and another in the stern pushing the craft slowly forward with long poles. In Free Port, they slept in the same bunkhouse they stayed at before, which felt like ages ago.

Even though Tec's canoe was transported on the barges, Katya asked that he leave it behind in the village, and instead selected two trim walnut canoes from the boathouse which were better at navigating upriver. The canoes were loaded with supplies—prepared food that didn't need a fire to cook, like venison jerky, bread, cheese—plus tarps, ropes, iron spikes for shelter. They also transported two identical bundles of goods, each wrapped tightly in oilcloth like a package, containing cast iron cooking pans, steel knives, wool blankets, rolls of blue denim fabric, cigars and pipe tobacco. Tec also made sure to find a place to stow his fishing gear.

The party was equipped with three rifles—Tec's, one for Katya, and a third rifle for Tory. Krystol wasn't armed, and didn't seem to mind very much. He was treating the whole excursion as a sightseeing trip. Because Krystol wasn't a formal resident of Steel Town, nor any of the Ten Towns, he wasn't permitted to be armed. It was Krystol's choice as he had been offered residency many times over the years and always declined, proclaiming, "I am a citizen of humanity." Katya rolled her eyes.

Before they embarked, Tec gave Tory a quick lesson on how to load and shoot the longrifle. They walked a good distance away from the settlement and came across the rotten hull of a wrecked riverboat along the river bank. Tec tacked up a sheet of paper with a circle and black dot at the center that he'd drawn in wax pencil.

Tory stood about twenty five meters away from the target, with Tec alongside, coaching her through the steps. First, she half-cocked the hammer of the flintlock. From the powder horn, she measured just enough for one shot using a small cup, which was then poured into the open gun barrel, saving just a little bit for the flash-pan. A patch of linen and the round shot were advanced down the muzzle using a special tool, a wooden sphere with two brass extensions of different lengths. Then she switched to the long ramrod to finish tamping the bullet all the way down to the end of the gun barrel. The *frizzen* snapped shut—a piece of steel struck by the flint to produce a spark, that also served as a cover for the flash-pan, keeping the powder dry from the elements.

As she went through these steps, she could not help but think of the magnetic gun she was certified to carry as a member of Audit, which would have sprayed a hundred high-velocity darts in the time it took to load a single round into the longrifle.

She cocked the hammer and raised the rifle, standing sideways to the target, her legs spread. Even though the gun was one and a half meters long, it was perfectly balanced, so it wasn't hard to hold pressed horizontally against her shoulder. She took aim with the sight at the end of the barrel, let out half a breath, and pulled the trigger. There was a click, a flash, and a *BANG* as the rifle recoiled against her shoulder and a sulfurous cloud surrounded her.

Tec paced over to the target and called out in amazement, "You hit the bullseye!"

"Must be beginner's luck!" she called back.

The sun was climbing in the sky, and Katya mentioned she wanted to get an early start. Tec figured Tory was ready enough. On the path back to the village, they passed the mouth of the Kiski where it silently joined the Allegheny on the opposite side. Tec looked over at the river longingly, and she could tell he was mentally traveling back upstream, back toward home.

She took the moment to hug him, whispering, "You'll be reunited with them."

Tec held her close. "We both will."

This far into the summer the river ran about a meter deep, but in any location could vary widely, in some stretches forming calm pools, and in others, tricky tumbling rapids. The river braided, presented gravel bars and midstream islands and side channels. The keel of the canoe acted like a blade, carving a path upstream to squeeze through narrow channels, yet was sturdy enough to grind across the pebbled bottom in the shallows.

With a continuous current of water coming at them head-on, traveling upstream was much different than going down. Taking a break from paddling meant quickly giving up hard-earned distance, plus the river had its own ideas on which way the canoe should go. Despite Katya's prowess as a canoeist, Krystol's halfhearted attempts at paddling—stabbing his oar at the water, taking frequent breaks to observe the countryside—meant she had to work twice as hard, and they often fell far behind. Any time Katya dropped out of sight, Tec grabbed his pole for a few casts. Soon fish were flopping around on the bottom of the canoe.

Tory for her part was glad to have as much space as possible between her and Krystol. Every time she glanced in his direction, he was staring back at her.

The summer sun blazed hotter than ever, and out on the river there was nowhere to escape it. They all wore wide brimmed hats like Leo the Agent, as well as long-sleeved flannel shirts which protected them from sunburn and biting flies, but made it stifling hot. The shouldering hills grew steeper, encroaching on the open sky, and any time the sun dipped behind the ridgeline, shadows brought sweet relief. Shortly after the sun set, it was as if a fever broke, and heavy dew blanketed everything.

They always camped on the west bank of the river, as the east bank was on Treaty Hunting Grounds. That first night they were all too exhausted to even build a fire, so they ate a cold meal, and numbly pitched tents, simple A-frames with a rope tied between two trees, an oilskin tarp draped over the line, pulled taut and staked into the ground. Katya assembled Krystol's for him, but Tory got the idea and waved off Tec's help. They smeared exposed skin with Tec's mosquito repellent and promptly fell asleep to the trilling and croaks of frogs.

"Only those with a Permit are allowed to set foot in the Treaty Hunting Grounds," Tec explained to her as they were paddling the next day. "And even then, they can only hunt in groups of two, with strict limits. No trapping, no building permanent shelters, only permitted equipment. The land is patrolled by the *Wardens*, who have been selected from among the Seneca and the Ten Towns because of their supreme outdoor skills. These are not men to mess with. They live year round in the Treaty Hunting Grounds, solitary, roving from place to place. If they catch anyone trespassing, poaching, exceeding the game limit—it's not just the hunters that are punished, but the whole town could have their

Permits revoked—which would be devastating. So Permits are only given to the most responsible residents who have proven themselves. Jace was starting down that path by volunteering out at Ninety-Three, until … well, you know."

On all of her journeys by river thus far, there had been sign of human habitation, a dock along the river, a glimpse of a roof on the hillside, a wisp of smoke above the trees. But here there was no one, pure wilderness. Bald eagles perched on dead tree branches and took flight when they came close. At one grassy bend in the river there were easily fifty elk grazing. Tory was astounded at the size of the animals, the sweeping antlers of the male bulls. The herd stood on the east bank of the river, protected by the Treaty—as if the elk knew it, watching them pass close by, unperturbed. Not that the party would even know what to do with the colossal animal if they bagged one—that much meat would easily swamp their canoes.

They set up camp the second night in a side valley alongside a beaver pond, underneath a willow tree. Katya was clearly frustrated at their progress, but was too much the diplomat to let it bubble to the surface. "This will be our last fire for a long time," she said. "From this point on, it's not safe, will act like a lantern attracting moths." She tossed on more pieces of driftwood, building a bonfire. "So let's enjoy it."

She brought out a bottle of whiskey and passed it around, and together they watched the blazing flames burn down into a pile of pulsing red-hot coals. The third-quarter moon had not yet risen and the sky was a river of stars above them.

"The Creator is generous with His gifts," Tec said.

Krystol snickered. "It's the one thing I've never understood about you people. Still believing in a supreme Sky Father. Look at all the different religions just in Steel Town. Isn't that alone proof enough that there isn't a god? If he's all powerful, why would he allow so much confusion among his believers?"

Tec bristled. "That's where you're wrong, Krystol. I see it just the opposite. After all that has happened these thousands of years, the message of a Creator who loves us, who became one of us, gave us His only Son to walk among us, to teach us how to live and love—knowing the whole time that we would reject that message. And yet He willingly sacrificed himself. Think of how many empires have come and gone, and yet our *Faith* has survived. To me, that's proof enough that it's real—realer than anything else. No, what I doubt is your *Science*, which promises prosperity but always seems to end in destruction and ruin."

"But science explains how the world works! Take this fire—it's the product of a chemical reaction of carbon and oxygen that produces heat. You can't possibly argue with scientific truths."

"You worship half-truths. No one doubts that Science is very good at describing things, breaking things into pieces, figuring out how the pieces interact. But every question is answered by another question. All your great theories—the Big Bang, Evolution—yes, I've read about them. They tell fantastic tales, but all stop short of answering the real question: *Why?*"

"Why is irrelevant. The universe doesn't *care* about anything. It just *is.*"

"You're just being defensive. Because Science can't prove why things happen, you act like it doesn't matter. Yet your actions betray you—Scientists are always racing from one thing to the next, always probing deeper, always believing the next discovery is the one that will unlock the mysteries. So you care very much about the *why.* But it's all around you, and you can't see it. There is no way all this is an accident."

Katya interjected to ask, "Tory, what do you believe?"

"I don't know..." she said. "There is no religion where I'm from—" Krystol gave her a knowing look, his lip curling ever so slightly. "But I can say this, even in a society entirely built on scientfic truths, there sure seems to be a lot of lies and deception ..." She suddenly caught herself, realizing she had dropped her guard. *It's the whiskey.*

The next morning Katya informed the group she was switching things up. She and Tory would take the lead canoe, and Krystol and Tec would be paired together. Both men began to protest but Katya cut them off, flashing some of the Chief's tone of authority. "How about you redirect all that passion for debate into paddling. See if you can keep up with the women."

Katya taught Tory subtle navigation techniques, like always looking upstream for sluggish current, guiding the canoe from one slow pocket to the next, in a zig-zag path, like hopping across stones. Katya's voice was carefully pitched just above the background noise of the river, so it didn't carry. The constant paddling and scanning ahead was a fully engrossing task, and Tory easily lost track of the passage of time, the hard work pushing aside any thought of what lay ahead, at the end of the journey.

For the most part, Tec and Krystol managed to keep pace with Katya, Tec too stubborn to let them fall far behind. The river was unpredictable, gravel bars and submerged rocks that threatened to gouge the hull or splinter a paddle, shallow rapids where they had to get out and walk beside the canoe, a grueling task, all the while taking care not to slip and twist an ankle on the slick river bed.

They were lucky with the weather, no rain, just day after day of heat and haze and blazing sun. To drink, they dipped cups right into the clear river water. At the end of the long day, Katya guided them to a campsite, hidden in a grove away from the river on dry ground. The canoes were dragged ashore, tied down and concealed. As the men pitched the tents, Katya led Tory to a deep pool where they stripped off their clothes and plunged in. After the initial full-body shock, the cold river felt deliciously refreshing. Though Tory couldn't shake the feeling Krystol was out there in the trees, watching.

One afternoon, as they paddled through a steep V-shaped canyon, they passed a giant wedge-shaped block of sandstone at the river's edge. Katya steered the canoe in close so that Tory could see squiggled images engraved in the flat surface of the rock—abstract shapes of humans and animals—almost completely weathered away.

"These rock carvings are from some of the earliest Seneca that inhabited this country," Katya said, then pointed to all the other names that had been crudely scratched into the rock in other places. "And those are from the ancient Americans, who defaced it."

Katya steeered them across the river to a little crack in the cliff wall, directly opposite of the carved rock, where a fresh spring cascaded into the river. She docked the canoe and hopped out, hefted the oilcloth parcel onto her shoulder and climbed up the bank, deposited the package in a big wicker basket hidden among the bushes.

"All right, hopefully that should appease them," she said as she climbed back in the canoe.

They camped a short distance further, on an island in the middle of the river. The next dawn was bright and clear and the humidity was down, a glorious morning on the water. Tory had been keeping track of the days, marking an X through each box in the calendar. Seven days had passed since they departed Free Port, and by Katya's reckoning, tonight they would be sleeping in beds under a roof in Oil Town.

The river curved in a horseshoe shape around a knuckled mountaintop. Rounding the bend, two stone piers rose from the water, all that remained of an ancient railroad trestle. Here, an iron chain was stretched across the entire width of the river, attached to the piers, hanging just above water level, blocking the way forward. Pieces of driftwood were snagged in the chain, dragging in the water like the teeth of a comb.

"Well this is new," Katya muttered.

Katya worked the boat up and down the line, testing it for slack, but the chain was much too heavy to lift it up and slide underneath. "Looks like we'll have to portage across that bottom land over there" she said, pointing to a marshy section on the west bank.

Just as the party beached the two canoes, a booming voice called out, "Hold it right there! We got you covered!"

Katya stood defiantly, peering into the forest to see if she could identify the source, but the echo in the steep valley made it hard to pinpoint. Something splashed out in the river and a green globe bobbed on the surface, drifting toward the chain—an unripe pumpkin. As they watched it float closer, there was the loud crack of a rifle and the squash exploded. Gunsmoke drifted from the trees out over the river channel, not far upstream.

"That's to show yinz that we're serious. And we know how to shoot."

"Impressive!" Katya shouted back, not flinching. "Heya, do I detect a Steel Town accent there? Because, you're talking to the Agent of Steel Town." She paused. "You know what that means, right?"

"We ain't governed by no Treaties!" the voice shouted back.

"What, you don't like the gifts we left you back at Carved Rock?" Katya scowled, "Rory and I worked out an understanding!"

"Rory ain't our chief no more! Now it's Clem. And he's expecting us to come back with … MORE!"

Katya gestured her companions to huddle. "This is a real pickle," she said. "I don't know how we get past them. And this horseshoe bend, they can easily take a shortcut over the ridgetop and cut us off downstream if we try to run…"

Krystol said, "Can't you just show them the Writ, let them know Steel Town will send an armed posse in response—"

"A piece of paper with a wax seal isn't going to do squat," Katya said. "They're *Pirates*. I doubt they can even read."

"So what are we going to do?" Tec asked.

"Give me a minute to think," Katya said. She removed her glasses and pinched the bridge of her nose. Then she suddenly looked up. "I've got it ... but you're not going to like it."

"I have a proposal!" Katya shouted at the treeline. "We'll give you the rest of our cargo! Plus two hostages that you can hold for ransom!"

Tec, Tory and Krystol looked at each other with wide eyes. Tec hissed, "What are you doing?"

"Trust me," Katya whispered back.

After a long silence, the Pirate shouted, "Why don't we just go ahead and take all four of you hostage?"

"Because who's going to carry your ransom demand back to Steel Town?"

Another extended break was followed by, "OK, deal!"

"Give me a moment to talk with my people!" Katya called out.

She turned and said matter-of-factly, "The hostages are going to be Krystol and me."

"WHA-A-A-A-T?!" Krystol cried out.

"Oh, don't be a ninny! Nothing bad will happen to us. In my experience they are all bluff, they aren't really that violent—well, maybe to pumpkins. We'll camp with them for a half-moon and it will all sort itself out. Besides, I want to see how the Pirates are organized so I can report back to Chief..."

"B-but I'm too important to be given as a hostage!" Krystol sputtered.

"That's exactly it. Once they realize they have captured a Scientist, they'll see a big prize coming and want to work out a deal to set us free."

"What about us?" Tory said. "Our mission?"

"You can return to Steel Town and take an alternate route—down the Ohio, up the Mahoning to Young Town, then over land to Lake Erie and by boat to Lake Town—"

"That will take much too long!" Tec protested. "And trekking across Buckeye territory runs the same kind of risks, let alone crossing Lake Erie, which by all account is treacherous to even the most experienced boatsmen!"

Katya didn't argue with him.

Tec continued, "No, we have to cut through the Treaty Hunting Grounds. That river mouth we passed about a day ago—that's the Clarion, right? I hunted in those highlands years ago, back when I carried a Permit. I can find our way north to the Seneca."

"Tec, by breaking the Treaty, you put not only yourself, but Flood Town at risk!" Katya warned.

"We've come this far, we're not giving up." Tec set his jaw.

Katya let out a deep sigh. "OK. At the mouth of the Clarion, there is a huge old sycamore, with a metal strongbox at its base, where hunters can drop messages. A Courier comes up river to Oil Town every half moon and will get the message. Let them know about the Pirates, the chain, everything you can. And if—when—you reach the Seneca, tell them too—"

"There has to be another way!" Tory said in desperation. But Tec and Katya's mouths were both fixed in straight lines as she handed him the wax-sealed Writ of Passage.

"Tory, please give Krystol your rifle and kit," Katya said. "I know, I know. But if he shows up unarmed they will immediately be suspicious of a trap. Because who would travel upriver without a gun?"

Reluctantly, Tory handed over the rifle. Krystol's face was even paler than usual, stunned as the reality of the situation sunk in. He grasped the gun limply.

"Now when we walk out—push off and paddle downstream as fast as you can. Don't look back and don't stop until you've reached the Clarion—even if it means traveling at night. These Pirates are fools, but even they aren't dumb enough to cross into the Treaty Hunting Grounds."

"Thanks for the reassurance," Tec said, deadpan.

Tec helped get the second bundle out of the canoe, keeping a small sack of food, his rifle and fishing gear in the hull. Then, as Katya and Krystol paced toward the trees, with rifles held above their heads in a sign of surrender, Tory and Tec shoved the canoe back into the Allegheny and started furiously paddling.

The thrash of their paddles, the thrum of her heartbeat drowned out all other noise, and before she realized it, they were well out of sight, around the horseshoe bend.

Only then did she realize she was crying.

The sycamore standing at the mouth of the Clarion was impossible to miss, easily forty meters tall, towering above the other trees, its canopy glowing in the setting sun. The strange peeling bark of the tree formed splotchy patterns in green, gray and brown, and the trunk was so wide, five people linking arms would be needed to encircle it. The strongbox had been wedged between two roots long ago, which had since grown and melded with the metal frame, fixing the box in place.

Lifting the creaky lid, Tec discovered papers in an oilcloth folio and a wax pencil. Tory looked over his shoulder as he scribbled in spidery cursive script, describing the time of the ambush as, *during the New Moon that follows Buck Moon*. He folded the paper in half and addressed the front *To the Chief of Steel Town. Urgent! Please Read!*

In the short period of twilight left before dark, they paddled up the Clarion far as they could. They didn't bother with food or setting up camp, just laid a tarp on the ground and collapsed asleep in each other's arms. At daybreak, they continued onward, wanting to put as much distance as they could from the Allegheny. Even though the hills looked the same, and the trees looked the same, something felt different here, as if the forest itself knew they were trespassing.

Whether it was the hot sun or lack of food, shortly after noon both of them hit a wall of exhaustion and couldn't go any further, and decided to pitch camp. Tec hunted for a flat patch of dry ground that wouldn't flood in a cloudburst, common this time of year. He used a long stick to beat the brush and poke under rocks to check for rattlesnakes, which were notorious in the Treaty Hunting Grounds. After a long internal debate, he decided that it was best to build a fire—he had to trust Katya that, even if there were Pirates pursuing them, they wouldn't dare cross the river. If they were to pass themselves off as two traveling hunters, it would look suspicious to camp without a fire.

While Tec set up the tents and collected firewood, Tory slipped into waders and headed upstream with a rod, hoping to catch a fresh dinner. This stretch of river was beautiful in the afternoon sun, golden slanted beams of light playing on the rippled surface and pebbled bottom of the slow-moving river. Tec had suggested a Green Caddis fly and sure enough, a hatch of those insects was rising from the water.

She waded out into the middle of the flow and cast upstream, reaching a deep pool beneath a cut bank, with an overhanging tree casting a shadow just where the riffle entered. Immediately there was a streak of yellow beneath the surface, a big splash—she had a trout on the line! In an instant she could tell—*this is much bigger than the one I caught on the Stoney Creek!*

Frantically, she tried to recall the techniques—keep the tip of the pole up, let it do the work. When the fish makes a run, don't fight it, just keep a finger on the reel to introduce drag. Slowly she worked the fish closer and closer to the bank, and then in one arcing motion lifted it out and up into the grass where it began to flop around. A rainbow trout, as long as her forearm. She hunted around until she found a firm branch of wood, and clubbed the fish once at the base of its skull to kill it.

A loud splash came from the river. She waded back out, cast a few more times and *wham!*—another fish was hooked. Again she battled it for what seemed an eternity, before it tired enough that she could get it up onto the bank. *This one's even bigger than the first!*

Once more she cast her line and a third fish struck! This one was smaller than the first two, but fought hard, thrashing the water. She was able to lift the trout out of the water without snapping the line, and caught it in her hand. She waded back in toward shore, barely able to contain her excitement. *Wait until Tec sees this catch!* She figured she'd play it cool, pretending like she wasn't having any luck, and let him stumble upon the monster fish on shore.

Then, just as she was about to climb up the bank, she saw a flicker of movement ahead of her. Something was creeping out of the bushes.

An enormous cat!

The animal was easily the size of a human on all fours. Being in the river must have disguised Tory somehow, because the cat paid her no attention as it sniffed and circled the two dead trout in the grass. The sun dazzled off its pale fur, flashed in its yellow eyes.

A short distance away there was rustling through the brush and Tec's voice called out, "Any luck?"

Before she could cry out in warning, Tec emerged from the undergrowth, fishing rod in hand. The cat startled, snarled, and in one fluid motion, before Tec even knew what was happening, leapt across the clearing and attacked. One giant paw raked across Tec's chest, knocking him backwards. In a flash the cat was on top of him, lunging for Tec's exposed neck—but as he fell his head hit a tree stump and twisted just enough that the teeth sunk into his shoulder muscle instead.

Tory had already dropped her pole and madly scrambled up the bank. Out of the corner of her eye, she spied the branch she had used to bludgeon the trout, grabbed it, and charged across the grassy landing. The cat sensed her approach, lifted its head to growl at her, its teeth red with blood.

And then Tory smashed into it, swinging the branch so hard it cracked in two over the cat's back. The cat somehow sprung vertically in the air, twisting its long body midair, landed on its feet—and in a blink, vanished into the forest.

"Tec!" she screamed, and dropped to his side.

Tec didn't respond—the blow to the head had knocked him unconscious. The cat's paw had shredded the front of his flannel shirt and one claw had carved a furrow into the skin that was bleeding freely. She pulled back his shirt collar to find deep bite marks from which dark blood welled up.

She remembered how Jace applied pressure, using his bandana as a bandage to stem her bleeding. Tec's wounds were so extensive, she realized that two different bandages were needed, one around the base of his neck, and another completely binding his chest. She quickly ripped off her colorful flannel shirt and sliced it into long ragged strips with her knife. She knotted the bandages as tight as she could, then collapsed to her knees in the grass beside him, dripping with sweat and tears. Tec remained asleep, his breathing weak and shallow.

She had no idea how long she sat beside him in the grass, gripping his hand tightly, not knowing when—or if—he would wake up. She knew she should be doing something, but was frozen to the ground. The sun dipped behind the mountain and bathed the valley in shadow.

Then suddenly there was a man's voice behind her.

"Mountain lion," he stated matter-of-factly.

Tory was too tired to do anything but stare. The stranger was a giant of a man, dressed in buckskin shirt and pants that showed off his bulging muscles and broad shoulders, with a knife and hatchet tucked into his belt. He leaned casually on his long rifle, his hat cocked back to reveal a tangle of rough-cut blond hair. His big square jaw was covered in stubble, his eyes were clear blue and seemed to consider the whole scene in front of him with amusement.

He strode over and squatted down beside her, examining Tec. "Sumbitch got him pretty good."

After a long silence, the man said, "He'll live. If he's lucky."

He glanced up at the dark silhouette of the surrounding hilltops. "But not out here. Come sunset, the wolves will come down."

He slung his rifle across his back diagonally, propped Tec up into a sitting position, knelt on one knee and bent forward as if fixing his boot, so that Tec's upper body slumped against his shoulder. In one motion, he rocked backward and effortlessly stood up, Tec's limp body draped over his shoulder.

"C'mon, follow me. My place is up the next hollow."

He glanced down at the trampled grass. "Nice fish," he grunted. "Bring 'em."

He carried Tec to a crude but sturdy shelter, partially set into the hillside, with exterior walls built of stacked creek-stone and caulked with mud and moss. The roof was a platform of fresh-cut logs covered with hemlock boughs. They ducked under an animal skin flap covering the front door. The interior was like a cave with no windows, a small fireplace in the rear set into a natural cleft in the rock, with a built-up chimney around it to protect the roof and timbers from catching fire.

He laid Tec on a rough cot in the corner, then turned to her. "C'mon. I've got an idea." Tory cast a worried look over at Tec. "Don't worry, he ain't going nowhere."

The man led her straight up the hillside behind the cabin, striding up the steep slope like he was climbing a set of stairs. Tory struggled to keep up, her feet slipped on the leaf mulch, tripped over tree roots. At the crest, the forest opened up into a little clearing, the surrounding trees ringed with wild grapevines.

The stench hit her first, like a wall. Then she saw it in the center of the clearing—the hulking corpse of an elk.

"Wolves brought this old bull down a few days ago."

As he approached, three giant birds with featherless heads beat their wings and awkwardly took to flight, circling around as they slowly gained altitude. A black cloud of flies buzzed around the carcass. He seemed unphased, crouched down, emptied a little leather pouch of tobacco while muttering something inaudible, then plucked things off the carcass.

"This should do," he said striding past her, over the lip of the hill, back toward the hut.

In the gloom he removed Tec's bandages with a sharp knife. "Learnt this from an old Seneca medicine man," he said. He took a pinch of tiny white maggots from the pouch and scattered them on the open chest wound and around the punctures at base of Tec's neck. The grubs began to wriggle.

"These little buggers clean out the wound," he said. "Now, we just gotta wait and hope he wakes up. And when he does—that he don't freak out."

"No, I'm pretty sure Tec will be fascinated. His craft is healing."

The man grunted, *"Healer, heal yourself."* That brought a chuckle out of him.

He introduced himself, "My name is Rollo Walker, from Oil Town. If you ain't guessed yet, I'm a Warden." He paused, then added, "I'll spare us both the charade and not even bother askin' for your Permits."

"We were traveling up the Allegheny and Pirates ambushed us," she explained hastily. "They took two of our companions hostage ..."

She found the wax-sealed Writ, but he waved it off. "I can hardly read. Ain't exactly a requirement for the job. How's about you just tell me where you was headed."

"To see John Cornplanter of the Seneca. We're carrying an important message for him. But now..."

From a pocket he found a another pouch of tobacco, like the one he had carried the maggots back in. He took a pinch and tucked it between his lower lip and gums, causing a bulge in his cheek. "I've been a Warden for going on ten winters now. Since my wife passed. It's been a long time since I seen a woman."

She was suddenly conscious of her bare arms, of wearing only a thin undershirt. Seeing the alarm in her eyes, he said, "You're right to be afraid ..."

Then, after a long pause, he continued. "But not from me. I know the missus and me said *'Til death do us part.* But her spirit's out here, watchin' over me, keepin' me on the Good Path."

He unsheathed his knife and drew the blade, looked at the steel thoughtfully, then reached over toward her. She flinched, but he merely grabbed one of the trout at her feet. In one motion he split the fish from gills to tail, scooped out the guts into a pile, then did the same to the second.

"I'll go get your gear and stow the canoe. Gonna toss this in the river," he gestured with a handful of guts. "Last thing we need is more critters slinking about. How 'bout you get a cook fire going."

Nearby was a stack of split wood covered by long strips of bark to keep dry, and a rock cairn filled with a tangle of hemlock twigs for kindling. She crept inside the stone hut to get the flint and steel from Tec's belt pouch. He was sleeping peacefully, though it was impossible not to see the squirming maggots in his open wounds without feeling nauseous.

Even though she had seen countless fires started by now, striking the flint and steel just right, keeping the charcloth lit while carrying it to the nest of tinder, proved to be a challenge. But soon enough she had a nice crackling blaze going in the fire pit.

Down in the hollow, in the twilight gloom, she saw a blue shadow moving against the dark backdrop of the forest. She looked around for something to defend herself.

But it was just Rollo returning with their equipment. He mumbled approval of the fire as he handed her Tec's rifle, propped his own against the front wall of the hut, and pitched the tarps as tents. She put on her second flannel shirt, a more subdued green-and-black checkered pattern, to which Rollo commented, "Better'n that fancy shirt from before, I could spot you clear across the valley."

He cooked the trout on a metal grate over the flames and they ate with their hands, picking the flesh out from the bones. Rollo finished by crunching the fish's head in his jaws, and seeing she wasn't going to, ate hers as well.

They sat for a while in the flickering darkness listening to the wolves howl and bark up on the surrounding ridgetops. "They smell the blood trail, but they know there's an alpha predator down in this hollow. They just are tryin' to decide if they're gonna do something about it."

He took a pinch of chewing tobacco and for a while he seemed lost in thought, like he was having an internal dialogue. Then he grunted once, as if a point had been made that he couldn't refute.

"So I'll get you up to the Treaty House at Buckaloons," he declared. "We'll have to cut across the high plateau, the hemlock swamps. But first, we gotta get your man back on his feet." He spit out a long string of brown saliva. "Cause I sure ain't carryin' him."

He offered her the pouch. *Why not?* she thought, and tucked a wad of the shredded leaves into her cheek, tasted the sickly-sweet juice that formed.

"Don't swallow—" Rollo said, but it was too late.

Suddenly her stomach turned. She spat out the tobacco, rushed into the bushes and vomited up everything.

13

Tec woke with a loud groan in the middle of the night, and Tory crawled out of her tent to go to him. In the pitch black of the hut, he was disoriented, but she sat on the ground next to the cot and in a hushed voice told him everything that had happened. He had no recollection of the mountain lion attack—the last thing he remembered was stopping to find a campsite. She held his hand as he drifted back asleep, and stayed awake the rest of the night beside him, listening to him breathe in the darkness, from time to time placing her palm on his forehead to check for signs of fever.

Before dawn, dim gray light filtered through chinks in the front door flap. Seeing the maggots in his wounds immediately triggered another bout of nausea, and she used every bit of her willpower to fight the urge to throw up. For the first time in a long time she missed her circlet, her mentor would automatically block any feelings of discomfort or pain.

Rollo had a crafted a solitary, rough hewn chair so he could sit to watch the sunset and the campfire, and when Tec woke later that morning, he felt well enough to come outside and sit in it. He draped a loose unbuttoned shirt over his shoulders, mainly to hide the wounds from view.

Rollo and Tec instantly got along. They brushed aside the lion attack as *just one of those things*, and plunged into an exchange of hunting and fishing stories. Tec naturally did most of the talking, but it was clear Rollo enjoyed listening and added a few tall tales of his own. Tory tried to follow along but quickly lost interest.

Eventually their conversation turned to the journey north. Rollo figured it would take them about a quarter moon—seven days—to cross over the mountains to the Treaty House at Buckaloons. But first Tec would need some time for his wounds to heal, and preparations needed to be made.

Rollo left at first light, only to return later in the morning dragging a yearling buck, still in its summer coat of orange fur with velvet on its antler nubs. He strung the deer from a tree branch and set about skinning it. That done, he went a good distance from the hut, further up the hillside, felled some mid-size trees with a handsaw and began constructing a frame.

"We're gonna pack in our food," he said, taking a break to gulp cold water from the spring-fed brook that ran down the hollow. "Sure, we could hunt our way up to Buckaloons, as you'll see there's plenty of game. But as you just learnt, out in these woods, once you've got fresh meat, you gotta figure out how to keep it."

"So while I'm building this smokehouse, how about you go back down to the Clarion, wiggle that rod and see if it's still lucky. And take a gun with you," he winked.

Tec accompanied her, sat on the bank with the rifle across his knees, wearing a hangdog look on his face, clearly wishing he was the one fishing. He kept calling out instructions, where to cast, what kind of fly to try—until she finally glared at him and shouted, "I think I saw a lion moving in that bush behind you!" He got the message.

On the third morning in Rollo's camp, Tec picked out the maggots, which had grown in size considerably. The chest wound appeared pink and clean with no sign of infection. Following Tec's instructions, Rollo

flattened the barb on a fish hook with the blunt edge of his knife, steril-
ized it in the fire, and stitched up Tec's chest, using fishing line as thread.
The shoulder bite marks didn't need stitches, had closed up on their own,
but they gave Tec the most concern. "Let's pray it doesn't develop into
lockjaw," he said.

The smokehouse was a simple box of cut logs with fresh hemlock
boughs as a roof. Rollo lowered the deer carcass from the high rope,
sawed strips of meat off and draped them on racks made from the
stripped green branches of the trees he had felled. He got a fire going in
the central pit and tended it throughout the day. Any fish Tory caught
were hung by their eye sockets and smoked whole.

By the fifth day, Tec was feeling limber and Rollo decided it was
time. "Don't worry, I'll get your canoe and gear back to Free Port, it will
be waitin' there for ya," he said.

Tec sadly left the waders behind but insisted on bringing the fly
poles in their cases. "They were my great-grandfather's."

Rollo touched the tomahawk-pipe hanging from his belt, "The
same."

Tec was only able to carry his rifle and the pole cases, anything
more would tug at the fresh stitches, so Tory shouldered the pack with
their gear. Rollo carried the smoked meats as well as some cups, a lidless
pot and cast iron skillet, his own rifle, and plenty of powder and shot.

After crossing the Clarion in a shallow section, they ascended the
mountain on the opposite side, a near-vertical climb. Tory's body had
grown accustomed to the gravity, but now the added load felt like an
enormous hand was pressing down on her, and she struggled to stay
upright. At the hill crest, her knees wobbling, she looked back down the
slope to the bend of the river only a few hundred meters below. *How am
I ever going to keep this up for seven days?*

As if reading her mind, Rollo soon located a strip of level ground, what he described as an old railroad, now completely overgrown by the forest and occasionally crossed by fallen trees they had to climb over or around. The railroad grade maintained a constant elevation, which let them avoid steep climbs into and out of the deep valleys to either side. "Be thankful for now," Rollo said. "More of them climbs is coming."

The morning was clear, with blue skies and fog down in the valleys, but by mid morning clouds began to develop, puffing up into tall columns. By late afternoon, thunder rumbled across the hills. The stormclouds were hit or miss, sometimes drenching the next valley while leaving them dry. Other times, the underbelly of the cloud moved overhead, the sky darkened, the winds gusted, and buckets of rain emptied on top of them. They huddled in the pines which acted like natural umbrellas.

As lightning flashed and thunder boomed all around, she said a prayer it didn't strike the tree they were under. Her mentor would have quickly displayed the miniscule probabilities, chided her for indulging in superstition. But she prayed anyway.

While the days were oppressively hot, at night the skies cleared, filled with glittering stars, and the temperature dropped sharply. Even wrapped in a wool blanket, she woke up shivering. The first night they camped in a strange area where the hills had been flattened as cleanly as if lopped off by a knife. "The ancient Americans called it strip-mining," Rollo said. "Just lift away the mountaintop like the lid on a box and take out all the coal inside. Some of these streams still run orange in color, from the sulfur run off."

Once they got into a cadence, all thoughts vanished and they just walked and walked, not saying much, stopping from time to time at a spring for water, or for a quick meal of smoked venison and trout. Tory's feeling of nausea never went away—she only ate small portions and struggled to keep it down. But she kept that to herself, not wanting the men to get all concerned. Her feet were red and raw at the end of a long day of walking, but luckily the soft leather of the boots didn't cause any blisters.

One morning they busted up a flock of wild turkeys crossing the grade, and as the big-bodied birds lumbered to get in the air, Rollo casually lifted his rifle and shot one right in the head. That night he roasted the bird over a spit and for the first time in days, Tory ate a full meal and then some, gorging herself on the juicy breast meat, gnawing a whole greasy drumstick down to the bone. Rollo smiled watching her eat, as if aware of her struggles but too polite to say anything. Tec seemed oblivious.

Rollo collected the bones and left-over scraps into a pot of water and set it over the coals. The next morning the fire was out but the pot contained a rich broth, with globs of fat floating on the surface. Rollo poured them each a cupful and declared, "Breakfast."

Tory took a big gulp, thinking of how good the roast turkey was the night before—but the moment the broth hit her stomach, a wave hit her and she was on her knees puking it right back up. "Turkey gizzard soup ain't for everyone," Rollo admitted.

Here atop the high plateau were clearings where wildfires had once burned, triggered by lightning strikes during dry spells, which had since regrown into meadows where hundreds of deer grazed in the daylight, and elk too. The briar patches at the edges of the meadow were swarming with blackberries, and they gobbled handfuls as they went. Tory came away with criss-crossed scratches on the back of her hand, but it was worth it—the tart but sweet berries stayed in her stomach.

"We're at the top of the world up here. Even the glaciers of the Ice Age petered out, not able to cross these mountains. The water can't make up its mind which way to go, so it just sort of settles in bogs and waits.

Maybe the best hunting in all the Treaty Lands—but it's just too damn remote. The animals here have forgotten about men as predators, you can practically walk right up to 'em."

They came to a point where the old railroad grade continued on in northeast direction, but Rollo declared, "End of the line for us." He pointed toward the northwest, where knuckled ridges of mountains rose and fell like waves, stretching to the horizon and beyond. "On the other side is Buckaloons."

Constant birdsong surrounded them as they walked through the leafy beech, oak and maple trees. Red-crested woodpeckers flitted from one dead tree to next, dutifully tapping away, and cicadas droned. Being out in front meant Rollo was on "web patrol" as he called it, meaning the first to walk through spiderwebs that crossed their path. Soon webs were draped all over his hat and shoulders, and Tec had to flick a couple of spiders off him, but Rollo didn't seem bothered.

Then as if they had crossed some boundary, the leafy forest abruptly gave way to all pines. The ground was clear of understory, covered with a soft mat of pine straw that muffled their footsteps. The hemlock boughs were almost purplish green, so dense they blocked out the sun and cast a perpetual gloom. All sounds vanished, save for the occasional bleak *caw caw* of a crow.

"These hemlocks were here before the Blackout," Rollo said in a hushed whisper, as if the trees were listening.

They camped along Tionesta Creek, deep in a gorge among massive pines that blocked out the sky and the waxing moon. The darkness seemed to swallow their little campfire. Even Rollo seemed on edge in this place. "I grew up along the Tionesta, downstream quite a ways, nearer to Oil Town, in a cabin among the hemlocks. My old man skimmed *rock oil*—kerosene—out of the natural springs. As a boy, my grandma, who was part Seneca, told me stories of a monster that lived up this valley called Flying Head. Just like it sounds—a big flying head, with bat wings and glowing eyes, that feeds on human flesh. Probably meant to scare me from running off into the Treaty Hunting Grounds," he laughed, then added soberly, "But still, the image sticks with ya …"

After another day's journey, up one long hollow, down another, they finally reached a hill crest that looked down on the ribbon of the Allegheny River. A village was located at the edge of the bottomland in a river bend, where another tributary joined. "Buckaloons means *Broken Straw* in Seneca," Rollo said. "Long before the Seneca, the Mound-Builders—the earliest people—lived right down there, ten thousand winters ago, on the edge of the melting glaciers."

He stood in front of them. "Before we go down, a few things. We ain't gonna try lyin' to 'em or making up some tall tale. There's nothing the Seneca hate more'n lies." He filled up Tory's pack with half the venison jerky and what was left of the smoked trout. "Be sure to give it to them as a gift. It's not much, but it will go a long way."

At the bottom of a long and rocky descent, a wooden footbridge crossed the Allegheny to an island mid-stream, and then continued on to the west bank. On the island, between the two bridges, a pair of poles with antlers mounted to the top stood like an open gate, and here Rollo stopped.

"End of my jurisdiction," he said. "Just wait here with me. They know we're here."

Soon two Seneca crossed the far bridge and walked out to meet them, carrying rifles. Their heads were shaved except for topknots, dyed crimson to match the red cloaks draped over their shoulders. One was an older man, the other a gangly teenaged boy. They stopped about ten meters away and simply stood there.

"Heya, String," Rollo said, addressing the older man by his English name.

"Heya, Rollo. Long time."

"It has been. As you can see, I've got two folks coming from Flood Town, named Tory Flood and Tec Anders. They were part of a party of four traveling under a Writ from the Chief of Steel Town, and were beset by Pirates on the Allegheny, down near Carved Rock. The other two were taken hostage. I encountered them on the Clarion."

"So you are handing them over with a Judgment," String said, as a statement not a question.

"No, I ain't," Rollo replied. "They have a message for Chief Cornplanter, and I decided to help them deliver it."

"But they have broken the Treaty by entering the Hunting Grounds," String said plainly.

Rollo shook his head. "The way the Treaty works, you have authority on that side, and I have on this. And I ain't gonna charge 'em with Trespass. I feel the hand of the Holy Spirit at work here, and I ain't getting in the way." He pointed at the two poles, "They cross that line, and they are covered under a Writ of Passage. You gotta decide whether you're gonna honor it or not. But my part is done and they are clear as far as I am concerned."

String frowned at this, but appreciated Rollo's logic, and nodded once.

"Go on," Rollo said to Troy and Tec, "Before he changes his mind."

Tory suddenly was filled with emotion and hugged Rollo tightly. "Thank you," she whispered in his ear.

"It's been a pleasure," Rollo said, then to Tec, "I hope your boy gets his Permit someday."

"And I hope he never crosses you!" Both men smiled and shook hands.

Tec handed the Writ over to String, who broke the seal and read the document. "*Gyantwachia* was here, but traveled on upriver this morning." The warrior turned to the teenager, "You should still be able to catch him at Kinzua. Show him the Writ and listen to what he has to say."

The boy removed his cloak, stripped off his shirt so he was bare chested and tied a bright orange bandana around his forehead. Then with a nod, holding the Writ like a baton, he took off running into the forest, nimbly leaping across fallen logs and around boulders that lined the river bank.

String pointed to a longhouse on the outskirts of the village. "You may stay in the Treaty House tonight," and gestured to the south facing door, which had a sign above written with the words *Steel* in English and *Gaisda* in Seneca.

Tory turned back to wave to Rollo, but he had already crossed the bridge and was climbing back up the mountain, disappearing into the Treaty Hunting Grounds.

String woke them at first light and gestured for them to bring their things and follow. The teenaged boy had returned sometime during the night, and now was waiting outside the Treaty House. He introduced himself as Deer Legs. At the river, a pair of canoes were tied up, finely crafted of lacquered black cherry wood, aged to a salmon color, with matching paddles. Deer Legs sat in the bow and String in the stern of one canoe, and Tory and Tec took the other. The people of the village came out to watch them depart, with a mixture of smiles and frowns on faces.

String pushed the pace and was pleasantly surprised at how Tory and Tec handled themselves, especially through a challenging set of rapids. By mid-afternoon, after some hard paddling, the group came to the remains of a gigantic earthen wall that once crossed the valley, now broken in two, as if an enormous bite had been taken out of the center. The river flowed through the gap, and they passed under the shadow of crumbling concrete towers. Beyond the broken wall, the valley opened up majestically into a broad floodplain framed by high wooded hills.

Another canoe was beached on a gravel spit not much further upstream, and they pulled their boats in alongside. String led them up the grassy bank into a forest glade where stately trees rose thirty meters tall and formed an arching canopy that reminded Tory of the vaulted ceiling of Liberty Cathedral.

John Cornplanter was unmistakable, standing straight with his shoulders held back, his plumed cap crowned with pheasant feathers and one single eagle feather rising vertically. He wore a black ribbon around his neck, as well as a necklace with a large silver medallion, a blousy shirt clamped by iron bracelets at his wrists, a crimson colored wool sash draped around his shoulders, tasseled buckskin pants and moccasins. The creased skin around his eyes gave the impression he was smiling.

His companion was tall and gaunt, with a mop of silvery hair brushed in a side part, and clean shaven except for bushy sideburns. He wore a strange costume, similar to a jumpsuit—a faded blue-denim work shirt with the sleeves rolled up, and matching blue jeans tucked into high leather boots. He stood awkwardly, hands on hips, elbows flared out, and gawked at them as they approached. He and Cornplanter made quite the odd couple.

"Greetings, Tory and Tecumseh," Cornplanter said in a warm voice. "I am John Cornplanter, and this is Barnabas, who is a visiting Scientist."

"You might be wondering about my name ..." Tec said, glancing over at String who was expressionless. "My parents and grandparents are Amish, but when your predecessor, Cornplanter the Preacher, came through town they got swept up in the spirit of the Native Revival. Most people just call me Tec."

Cornplanter grinned. "I can relate. My mother came from Glass Town and named me after John, the Gospel writer." That brought a smile to even String's dour face. "But if you don't mind, I like the sound of Tecumseh."

"We've come a very long way to meet you," Tec said.

"I'm sure there is much to tell of your journey. You have arrived at a fortuitous time! We are discussing these young trees," he pointed at a set of saplings scattered throughout the understory of the mature trees. "Barnabas, why don't you explain more."

Barnabas spread his arms in a wide arc, gesturing to the tall trees overhead. "You may not realize it, but you're looking at *Ulmus Americana*—the American Elm. These were once the majestic king of American trees, but in the century before the Blackout, all were wiped out by a plague, a fungus carried by wood-beetles, carried in on ships from across the sea. The American Elm was considered extinct by scientists. But then, all these centuries later, the Seneca discovered this stand of elms growing in this valley. In fact, it's why I came up here." Barnabas got a wistful twinkle in his eyes. "You could say it's my life's work, to restore the elm trees ..."

"Ah, Barnabas, my friend, you neglect the larger story of this valley, in which the great elm *ookohatah* plays an important part. Do you mind if I tell it?"

Barnabas deferred, and Cornplanter picked up the tale. "We live in a haunted land, filled with the ghosts of the many millions who were swept away by the Blackout so many winters ago. Just dig down a few feet in the soil and you will find signs of them, their plastic trinkets, and often their unburied bones too. Tecumseh, I understand you are a farmer who plows the soil, so you know this well." Tec nodded solemnly. "But not here. Not in this valley …"

"Before I tell you why, though, I have to go even further back, to the time when my namesake, the original Cornplanter, had his longhouse in this valley, not far from here. After the First American Revolution, he traveled all the way to Philadelphia to meet and exchange letters with the new American president, George Washington. A great Treaty was signed at *Canandaigua*, promising these lands were the Seneca's—*forever*. Of course, we know the history, the land was whittled down and parceled out and swindled away. Yet despite it all, this lone stretch of valley along the Allegheny remained intact, the home of the Seneca."

He frowned. "The Americans believed above all in *Progress*, and to them that meant *dominion* over nature, making the land more *productive*. They never met a river they didn't want to dam, a swamp they didn't try to drain. And so their *Engineers* came up with an excuse, some nonsense about *flood control*—" which brought a sharp laugh from String "—and built that dam you passed on the way upriver. They seized this land, breaking the Treaty of Washington, moved the Seneca out of their towns and off their farms. In the name of flood control, they flooded this entire valley. Where we're standing once was under water as tall as these trees. They called the dam *Kinzua*."

"And then came the Blackout," he said. "The Americans' *Progress* caught up with them, and it came with a terrible price. Best we can figure, over time the spillways clogged up with silt, and some great storm caused the water to go over the crest, causing the dam to bust open. That wall of water must have swept everything from its path, all the way to Steel Town—"

"Like the Johnstown Flood!" Tory exclaimed.

Cornplanter nodded with appreciation. "With the water gone, a new forest sprung up ..."

Barnabas interjected with excitement, "There must have been elm seeds buried in the mud, that somehow survived all that time! This is perfect habitat, elms thrive in floodplains like this ..."

"Much like the Seneca!" Cornplanter laughed. "Now, to our purpose here today—"

Again Barnabas couldn't contain himself and jumped in again, "We are going to transplant some of these young elms over the divide, into the Genesee River watershed."

"Yes," Cornplanter said, taking the interruptions in stride. "But we Seneca are sensitive to being moved against one's wishes. So I'm going to spend some time with these elms, to see which are freely willing to go." Barnabas rolled his eyes a bit at this, but wisely kept his mouth shut. "If you can permit me a few moments..."

Just then a blue jay swooped in, lighted on a branch of one of the saplings, causing the thin tree to sway. The bird cried out loudly—*jeer jeer jeer*—and then flitted away.

"I think we have our first volunteer!" Cornplanter said with a smile. He crumbled some tobacco onto the ground at the base of that tree, then tied a thin band of purple and white shells around the trunk to mark it.

"This may take some time," String said.

The rest of them headed down to the river to give Cornplanter some space, and String started a cook-fire on the gravel beach. He had brought along a basket of fresh corn from the village, which he half-peeled to remove the silk, then soaked the ears thoroughly in the river and laid the wet husks directly on the coals to roast.

After a while Cornplanter came down from the forest to join them. They let the corn cool, peeled away the burnt husks and ate. Tory watched the men to figure out how to hold the corn cob with both hands and bite into the kernels. The taste was incredible, like a burst of sunshine. Sweet juice ran down her chin, but she didn't even notice. Tec had the presence of mind to pass around the venison jerky and smoked fish Rollo had given them at the bridge, and there were nods and grunts of appreciation.

After eating, Tec broke out his fishing rods and gave an impromptu demonstration of fly-casting to String, Deer Legs and Barnabas, while Cornplanter stayed back with Tory. Cornplanter packed his toma-hawk-pipe with tobacco, lit it with an ember from the fire, and leaned back into the grass, propping himself up on one elbow. After a few puffs he passed the pipe to Tory. She noticed the sharpness of the blade on the underside, glanced over at the men by the river, standing a good distance away.

"So let's talk about this message," Cornplanter said.

Tory took a little draw and was careful not to inhale, just letting the smoke sit in her mouth before breathing out. She returned the pipe to Cornplanter, then removed the documents from her satchel—Levi's calendar, and a map that Asha had drawn. She explained their belief, that the message told the time and place of the arrival of a water ship from Mars. Cornplanter's reaction to hearing the news was impossible to read.

"I'm sure Barnabas can verify all this if you need it," Tory said in a rush. "We were traveling with a Scientist of our own … but he and our Agent, Katya, were captured and are being held for ransom by Pirates."

"Ah, the Pirates. We'll have to do something about them … But I know Katya well, she can handle herself. In fact, I'm more worried for the Pirates than for her!" They both laughed at that thought.

"Tory, may I ask you something?" Cornplanter said. "Are you happier out here, now that you're outside the Belt Wall?"

The question caught her off guard, but after a pause, the words came gushing out. "I had no idea how beautiful, how rich everything was going to be. They never told us. I was ready for an environmental catastrophe, tribes of cannibals ..."

Cornplanter chuckled. "Sorry to disappoint you!" Then he grew serious, "Why do you think the people who gave you this message sent it? To what purpose? And why to me?"

"I don't know. It must be important that *you* know about the water ship coming ... but honestly, I have been trying to figure it out and can't."

He nodded, lost in thought. "This information is too big for one person. Being given the name *Gyantwachia* is an honor—but I'm not not a *President* or a *Ceasar*, like the ancients. I'm one chief among many, and we Seneca arrive at our decisions through consensus."

He took a long draw on the pipe. "And even if the Seneca are of one mind, any action we take—or don't take—will affect other people. The Ten Towns. Our brothers and sisters who live along the Lakes—the Onondoga, Mohawk, Huron, Ojibwe, and Cree. Should they not know of this as well?"

He sat up and his eyes flashed. "What is needed is a Great Council. Gather the different tribes, share this knowledge, and come to a collective decision."

He stood and it was as if a silent signal was sent to String and Deer Legs, who turned and came trotting over. Barnabas followed. Tec looked around puzzled, seeing his audience had vanished.

"Here's what I propose. We are going to send our fastest scouts out to the Ten Towns, to the people of the Lakes, bearing a message of Peace, asking them to send representatives to join a Great Council."

"We will gather at this place, just northeast of Lake Town, on the border of our territory. It is neutral ground." He pointed to a place on at Asha's map on the shore near the X in Lake Erie. Tory stared in disbelief.

That's not far from the secret landing zone!

"I myself will journey to Lake Town, to talk to their Captains, given how close they are to this event. The Sturgeon Moon rises tomorrow night… so we'll commence the Great Council on the new moon after the Harvest Moon. That should give time for people to arrive."

Tec had come over and caught the last part, and asked, "But what if it's a trap set by the Martians? The Steel Town Council thought so…"

"You raise a good point, Tecumseh …" Cornplanter said, his brow furrowed. "There so is much we don't know about the Lost Tribe of Mars."

On an inspiration, Tory dug out Niko's book from the backpack, where it was wrapped in a square of oilcloth, and presented it to Cornplanter, "Here's a book you should read, by the Librarian in Steel Town. His research has uncovered the events leading up to the Blackout."

"O-ho, what a gift!" Cornplanter exclaimed. "We've passed down many stories among our people for thousands of moons, and are still trying to make sense of what happened so long ago. It will be interesting to compare to this Testament."

Cornplanter straightened to his full height and addressed Tory and Tec, "I want to thank you both for your bravery and your insight. I am inviting you to stay as my guests at Chautauqua until the Great Council. Tecumseh, given that you're already here, in my message to Flood Town, I'm going to ask permission that you serve as its representative."

"Dear old Verna will love that!" Tec laughed.

"Deer Legs, camp here tonight with them, and in the morning, lead them to Chautauqua. Please ask my wife to help them settle into the Guest Lodge, and bring supplies from our village." The boy nodded.

He turned to String, "Come, let's go back to Buckaloons. We have many preparations to make."

Barnabas looked a bit lost, but Cornplanter reassured him. "Stay here tonight with the others. We'll send people and carts in the morning to start moving the elms. Don't worry, my friend, this is just as important. Maybe in the course of time, even more so."

And in an instant Cornplanter and String were in a canoe headed back down the Allegheny. "He's an impressive man," Tec observed.

Tory remained quiet, fidgeting with her silver necklace, and watched as the canoe passed through the gap in the distance and out of sight.

The way to Chautauqua followed an established foot-path that ran northwest across the rolling country, crossing through a mix of forests and meadows. The path was so much easier than the journey across the rugged hills of the Treaty Hunting Grounds, and yet Tory struggled to keep pace with the two men, and was sure she slowed them down. She felt the tug of gravity in her very bones, and wanted nothing more than to lie down in the ferns, in the tall grass, and sleep.

At sunset they crested the hill overlooking Chautauqua, a jewel of a lake nestled among gentle hills, with a picturesque village along the shore, fires burning bright in the twilight. To the east the Sturgeon Moon rose, bloated and orange in the late summer haze.

Tory couldn't help but think back to that first night when she arrived. This would be the third full moon since then—about ninety days on Earth. *The idea was that I'd get stronger the longer I was here—not weaker!* She knew she needed her stamina back, for what lay ahead.

Deer Legs ushered them into a longhouse situated on a bluff over-looking the lake, then jogged away toward the village further down the shore, to find Cornplanter's wife. Inside, the space was big enough to sleep twenty, and felt like a cavern with just the two of them. Tec busied himself lighting a fire in the central hearth.

Finally Tory spoke up. "Tec, I have a confession to make …" She sighed deeply. "I'm not feeling well …haven't been feeling well …for some time now."

"You're not that good at hiding," he replied. "I've noticed."

"My stomach is always upset. And now, I see that bed and just want to lie down and sleep. I think I may have caught some disease …"

"I'll go find some wild ginger and make you some tea that will help your nausea. But Tory—you should have told me earlier! Remember how you said we have to trust each other?"

She hung her head, "I know. It's hard for me to open up."

He enfolded her in his arms and she slumped against his chest. Under his shirt, the raised bumps of the stitches pressed against her cheek. They stood there for a long time, and he gently stroked her hair.

Then a thought struck Tec and he asked, "When is the last time you had your *time of the moon*. Your menstrual cycle?"

She was puzzled by the question. "I-I haven't. I don't. I was put on fertility control since … shortly after puberty, and it suppresses … that aspect."

Tec's face screwed up, like he'd tasted something bitter, but then he composed himself. "But since you left the Belt Wall, have you taken any of this medicine?"

She had a flashing image of the empty med bulbs floating in zero gravity, flushing them out the airlock.

"No, I haven't."

"Well that explains it!" Tec exclaimed.

She looked at him blankly.

"Medicines wear off. The way you are feeling—the tiredness, the nausea. You aren't sick, Tory. You're *pregnant!*"

14

Staying at the Guest Lodge felt like being in a cave. Though the longhouse entrance faced east towards the rising sun, their beds were at the far end, in the cozy gloom, the only sound the hissing red coals in the hearth. In the dim early light, she heard Tec puttering around, but she rolled over, burrowing deep beneath the fur blankets. All she wanted to do was sleep.

By the time she did get up, she was surprised to find how high the sun was in the sky. Tec was outside to greet her with a steaming mug of ginger tea, and they sat side by side on the slope-backed *adirondack* chairs, watching the wisps of fog rising from the lake, the sunlight illuminating the trees on the far shore.

The Guest Lodge was located on a triangle-shaped peninsula that jutted out into Lake Chautauqua, forming a pinched channel that was only three hundred meters wide. North of the narrow point, a scenic bay opened up, ringed by a few hills, at the foot of which lay the Seneca village, eight longhouses encircled by a wooden stockade. Canoes lined the gravel shore, and from time to time people paddled out onto the lake, waving to them as they passed.

"Please let me know when you're ready to talk," Tec said after a while.

Tory nodded, breathed in the fragrant steam from her mug, but remained silent, watching the boats.

Around mid-morning, Cornplanter's wife, who was named Soon, walked the lakeside path from the village to the Guest Lodge, circling around the corn fields and orchards that lay in between. She was accompanied by Deer Legs, who called out "Heya!" as they approached.

Soon was strikingly beautiful, though she did little to embellish it. Her hair was held back in a simple braid and she wore a patterned blanket as a shawl over her shoulders against the morning chill. It was impossible to tell her age or what her relationship was with Deer Legs. *Is she his mother? Older sister?*

She unrolled a black bearskin on the ground and arranged the various items that Deer Legs brought for them, ears of corn, smoked fish, apples, dried berries, yellow thumb-shaped potatoes. She also brought a sampling of books from the village library. One book caught Tory's eye, with its bright green cloth cover and illustrations of birds inside, *The Everglades: River of Grass.*

Soon smiled but did not speak to them—though it didn't seem to be because of any language barrier or taboo among the Seneca regarding outsiders—she just was a very quiet person. Deer Legs did not have that problem. Normally used to having to hold his tongue and listen while his elders spoke, now he became a babbling fountain of information.

"This wild rice comes to us in trade with our brothers and sisters the Ojibwe, who live along *Gitchigumi* far to the west," Deer Legs said, gesturing to the items on the blanket. "... and these baskets come from our brothers and sisters the Mohawk who live to the east by *Kaniatarowanenneh*—you can see how the splints of black ash are woven together to make this pattern, with braids of sweetgrass used for embellishment. These are really prized baskets, I can tell you!"

Tec pointed to the smoked fish and said, "How can I help catch?"

The next morning, Soon and Deer Legs arrived paddling a beautiful canoe with a distinctive hooked nose at the front, bowed out wide in the middle. "This is Cornplanter's canoe," Deer Legs called out as they came into shore. "A gift to him from the Ojibwe. They are the masters of crafting birch-bark canoes. The hull is made of birch bark, the cords from spruce roots, the frame from white cedar." He thumped his paddle against the side to show how sturdy it was.

Deer Legs leapt over the side into the shallow water, while Soon gracefully exited the front onto the rocks. Tec helped carry the canoe ashore and immediately spied the massive fishing pole resting inside, easily two and a half meters long.

"May I?" he asked, and Soon nodded. Tec hefted the mighty pole with a sense of awe. "Hickory wood," he observed. The shiny metal reel went *click-click-click* as he turned the handle. Deer Legs opened a case which contained hand-carved lures, each one painted brightly to look like a bait fish, with three sets of giant treble hooks dangling below.

"You ever fished for muskie before?" Deer Legs asked.

"It's been a lifelong dream of mine," Tec said. "I've read all about it."

"Reading and doing aren't the same," Soon said aloud, startling them all.

Deer Legs took the opportunity to explain, "Soon is a legendary fisher. The big muskies are notched on a measuring post by the shore, and she has caught the biggest. That's her pole, her lures, she carved and painted them herself. And that reel there was crafted in Steel Town, to her design."

Tory saw the giant hoop net and hammer-like club lying in the canoe. "How big *are* these fish?" she asked, a little concerned.

"You will see," Soon said.

Tec said, "As someone who ties his own flies, I am amazed at the craft involved with these lures, Soon."

"And I have heard about *fly-fishing*, but have never tried," Soon replied. "Maybe we can teach each other?"

For some reason Tory felt her cheeks getting hot, and she blurted out, "I know how to fly-fish too, and have caught a lot of big trout!"

Soon looked down at her feet, nodded to herself, then smiled warmly, "I'm sure you have. You know, fishing for muskies is not for one person. Tecumseh will need you out on the lake as well. You can learn together."

"Oh—" Tory sputtered. *What just came over me?*

At dusk, Tec dragged Tory along with him to the marshes along a nearby creek, to catch frogs. Tory's job was to shine the hooded kerosene lantern, which froze the frogs in its bright glare, while Tec sneaked up and tried to grab them. Some of the times he was successful, but most attempts he came up empty handed, and often tumbled into the muck. Tory found the entire process very entertaining.

Tory slept in late again, creeping out of bed just in time to meet Soon and Deer Legs on their morning visit. At breakfast, Tory devoured a whole skillet of scrambled eggs and venison sausage, her appetite fully restored and making up for lost time. Afterwards, Tec and Tory took Cornplanter's canoe out onto the lake.

They started fishing in the shallower water below the narrows, hugging the shoreline. One of the covered Mohawk baskets shimmied side to side from the live frogs inside. When Tec cracked open the lid to grab a frog, another one inevitably squirmed out and jumped around the canoe. Tory laughed out loud as Tec tried to nab the escaped frog with his free hand, still holding a wriggling frog in another, all while avoiding tipping the canoe. Finally the runaway frog leapt to freedom over the gunwale, landing with a *plop* into the lake.

Tec hooked the captive frog through its upper lip and cast it out on the long pole, and in no time he had a bass on the line. He gave her a significant look, as if to say, *See?*

The bass was a round, stocky fish, drab green in color, with a large gaping mouth. The fish fought hard, but Tory found it ugly compared to the sleek form, rainbow coloring and red spots of the trout she'd caught.

Once Tec caught enough bass to supply dinner, he let the rest of the frogs go. But instead of returning to shore, they paddled further north, into the upper bay. Soon told them how the muskie—which sometimes she called *jighoses*, which meant *long face* in Seneca—loved the cold depths, but as the nights turned cooler, would come up into shallower parts.

While Tec fished, Tory delicately turned around to face the stern and lowered her body into the hull of the canoe, propped her back against the bow seat, and cracked open *River of Grass.* The book was about a vast swamp located at the southern tip of America, home to countless species of exotic birds, and told the story of how Engineers—*the same ones that built the dam at Kinzua!*—tried to drain the Everglades for farming and development, with disastrous results.

She was surprised to read the name *Okeechobee,* which she recognized from her years working in Reclamation. For centuries, AIs tried to devise a way to tap that large source of fresh water, which lay only a slight deviation south of the tankers' regular flight paths. But the lake was too shallow, less than three meters at maximum depth—the intake nozzle would get stuck in the mud at the bottom. Other lakes on the other side of the planet, like *Baikal* and *Tanganyika*, were also considered, but the predictability of the long-established routes won out in the final analysis, and so the Great Lakes remained the sole source of water for Nubai.

Tory hoped the book could distract her, but found herself reading the same lines over and over again. Her thoughts kept circling around the same thing: *I'm pregnant.* She pictured the AIs in a frenzy over the news, running scenario after scenario, and laughed quietly.

But Tec heard her, and after hours of no action, took it personally. "I see why they call muskies *The Fish of Ten Thousand Casts!*" he said, dejected.

By late afternoon they arrived back at the Guest Lodge, exhausted from the long day. Tec prepared a meal of cooked bass, fire-roasted corn and potatoes, and wild rice. Then after dinner, Tec built a fire in the outdoor ring and they huddled close under a fur blanket and stargazed. In the cold sky, the stars appeared even more brilliant, the glittering braid of the galaxy like a rope she could reach up and grab.

The next day it rained, and they spent the day inside in bed together, reading and napping. Tory rested her head against Tec, using his stomach as a pillow, and Tec ran his hand through her hair, which had grown out and was now longer than she'd ever worn it. But they didn't talk about what was on their minds.

Each day they canoed to a different location, let the boat drift with the wind and current. Tec always had a theory why this particular location, the current weather, were perfect for catching muskies. Then, after many casts with no luck, he would revise his statement to why the conditions were actually terrible.

One afternoon out on the boat, Tory glanced up from her book, watched as Tec cast the long pole, listened to the *click click click* of him slowly reeling in the line, the *whirrr* when he cast it back out. Puffy white clouds drifted across the blue sky. With the arrival of colder nights, and shorter days, the trees on the surrounding hills had lost their vibrant green, now faded to an olive color, the crowns of some trees hinting yellow and red. A chilly breeze crossed the lake and made her wish she had brought a blanket.

"Tec, I can't stop thinking something bad is going to happen," she said, breaking the silence.

Tec stopped reeling in the line. He grinned at the sight of her sprawled out in the hull of the canoe, the book resting on her chest, like she was napping in a hammock.

"Tory, you completed your mission. The message has been delivered to John Cornplanter! He's assembling the leaders of the First Nations and Ten Towns—a lot of wise people—well of course, excepting myself," he winked. "But the weight of the decision, of what to do next, is off your shoulders. You can turn your thoughts to other things …"

It was quiet for a while and he made another long cast into the deep water. "Can I ask you a question?" The lake lapped against the side of the canoe. "Will you come back with me?"

Tory stared at the clouds drifting overhead.

"I want to," she said.

"That's good enough for me."

As he resumed bringing in his line, the reel stopped turning and the tip of the stiff pole bent, a sign of being snagged on a submerged tree stump. Tec muttered to himself for letting the lure sink too deep while he was busy talking to Tory. "Soon will not be happy if I lose one of her lures …"

Then the pole nearly jumped out of his hands.

"I hooked a muskie!" he yelled.

The force of the strike put Tec off balance, and as he tried to brace himself, his shin jammed into the gunwale. For a precarious moment, the canoe rocked side to side and nearly toppled. But Tec crouched down, lowering his center of gravity, and Tory was already laying in the bottom of the boat, so the wide-bellied canoe quickly balanced out.

In the water nearby was a furious thrashing and the entire pole—which had seemed unbendable—was now bowed so sharply it looked like it would snap. It appeared Tec was wrestling with an an invisible hand trying to yank the pole from him, jerking it from side to side. He hooked the butt end of the rod under his arm, wedged against his ribcage, so he could reel with his free hand.

"Get the net!"

Tory scrambled to place the long-handled hoop net in the water. A pale green shape flashed underwater and at first she thought it was a log of driftwood until it started writhing.

"Get the net around it!" Tec shouted.

"I'm trying!" Tory yelled back at him.

In an instant she saw a chance to slide the billowing net under the fish and scooped upward. A monstrous, dripping, twisting shape took form in the mesh of the net. The thing weighed nearly twenty kilos and Tory had to strain with all her might to get it over the gunwale.

The muskie slid out of the net into the bottom of the canoe, and she hopped over her seat to get out of its way. The Seneca name *long face* was accurate—the fish had an enormous jaw that jutted out in front and stretched back all the way behind its eyes, filled with razor-sharp teeth. Its body was long and snakelike, greenish-yellow, with blood red fins. It flopped around violently, leaving a streak of slime across the cover of Tory's book. Tec wasted no time grabbing it through one of its gills, finding the club, and whacking it hard once, twice at the base of its skull, killing it.

For a long time they just sat in the boat, breathing heavily, looking at each other and the muskie in disbelief. Then Tec let out a whoop that echoed across the lake.

He didn't bother going back to the Guest Lodge, but instead made a beeline for the Seneca village. He marched up to the front gates of the stockade, laid the muskie down in the grass. "To thank you for your generosity!" he called out.

Villagers came out to see, and several of the older men and women nodded in approval. Soon was given the honor of carrying the muskie down to the measuring post. Tory had no idea how a slender woman like Soon could catch muskies, but changed her mind after seeing how effortlessly Soon held the fish one-handed by its hook-jaw against the post, while Deer Legs stretched the tail down to touch the dirt. The muskie was just a finger's width shy of the notch which marked Soon's record.

The assembled crowd cheered and laughed and some patted Tec on the shoulder, pinching their fingers to show "just that much." One of the elders said to him, "It is better not to measure the fish. Then, when you tell stories, you're not lying if it happens to keep getting bigger." More laughs.

A bonfire was built on shore and a feast prepared in honor of the catch. Everyone in the village, including the children, shared a bit of the muskie's flesh. From that point on, some sort of barrier was broken. Although they were never invited inside the stockade, a steady stream of villagers came to the Guest Lodge throughout the day, to chat, exchange stories, share their crafts.

The way the Seneca grew corn was much different than the straight, orderly rows that Tec was accustomed to planting on his farm. Here, the corn stalks were scattered about, spaced at a distance from each other, and planted alongside green beans, whose tendrils climbed the corn stalk like a trellis, and pumpkin vines, which radiated outward in a circle along the ground. "The Three Sisters," this method was called, *jo-hay-ko*.

Tec gave lessons on how to tie flies and cast a fly rod, and had long discussions with some of the elders about the healing properties of various herbs and plants, which often led to foraging expeditions into the surrounding woods. They went on long hikes, hunting for rabbits and grouse along the way, Tory using a rifle borrowed from Deer Legs. Tec didn't go back out muskie fishing, and when she asked why, he smiled, "My father had a saying, *Always best to quit while you're ahead.*"

Each night before bed, Tory drew an X through another day on the calendar. The days, which had seemed in abundance when they first arrived here, began to dwindle to a handful.

One evening at sunset, three of the village elders arrived wearing weird carved wooden masks, the long twisted faces painted crimson with streaming white hair. These were the medicine men wearing *False Faces*, and they invited Tec to join their Sweat Lodge that night, which was considered a great honor.

After he departed, she built a small fire outside along the shore. The sound of chirping crickets was nearly deafening, but she didn't mind, actually found it calming. The Harvest Moon rose full and pale yellow, washing out many of the stars, but Mars still appeared as a tiny dot. So far away, yet it gleamed like a red eye, its gaze fixed down upon her. She idly rolled the silver pendant of her necklace through her fingers.

When he comes back I'm going to tell him.

The temperature plummeted and the flames burned low. Even wrapped in the fur blanket, she began to shiver. After a while, she gave up waiting and went inside, crawled into bed. When she got up to pee in the middle of the night, the other side of the bed was still empty.

The next morning when she woke, Soon and Deer Legs had already arrived at the Guest Lodge, and Tec was with them. All wore somber expressions.

"It's time," Soon said.

The journey from Chautauqua to the shore of Lake Erie was an easy morning's walk, which was a good thing, because Tory didn't think she had a longer trek in her. Every bit of her body felt like there was extra weight pushing down.

In a few short days, the countryside had completely transformed. The trees were ablaze in bright reds, oranges, and yellows, while the meadows were fringed with purple aster and yellow goldenrod. The rolling plateau ended in an escarpment that provided a breathtaking view of Lake Erie. Chautauqua had seemed a large lake, but from any point the opposite shoreline was always visible. Here the blue lake stretched out of sight, from horizon to horizon. Tory felt dizzy seeing such a huge expanse of fresh water. *No wonder they send the tankers here.*

Below the natural ledge, a ribbon of flat ground hugged the shore, checkered with forest, meadows, marshes, and neat rows of grapevines. Far to the south, a peninsula extended out into the lake, and at the tip stood a light house that Deer Legs called the Flash Light. A ship with tall wooden masts and furled sails lay at anchor just off shore. "The delegation from Lake Town," Deer Legs remarked.

They arrived at the campsite to find Seneca and Lake Towners working together, building *wigwams*. One group harvested black ash saplings and cattail rushes from a nearby bog, another stripped the bark from the trees, a third wove the reeds into mats. A circle was etched into a cleared patch of ground using a rope tied to a central stake, with anchoring peg-holes dug around the circumference. The saplings were bent into the shape of an arch and formed the ribs of a dome that was then thatched with the reed mats. Strips of bark were tied in a ring around the smoke vent at the top. When finished, each wigwam could sleep four people comfortably, six snuggled close.

The Mohawk and Onondoga arrived shortly after, dressed in ceremonial clothes similar to the Seneca, wearing their formal *gustoweh* feathered caps, the Mohawk with three eagle feathers raised vertically, the Onondoga with two—one pointing straight up, the other tipped off to the side—in contrast to the Seneca, who sported a single straight feather. Cornplanter greeted them with warm familiarity and they spent some time smoking pipes.

Glass Town came next, overland from the west, escorted by Onondoga guides, with the Amish from Lancaster not far behind, riding fine draft horses. The Huron, Ojibwe and Cree approached from the northeast in elongated birch-bark canoes that held six people, all of whom paddled, three to a side stroking in unison, cutting through the wind-blown waves on the lake. Some wore traditional dress—buckskin shirts and leggings and moccasins—but most wore blue jeans and flannel shirts, and hats with a stiff bill that shaded their eyes.

Another tall ship from Lake Town appeared from the southwest, its stacked billowing sails like a fast-moving cloud against the horizon, bringing the delegations from Young Town, Wheel Town and the most distant town, Falls-of-the-Ohio. These groups had journeyed by steamboat up the Ohio and taken the overland route to Lake Erie—the same path Katya suggested when the Pirates had them cornered. Tory felt a sudden stab of guilt. *Where are you, Katya?*

People from villages scattered up and down the the shoreline of Lake Erie stopped by the campsite, to see what all the commotion was about. They brought bottles of wine from their vineyards, catches of walleye and bass from the Lake, and were invited to join the bonfires at night, the singing and dancing and exchange of stories.

During the afternoon, teams were picked to play a match of *lacrosse*, a game where all the players carried sticks with a hooped basket at the end, trying to advance a wooden ball down the field and into the opposing team's net. The men stripped down into loincloths and undergarments, and the women watched from the sideline, placing wagers on each team.

In the first couple of matches, the teams were aligned, the First Nations against the Ten Towns—and the Natives won easily. But then an alternating selection occurred between two captains, and the teams became balanced. Several young men from the Ten Towns were picked highly in the draft, based on their fierce playing style in the first round.

Lacrosse was a brutal, violent sport played under the bright sun. Players from both teams emerged bloody and nursing wounds. And smiling too, with arms around their opponents. Luckily Tec was considered too old to play, but he had no problem joining afterwards to drink a cup from the casks of beer that Lake Town supplied.

Just before sunset, the parties from Coal Town, Oil Town and Steel Town arrived together in a large contingent. It was easy to recognize the short and stout Bruno from Mount Washington, with his close-cropped head and long goatee, walking with a certain swagger to show off the muscles of his bare arms. Six Seneca accompanied them, decked in war-gear, tomahawks hanging from their belts, their faces painted in red and black. Everyone was armed with rifles.

In the middle of the marching column were nine disheveled men with their hands bound in leather cords and heads bowed, looking like they hadn't eaten well in a very long time, nor bathed either. Katya was walking behind them, flashing a beaming smile. She waved a cheerful hello when she saw Tec and Tory in the crowd that had gathered. Krystol was there too, huffing and puffing, waddling as if his inner thighs were chafed, and altogether looking out of sorts. Tory noticed the long rifle she had given him was slung over his shoulder.

The prisoners were brought before Cornplanter and the others gathered around. String stood at the front of the Seneca warriors. "We captured these Pirates not far from Carved Rock. As you suggested, we sent There-He-Goes with his Permit ahead through the Treaty Hunting Grounds. He met up with the parties from Steel Town and Coal Town who were coming up the Allegheny."

"Our courier found the message Tec left in the drop-box, and so we brought ten militia with us just in case," Bruno supplied. "There-He-Goes had a good plan—we kept going up the river as normal, letting our boys out on shore before we got to the big bend at Carved Rock, so they could climb up to the mountain top. When the Pirates tried to stop us at the old bridge, your Seneca warriors swept down from the north, and our militia had them pinned from above."

String said plainly, "They surrendered."

"These Pirates steal your trade as much as they do ours," Bruno said. "So we brought them here, to the great and wise Cornplanter, so you can decide their Judgment."

Cornplanter bowed his head silently in acknowledgment. He walked along the line of Pirates who huddled pitifully, taking a moment to stop and look at each man.

"I'm sure you have all heard tales of our ancestors, the *Haudenosaunee*, the Six Nations, the people of the Longhouse, who the ancient Americans called *Iroquois*. They were legendary warriors, had no fear, and woe to any enemy they might encounter! Those defeated in battle were scalped—many while still alive. But the dead were the lucky ones. Captives would be brought back to the village and forced to run through the *Gauntlet*, a row of people that would beat them with sticks and clubs. And that was just the beginning. The Haudenosaunee were masters of torture, would peel strips of skin from flesh, remove fingers, and finally burn their enemies alive."

Some of the Pirates were visibly shaking in fear, but others arched their back and stood defiantly.

"People were arrogant and full of hubris back then—the Haudenosaunee included—thinking that a slight, a disagreement, a trespass justified the taking of human life. But we have the wisdom—and burden—of hindsight. There simply aren't enough of us left to indulge in that childish view of the world."

He continued, "I don't know what decisions led to you to abandon your home and take up a life of Piracy. You'll have to answer for that to your Creator. But in the here and now, listen to my words and my Judgment."

He paused for effect, then said, "Each of you will be sent to a different village among the Seneca. You'll live and work there for two winters. Not as slaves, but as free men. After that time, if you want a Writ of Passage to travel outside Seneca Nation, I will grant it. But if you want to stay, marry a wife, become a part of the community, you will be welcomed."

There were some raised eyebrows, exchanged looks, but the elders among the First Nations, who stood at the front of the crowd, nodded in approval. One of the Pirates stepped forward and fell to his knees. "Thank you, Chief Cornplanter. Thank you!"

Tory and Tec settled into the "Flood Town" wigwam, a surprisingly large space that felt empty with only the two of them. This was her first opportunity alone with Tec all day, but all Tory wanted to do was lay down and sleep. But she mustered the energy to say, "I missed you last night."

"I'm sorry about that," Tec said, preoccupied with unpacking their gear. "I had no idea the Sweat Lodge would go all night."

"I waited up. I wanted to talk ... about things."

Tec stopped what he was doing and turned to her, but before he could respond, there was a rustling at the door, and Katya popped her head in. "Hope I'm not interupting," she winked.

She had a bottle of whiskey with her and cups. "I heard the news from John Cornplanter! Congratulations! I am so happy for you."

Tec took a pour, but Tory declined. "Yeah, the whole not-drinking thing, might be why I haven't traveled down the 'mom' path yet," she laughed.

Katya launched right into a tale about about her time in captivity with the Pirates, which mostly involved loafing about, beating them at cards, and listening to Krystol complain. She was riveted to hear Tec tell of their journey across the Treaty Hunting Grounds, and cringed at the sight of Tec's still-healing scars.

Just as Tory thought the visit was winding to a close, Katya said, "It's a bit crowded over there at Steel Town camp, and I could use a little time apart from our good friend Krystol! OK if I just stay here?"

"Of course," Tec said, and went out to find another bedroll and blanket for her.

When he was gone, Katya asked, "Hey, you all right? You've been quiet."

"Just tired."

The next day—the final day on the calendar before *October 13*—passed much like the previous, with greetings and the exchange of stories and small tokens. Tec was in his element, talking to just about everyone, interested in every topic. Tory found it tedious, but did her best to appear as if she were listening, nodded, and answered questions when asked.

As the sun slowly crossed the sky, Tory began to worry. There seemed to be no sense of urgency among anyone. After another match of lacrosse began, Tory sought out Katya in a panic. She was engaged in a heated round of betting on who would score next, and stepped away to hear Tory.

"When is this Great Council going to start? The water transport is scheduled to arrive tomorrow morning! Can't you talk to Cornplanter?"

Across the field, Cornplanter stood quietly, arms crossed, watching the back and forth of the match. Deer Legs was heavily cross-checked from behind, then was helped to his feet by two men, one from Steel Town, the other a Cree.

"I think he knows what he's doing," Katya said.

As the sun dipped toward the horizon, its dazzling twin reflected in the clear lake, a drum began to beat. One by one, the delegations entered a central circle, with benches around a fire pit stacked high with unlit driftwood. The surrounding trees glowed orange and yellow and red in the last light of day.

The Great Council began with the *Thanksgiving Address*, delivered in turns by Cornplanter and two other chiefs from the Onondoga and Mohawk Nations. The long speech gave thanks to the Earth, the waters, fish, the fields, berries, the Three Sisters, medicine herbs, trees, animals, birds, the Four Winds, lightning and thunder, the Sun, the Moon, the Stars, the teachers who had gone before, and the Creator. After each stanza, a refrain was repeated, "*Now our minds are one.*" The recital stretched on and on, taking almost as long as one of the Amish hymns from the Ausbund.

Next, introductions were made, where members of each delegation stood, stated their names, their tribe or town, their craft—which took a long time with such a large assembly. As this went on, night fell and the central fire was lit.

Finally the welcome ceremony concluded, and the circle was opened to discussion. By now, everyone was familiar with the deciphered message, and were in general agreement that it must be about the arrival of a Martian water transport ship.

An Ojibwe confirmed, "We have seen what you describe, out on *Gitchigumi*—always at night, always when there is an aurora. Great bolts of lightning flash, outlining the shadow of a giant rope coming down from the sky."

A Captain of Lake Town added, "Yes, our fisherman have reported much the same when out on the lake at night, though most people took it as a sign of having too much to drink!" Everyone laughed at her joke.

After the laughter died down, one of the stoic Cree said, "We too have seen this on *Winnipeg.*"

A delegate from Glass Town asked, "But why here?"

The scientist Barnabas, who had joined as a guest of Cornplanter, spoke authoritatively, "The Great Lakes of North America were formed after the glaciers receded in the Ice Age, 12,000 years ago. They are the source of nearly all the freshwater on this continent—"

Not to be outdone, Krystol interjected, "There's an advantage of refilling from the Great Lakes, which are so big and wide open. The intake hose—the 'rope' as you called it—likely creates a drag in the atmosphere that causes the hose to drift for miles across the lake surface while taking in water. Plus they can rotate between the lakes, avoiding a predictable pattern."

People looked at him blankly. Then Katya spoke, "Back before the Blackout, the Great Lakes were where Mars got its water. It makes sense they still use the same routes." Katya leaned over to Tory and whispered, "See, I was listening when you read Niko's book to me."

Bruno from Steel Town said, "So, we know a great rope is going to come down from the sky tomorrow morning over the lake out yonder." He twinkled his fingers above his head. "What do yinz intend to do—climb it?"

The Captain of Lake Town inquired, "Steel Town brought kegs of gunpowder, if I'm not mistaken?"

Bruno replied, "Yes we did."

"I have an idea—" she said. "What if we lashed the kegs into one of our long floating nets. And when the ship drops its hose, we can sail out in front of it, place the net in its path, so it tangles up their pipe. Then, when it lifts into the sky—"

"The lightning will ignite it!" a delegate from Oil Town completed her thought.

All eyes turned to Krystol, who shrugged, "It could work. It sounds pretty complicated though, lots of ways it could fail ..."

An Amish Elder from Lancaster was alarmed hearing this talk. "What if instead we just do nothing? Let their ship come and go in peace."

A delegate from Young Town stood up, "Because we can send them a message. We're not going to be dominated—ever again!" He smacked his fist into his palm for effect.

The Onondoga chief asked out loud, "Why do they deserve having their water shut off? There is plenty of the lake to share."

"We know the Martians were responsible for the Blackout!" a delegate from Coal Town cried out.

The Mohawk chief replied, "But that happened hundreds of winters ago, to our ancestors, who have long stopped caring about the wrongs that were inflicted upon them. We here today have no grievance with the Martians."

The Amish Elder of Lancaster added, "In fact, we may be creating a new one."

Tec was surprised as anyone to hear himself speak. "We know their intentions aren't good! And why? Because the Martians know we are down here, know our struggles, but have never helped."

"We don't need their help!" the Young Town delegate shouted.

Tec replied, "From Niko's book, we know the Martians have access to powerful medicines—*a way to cure cancer!* Yet they have never offered it to us."

The chief of the Huron grudgingly agreed, "No one with a pure heart would withhold medicine from the sick."

Tory squeezed Tec's hand in support when he sat down, knowing he was talking about his wife Lara, and he mouthed the words back, *Thank you.*

Cornplanter spoke, "Perhaps this is what they want—to provoke us. They *want* us to take some action. Otherwise, why would they reveal the arrival of their water ship to us? I also read the book written by Nicodemus, the Steel Town librarian, about the fall of America. It made clear the water ships are the greatest vulnerability of Mars."

Bruno threw up his arms. "See—it's a trap! All along I've been saying that."

"Perhaps the suggestion of our brethren the Amish of Lancaster is worth heeding," Cornplanter said. "We do nothing, and let the ship pass."

A long silence followed.

Then Cornplanter rose. "So I put it to you now, my brothers and sisters, who have journeyed so far to participate in this Great Council together. Are we in agreement? We will take no action tomorrow. We will let the Martian ship come and go in peace."

Everyone around the circle nodded their head, said yes.

He acknowledged the vote, then continued, "Please, if you have a disagreement, a different thought, raise it now. I promise we won't quit this circle until *all of us are of one mind.*" He stressed the last part.

No one spoke.

"So it is decided."

It was well into the night before Cornplanter was able to detach himself from the celebration that broke out after the Great Council had concluded. He sought out Tory and Tec, and invited them back to his wigwam. Soon was inside already and had a small fire going, and Deer Legs brought in a bottle of icewine, chilled in a nearby brook. "This is a local specialty," Deer Legs informed them. "They let the grapes stay on the vine until it freezes, and then they harvest. Makes for a very sweet wine—"

"Tory is not drinking," Tec said, gently patting her stomach.

Tory flinched a little at his touch. "It's all right," she said. "I can pour the cups. Deer Legs, go have fun with the others."

The boy eagerly ducked back out under the entry flap of woven rushes.

The wine bottles had a glass top, rubber ring and metal clamp that sealed them tight. She popped the hinge open, and then knelt down to pour the cups. With her back turned toward the others, she reached up to her silver necklace and discreetly gave the pendant a half-twist, which caused it to slide open. A tiny white pill slid out into the palm of her hand.

She poured the glasses and handed them out, giving the last cup to Cornplanter, and then sat down in the circle near the entrance next to Soon. Cornplanter smiled at his wife, his new friends around the fire. He was about to raise a toast when suddenly Tory spoke up, interrupting him.

"Before we go any further, I have something to say."

She held up the little white pill from the palm of her hand. "You see this? It's poison. It was meant to kill you, John Cornplanter."

She tossed it into the fire where it vanished with a hiss.

Tec gasped audibly, but Cornplanter reacted evenly, only narrowing his eyes. "There is more you wish to tell us."

She felt their stares burning into her. "Where do I begin?" she said, her voice shaking. "How about with my name—it's actually pronounced *Taurii*." She said it slowly to stretch out the strange vowels. "Taurii Six-Three-Six." She sighed deeply, and looked down at the ground. "And I'm not really from the Belt Wall …"

She tried to make eye contact with Tec but she couldn't bring herself to, and her eyes welled up in tears. "I'm … I'm from Mars. They are the ones who sent me here on this mission."

Tec looked like he had been punched in the stomach, all the blood draining from his face.

"But how did you get here—to Earth?" Cornplanter asked, astounded.

She pointed up at the hole in the center of the wigwam. "I came in on one of the water transport ships. The previous one, five months—moons—ago. I jumped from low orbit and fell softly to earth using a parachute."

"*Skywoman*," Soon said quietly. A look of shock crossed Cornplanter's face hearing that name.

"How were you chosen for this mission—did you volunteer?" he asked.

She laughed once, bitterly. "That's not how things work. When I was young they determined I was different, on a genetic level—you understand? I never got the modifications and upgrades as everyone else. I was recruited into *Audit*, their secret police. And when it came to this mission, the fact that I still look human … I guess I became the obvious choice."

"When you say *still look human* … what do Martians look like?"

"Different. Much different. It's hard to explain."

"But why did they send you to ... kill me?"

"For a long time, I didn't understand. But then at the Council, when Lake Town proposed attacking the ship, it suddenly clicked. They *are* trying to provoke a conflict—although why now is still a mystery. It was wise decision not to take the bait. But just think if you were killed, of the reaction among the others..."

"There would be a rush to avenge me."

"You see, this is how the AIs work! They thrive on complexity, enjoy playing games within games. They correctly anticipated that the message would assemble people together, that the water ship would be a tempting target. They think you are full of bitterness and hatred, even after all these years, looking for any chance at revenge. Though even with the right conditions, they couldn't be certain it would provoke an attack. But killing *you*—that would provide the spark."

"The *hay-eyes* you speak of—they are the intelligent machines I read about in Nicodemus' book, right?"

"Exactly. They are relentlessly running simulations, branches, probabilities, trying to predict and alter the future course of events. But sometimes they miss the simplest things. Like me meeting Tec ..."

Tec had been dazed throughout the entire discussion, but hearing his name snapped the spell. Suddenly his face grew red and expression twisted in anger. He stood up abruptly and spat out, "So it was all a lie–!"

Before Tory could answer he had stormed past her, out of the wigwam.

Tory jumped up to follow, but Soon stepped in front of the exit and placed a gentle hand on her chest. "Stay. For a moment."

Numbly, Tory sat back down on the ground. Cornplanter leaned in, his eyes glittering in the fire. "One thing that struck me, when you talked about the Martians. You never used the word *we*."

"I-I don't feel anything toward them anymore. I don't know if I ever did."

Cornplanter watched the smoke rising through the hole at the top of the wigwam. "Everyone has told you what to do, since you were very young. And based it on half-truths and tricks."

Soon knelt beside her, took her hand. "Tory, what do *you* want?"

The words came out in a flood. "I want to stay here. I want to be with Tec. I miss Sara so much. Even Jace. And even though I didn't think it was possible—I ... I want to be a mother."

"Have you told him this?"

"I've been afraid of what he would think, if he knew the truth about me."

"Now he does."

"I am so ... *ashamed*," she whispered, breaking down into tears.

Soon held her in her arms for a long time, as Tory's body was wracked with sobs. Finally, she let out a long shuddering sigh and regained some of her composure. Soon ran a soothing hand through her hair.

"Now you can go and find him, Tory."

"Just be honest," Cornplanter counseled. "Don't try to explain it away or make excuses."

"Ask for his forgiveness," Soon said.

Tory nodded and stood up, tears still trickling down her cheeks.

Outside, the night had turned very cold and a steady breeze blew in from the lake. The ghostly green curtains of an aurora pulsed in the sky—right on schedule, in advance of the arrival of the water transport. Crowds of people were gathered around the various campfires scattered throughout the forest, and she didn't know where to begin to look. She asked herself where Tec might go when upset—and as soon as she thought it, she had an answer. *Down by the water.*

Tory glanced back once to see two silhouettes in the open doorway of the wigwam, Cornplanter and Soon, holding hands, watching her go. Then she walked along a newly-trod footpath that cut through the tall grass on the bluffs, and climbed down onto the rocky beach.

The aurora reflected off the wavetops, creating a shimmering display. The beacon of the Flash Light glinted brightly on the southern horizon. The crashing waves cast a frigid spray and she wrapped her arms around her sides. She searched up and down the coast without seeing anyone. But when she turned to take the trail back to the campsite, a dark figure was standing there.

"Tec?" she called out.

The figure stepped out of the tall grass and in the eerie glow she saw it wasn't Tec at all—*it was Krystol!*

He was carrying the rifle. In fact had it pointed toward her.

"Interesting finding you out here tonight. Admiring the aurora?" Krystol sneered.

"What do you think you're doing?"

"I could ask you the same question ... but then we both know the answer. I'm not sure what your message hoped to accomplish—it certainly caused a commotion. But one thing I'm sure of. There is an escape ship somewhere around here, ready to whisk you away ..." He held the rifle awkwardly, but gave every impression he knew how it worked.

"... and you are going to take me with you."

He lowered the barrel, so it was pointed toward her belly.

"Understood?"

15

Tory had enough time to examine the Atlas at the Carnegie Library to know the landing zone had to be northeast of the campsite. Now she just had to find it. But looking at a map and wandering outside in the dark were two very different things. Given that a drone shuttle would need a flat, clear spot to land, it stood to reason the *LZ* would be situated along the shore. But Lake Erie had a *lot* of shoreline. *Could the AIs have been more cryptic*? She cursed them under her breath.

Games within games.

The weird light of the aurora helped her pick her way among the rocks of the beach. With the plummeting temperature, wind and waves, a rime of frost formed around the edges of the stones and she had to take extra care with her footing, so not to slip. Krystol paced behind her, keeping her at a distance, keeping the gun trained on her. They didn't talk. She thought about trying to make a break for it, but out on the wide open shoreline, there was nowhere to run.

They walked for a long time, easily five kilometers, and with each step, Tory was becoming concerned she had misremembered the message. She was positive the instructions read *SE,* southeast. *But could it have been SW?* There were a million details to absorb in training, so easy to overlook some little item.

And what would Krystol do if this journey ultimately led nowhere? *Can I trick him, get close, wrestle the rifle away? He outweighs me by a lot, but he is soft …*

They had to circle around a large moraine boulder that blocked the way forward—and just as she was convincing herself this was the right opportunity to turn on Krystol—she saw the shuttle.

The transport was dome-shaped, much like a wigwam, raised a meter above the ground on four legs. A ring of multi-directional thrusters was mounted on top, and a forward observation bubble protruded in the front. The glossy black outer shell hissed and ticked, cooling down after entry from orbit. A dim blue light glowed inside the open cargo door, and the boarding ramp extended down to the ground, ready to welcome her.

Krystol let out a high-pitched gasp, which she thought was because he was seeing the Martian ship for the first time. But then she realized why. *We're not alone!*

Two shadowy figures lurked at the treeline, standing still against the backdrop of swaying branches. They were very tall, well over two meters, clad in exoskeleton suits made from the same reflective black material as the hull of the drone shuttle, and approached awkwardly, sluggishly, as if they were submerged in water. Their bulky helmets were supported by stiff neck collars, and the tallest one had an array at the crest that looked like a spiked crown. Little blue lights flicked on inside the helmets and their faces became visible through the face shields.

"Wen Prime," Tory said, trying to sound casual, "I didn't expect to see you here."

"You know I leave nothing to chance." The tinny voice came from a small speaker set in the throat collar.

Tory pointed to their crown-helmet, "Did everyone finally come to their senses and declare you king?"

"Very funny," Wen Prime said. "Do you know I had to have my horns cut off to fit inside this contraption?" The thin strip of their circlet was just visible across their brow and flashed orange in annoyance.

"The AIs outdid themselves this time. The helmet deflects the electromagnetic pulse, and these antenna have enough signal to maintain short-range comms with the shuttle. And of course we can't be breathing Earth air and risk catching any nasty viruses..."

Now that they were closer, Tory saw the disc joints extruding from the hard suit at the shoulders, elbows, hips, knees—and similar smaller rotors at the wrist, knuckles, ankles. Yet even with all the mechanized support, it was clear they were struggling with the increased gravity.

"You realize the Defense Network isn't needed anymore. No one here has had electricity for ages."

"And we intend to keep it that way," Wen Prime said. "Besides, the aurora instills a certain sense of awe, wouldn't you agree? But I forget my manners. Let me introduce Cadet Vega 643. They are new to Audit, I recruited them myself. Young and impressionable. And *very* good at taking direction."

In the dim helmet light, Vega had a fish-like appearance, devoid of expression—but their circlet shone clear blue, which signaled *I'm concerned.*

"Vega, this is Taurii 636, one of the finest Operatives that Audit has ever produced. You should feel lucky to meet her, and follow her example. Now Taurii, it's your turn. Please tell us about your guest tonight."

"This is Krystol, the scientist who deciphered your message."

"Oh wonderful! The whole message-thing was a bit over the top, I thought, but you know how the AIs can get when they lock onto an idea." Wen Prime turned to Krystol and bowed slightly, stiffly because of the suit. "It's nice to meet you."

Krystol was too stunned to speak and just made a glottal sound.

"Well, Taurii, it seems we have a lot to catch up on. We detected an x-ray burst from your necklace when it was activated a few hours ago. So tell me, I'm curious how quickly this John Cornplanter died. The AIs assured me the poison would act in under thirty seconds—"

Krystol suddenly found his voice, "B-But Cornplanter's not dead! I saw him saying goodnight to Tory as she left his hut. He looked fine!"

Wen Prime stared at her. "So. Not dead."

Wen Prime turned to Vega and said, "I know how much you were looking forward to a skirmish with the Earthlings, but sadly, it looks like we're going to be disappointed."

"They *were* planning an attack, but Cornplanter talked them out of it!" Krystol supplied. "Their idea was to attach kegs of gunpowder to a submerged net, sail out in front of the water intake hose, with the hopes the net would get tangled up, and the gunpowder ignited by static electricity as the tube was being raised back into orbit ..."

"Really—? That is quite interesting ..." Wen Prime paused for a moment, then said. "AI estimates a 5% probability of success, with a 1% chance of inducing critical system failure. That is significant. Thank you, Krystol for this information—a new vulnerability we weren't aware of! You certainly have brought a bounty of gifts to us tonight."

Krystol kept talking in a rush, "I have more! When she left Cornplanter tonight, instead of coming here, she ran off instead to find her *lover*, Tec Anders." He said it with scorn.

"Wen Prime, let me explain—" Tory said, but they raised a hand.

"Please continue, Krystol," Wen Prime said, strangely eager.

"Do you realize that she is ... *pregnant* with his child?"

In all the time Tory had known Wen Prime, she had never seen them smile. She wondered if possibly the caprine muscular structure of their face prevented it. But they were grinning now. In the blue helmet light they looked absolutely sinister.

"Oh Taurii—I always knew it was you!" Their circlet flashed an intense purple, a rare slip for Wen Prime, which meant *I'm happy.*

"I can't tell you how much the Founders and the meddlesome C-suite doubted this entire mission. If I could show you the probabilities the AIs ran ... here, let me pull them up ... *Perishes on re-entry, 50% ... Killed in first encounter with humans, 12% ... Dies of illness, 11%.* Altogether when you sum them up, the chance of success was under 1%. Well under. It goes to show you how desperate they are, that they greenlit the mission anyway ..."

"What are you talking about?" Tory said.

"Forward Simulation Branch 2833-C. Except it's not a simulation anymore, it's a certainty."

Tory stared blankly.

"At the Founders' meeting it was discussed—weren't you at all curious?"

"I was too terrified to pay attention."

"Ha! Fair point. And the AIs did insist on keeping you in the dark. Well, 2833-C concerns the viability rate of each sequential cohort. Historically, there's always been a high error rate, but nearly sixty years ago, an anomalous trend was detected—which was flagged as its own branch in the simulation, 2833-C. But it's only been getting worse. Only 10% of the latest batch of embryos survived in vivo, well below the replacement rate necessary to keep the population stable."

"But what about the Starship project, colonizing Proxima Centauri?"

Wen Prime laughed. "A fiction to keep people preoccupied. You can't escape the laws of physics! There's simply no way to build the engines required to cross that distance, let alone keeping a multigenerational population of colonists alive in a sealed tin can. No, I'm afraid we are all stuck here in this little backwater Solar System ... The problem is, Martians are no longer able to survive here on Earth. If it weren't for this suit, I wouldn't be able to even stand up in this gravity."

Then Wen Prime became agitated, another first. "Don't you see? We pushed the genome too far! All the upgrades and tinkering and modifications—and for what—survival? No, mainly for *status* and *fashion*. The consequence is, we can't reproduce anymore. Nubai is dying, Taurii—it is a just a matter of time."

Wen Prime paused for a long time, then said quietly. "Unless ..."

"Unless what?"

"The cell line were able to be rejuvenated, a new set of genes introduced into the pool."

Tory gasped out loud.

"Yes, that's where you came in. Very early you were identified as having all the genetic markers that had the closest similarity to a base human genome. Which meant, the best possibility to reproduce. We just needed to find a way to fertilize your ovum."

"My mission ... *that's* what it was all about?"

"All that mumbo-jumbo about you being a Variant, that you had to remain a biological female—all part of the plan. We couldn't risk having anything tamper with your genome. And to build up your skeleton, your musculature, to prepare you for Earth gravity, we had you work in Reclamation—"

"Wen Prime, you're talking about my whole life!"

"But didn't I always tell you that you were special? Look Taurii, you will be treated as a hero back in Nubai. Permanent membership in the Founder's Club! Hell, *breasts* may even come back in fashion—"

"But what about me?" Krystol sputtered. "I've done everything I can to help make your mission a success! I decrypted the message. I helped bring her to Cornplanter. And tonight, when she was about to *escape*—I delivered her here to you!"

"What is it that you want, Krystol?" Wen Prime asked, their goat eyes narrowing.

"I want to come with you! My whole life I've wanted to see what Mars was like. *Please,* take me with you!"

Wen Prime was thoughtful for a moment, considering the request. Then they drew the mag-gun from their belt and sent a high-velocity dart through Krystol's forehead.

He had a puzzled expression, then slumped forward, the musket clattering to the ground.

"Vega, would you be so kind and fetch me that weapon? And those various pouches."

It took some effort to get the powder horn, loading ball, and kit off of Krystol's body, and while doing so, Vega tried their best not to look down at the back of his head, most of which was missing.

Wen Prime examined the long rifle closely, paying special attention to the flintlock mechanism, the octagonal barrel, the wood stock. They tried to gauge the weight of it, even with the suit mechanics compensating. "Incredible," they said. "Who would have thought they could still manufacture a firearm like this."

Wen Prime glanced over at Tory, "This piece will look magnificent mounted on the wall above my bed, don't you think?"

"Wen Prime," Vega meekly interjected. "We're only minutes away from the beginning of morning twilight."

"Yes, I can see the ticking mission clock as well as you. All right, why don't you stow this in the shuttle," handing Vega the rifle, "and bring back the med kit. Time to see what Taurii's been up to."

Vega entered the shuttle and returned lugging a hardened case, which they set down near Tory. "Hold out your arm please," Vega said in a shaky voice. They placed a handheld device against her forearm and there was a sharp pinch. A vial full of her blood was extracted and inserted into a slot, as a centrifuge whirred to life inside.

"Here come the results," Wen Prime announced after a few moments. "Well, congratulations are in order—you *are* pregnant! And let's see ... wow, your metabolic panel is off the charts. You are in prime health ... no sign of any contagious viruses. Which is good news, we won't have to hermetically seal you inside of a case for the trip home. Once we're back on the fast packet, we'll take a stool sample—I'm sure there's an interesting story to be found in there..."

Wen Prime was famous for their dry wit. She had forgotten how exhausting it was.

"But what about my—" She caught herself. "You know," she said, pointing to her stomach. "How will it survive space travel?"

Wen Prime waved their hand dismissively. "Don't pay the fetus any concern. All we need to do is harvest the new cell line, then you won't have to be concerned with it any longer."

A blue glow was lightening the sky to the east and caused the shimmering curtains of the aurora to fade from view. Further down the shore to the south, little glints of light flashed along the shore.

"Looks like they've noticed your absence," Wen Prime observed.

"Should we move the shuttle to somewhere less conspicuous?" Vega asked.

Wen Prime waved off the suggestion, their circlet flashing orange in annoyance. "We realize that daytime refills are rare, for all the obvious reasons. But for today's purpose, we want everything in full view, including the shuttle, so they can understand what they are up against. What are they going to do, fire muskets at us?" Wen Prime laughed.

Tory shivered, and Wen Prime took notice. "You must be freezing out here!" They turned to Vega and said, "Let's get Taurii into the shuttle and give her a circlet. I'm sure she's missed her mentor."

As they walked toward the open bay door, Wen Prime added, "Oh, and Vega, please strap her in tight, just in case she has any ideas of running away again."

The interior of the shuttle was oval shaped with a modular seating area. An open arch led to the forward observation pod. Vega showed her to a seat, clamped a harness down that buckled between her legs and locked her in place. The cargo doors closed.

Wen Prime and Vega removed their cumbersome helmets. "We've got about thirty minutes until the refill operation commences," Wen Prime said. "Now if you'll excuse me, the Founders are quite anxious to receive a status report. I'm going to take the call via tightbeam in the forward pod. But first ..."

Wen Prime towered over her, slipped a circlet down over her temples. She felt the gentle magnetic snap of the nodes connecting. "Welcome home," they breathed into her ear.

She experienced the familiar electric rush as her mentor came online, and columns of icons and widgets began appearing around the periphery of her vision.

But something was different—normally the presence of her mentor felt like an extension of her, something she wasn't even conscious of, as familiar as the skin on her hands. But now she could sense its ... *otherness* inside her head, as if coated in a cold, slimy gel. A feeling of nausea swept over her.

Her mentor seemed unaware of anything out of the ordinary— eagerly showing her a map with the location of the shuttle, the orbital path of the water transport, a spinning operation clock. An alert popped, that due to lack of connectivity, only limited local AI resources were available. During a routine diagnostic scan of her vitals, another alert icon flashed: *Anomaly detected!*

The notification had an audio stream attached, which as she listened in, made no sense whatsoever, like a rapidly pounding drum. Then she realized: *it's a heartbeat!*

Her mentor provided the highest-probability explanation: Tory had been infected by some kind of parasite. Emergency medical procedures were needed immediately.

That's the baby, she thought to herself in amazement, and just sat and listened to the thrumming for a while.

Suddenly it dawned on her, her mentor didn't react to that thought. She could see her reflection in the viewport on the cargo doors to her left. To her surprise, her circlet was glowing pink, *I'm calm*—though she felt anything but at the moment—instead would have expected an anxious green.

Am I doing this—? she wondered.

For a moment she allowed her thoughts to drift to Tec, of his boyish charm, how the corner of his eyes crinkled when he smiled, the way his rough hands felt, his arms around her ... how patient he was with Sara, and how he showed Jace what it meant to be a father and a man. An overwhelming feeling welled up inside her—*I'm in love with Tec.* All she wanted to do was be near him once again. And then a sudden stab of dread struck her, that everything was about to be taken away from her—forever. And that in turn triggered a simmering feeling of rage at the unfairness of it all.

She glanced over at her reflection in the viewport, and her circlet still registered a steady calm pink.

It can't read my thoughts anymore!

Instead, her mentor was busy suggesting that she join a livestream of the water transport, as the intake hose descended over Lake Erie. As with all mental projections, it was hard to get the right sense of scale, but even with that distortion, the fully deployed hose was more massive than anything she'd seen before. A black line curved up and up until it vanished in the pale dome of the morning sky. The rising sun glinted off the braided-metal skin of the tube as it dipped toward the surface of the water.

Suddenly there was a flash and a jagged arc of lightning leapt up from the lake to strike the nozzle, and then another, and another. Crashing booms of thunder were audible inside the shuttle, like bombs exploding outside, even causing the thick plexiglass of the viewport to vibrate.

When the intake hose penetrated the lake surface, the barrage of lightning halted. High above them in orbit, the transport ship opened the aperture of its main tank to the vacuum of space, and the pressure imbalance caused the water to get sucked up, like a gigantic drinking straw. The lake surface around the hose began to froth and churn and swirl.

Wen Prime popped their head back in to the main cabin to say "It's go time."

"Prepare for liftoff," the drone shuttle AI intoned.

The ring of thrusters above them ignited and the shuttle lifted vertically, tilted slightly forward, and flew out over the lake toward the distant intake hose. The mechanical collar—the place where she had stowed away while waiting for her launch window—was visible even at a distance, a thick band around the tube about fifty meters above the water.

Her mentor helpfully displayed a schema of the short flight path, covering the twenty five kilos in less than ten minutes. Upon approach, the shuttle would raise its nose up and the extensible legs would latch on to the collar, like a tick fastening on to a leg. The interior cabin seats would reorient and a second bay door, in the floor, would provide access into the mechanical collar. Once the refill was complete, the tube would be reeled in slowly, like a giant fishing line, carrying them along with it back to the orbiting transport ship.

The drone shuttle AI chimed, "Two watercraft detected, heading on bearing to intercept intake hose."

From up front, Wen Prime shouted gleefully, "It looks like they are trying to come rescue you, Taurii. We may have that skirmish after all!" They spoke to the drone shuttle AI, "Give us a scan and assess any weaponry aboard."

The two tall masted ships from Lake Town were under full sail, their bows rising and crashing through the waves on the lake. The image zoomed in and panned across the deck of the first ship, superimposing a yellow outline over crew members carrying rifles. As the scan focused on the second ship, Tory caught a glimpse of Tec on board, leaning against the forward rail, as if willing the ship to go faster.

Her heart leapt in her chest—and she stole a quick glance over at her reflection. *Still calm.*

"Only weaponry aboard: hand-held ballistics. Do not possess range, muzzle velocity nor ammunition to penetrate shuttle hull or titanium sleeve of intake hose," the shuttle drone AI informed.

"What, no cannons?" Wen Prime said, disappointed. "Well, no matter, we can always splice those in afterwards during final edits. If we're lucky, we may have the start of a new streaming series in the making…"

The shuttle drone AI said, "Attack plan: descend to altitude fifty meters, providing angle for high velo mag-gun to penetrate wooden hulls below water line. Risk … 0.01%."

"Do it," Wen Prime said.

The shuttle banked sharply, changing course and accelerating toward the approaching ships. In the seat across from her, Vega's face looked greenish, but it was hard to tell if that was from the high-G maneuver, or just the natural sheen of their skin.

"Vega," she whispered. "I need your help. That last turn … the strap is really cutting into my stomach. The harness is too tight, can you adjust it?"

They stared back at her with blank fish eyes.

On a gamble, with a little inward mental flick, she instructed her mentor to project *I'm scared*—and it worked! Her circlet glowed yellow.

"Vega—it's crushing the baby!" she said urgently. *"Please help me!"*

Something registered in their head, and they crossed the aisle, knelt at her side. They began awkwardly fiddling with the buckle between her legs, and Tory raised her hands above her head so they could lean in and have more room. Vega's circlet projected a deep blue, *I'm concentrating.*

At the moment she heard the click of the harness lock opening, she interlocked her fingers and hammered down with both hands as hard as she could, striking a blow at the back of Vega's exposed, fragile neck. There was a crunch and Vega collapsed to the floor of the shuttle, their circlet fading to flat gray.

In the observation pod, Wen Prime leaned forward in their seat, face pressed close to the plexiglass, completely preoccupied with the two ships, now less than five hundred meters away.

The shuttle drone AI said, "Targeting … pitch and yaw of waves requires additional calibration … estimate twenty seconds to fire."

As Tory slid out of the seat harness, her mentor scolded, "Passengers must remain seated during attack manuever." Tory paid no attention to it. She hurried to get the musket from among the equipment cases where Vega had stowed it.

The med kit dislodged in the process and clunked heavily to the floor. That got Wen Prime's attention. They turned to look back into the main cabin to see where the sound came from, saw Vega sprawled on the ground, saw Tory with the rifle in her hands.

"Taurii, wait! What are you doing—?"

As Wen Prime spoke, they reached for the mag-gun on their belt and smoothly drew it, raised it toward Tory. But Tory already had the rifle lifted and leveled. There was a flash and a loud *BOOM*. Gunsmoke filled the main cabin.

The bullet caught Wen Prime in the throat and toppled them over backward. The mag-gun fired on full auto as they fell—sending a burst of high velocity darts ripping through the ceiling of the cabin.

The shuttle lurched sideways.

"Alert!" the shuttle drone AI chirped. "Outer hull pierced. Thrust malfunction in nozzles six, ten, fifteen, and sixteen."

And a moment later, "Two crew members offline."

And then again, "Probability of full engine failure: 66%. Emergency override: ending attack routine, returning to shuttle dock."

Her mentor, still clueless as to what was happening, blithely alerted her to a change in flight path. The animated diagram showed the shuttle disengaging from the two ships, gaining altitude and returning to the mechanical collar.

She raced over to the cargo door and pulled hard against the latch.

"Exterior doors may not be opened during flight," both the shuttle drone AI and her mentor squawked at the same time.

With every ounce of authority she could muster, she yelled, "I am Operative Taurii 636!" She glanced at Vega sprawled on the floor and the pool of blood around Wen Prime. "I'm the ranking officer on this ship, and I'm ordering you to open this door. *DO IT NOW!*"

For agonizing seconds the shuttle hovered, wobbling and lurching from side to side as the shuttle drone AI struggled to process all the events happening—it simply lacked the computational power to handle this level of dimensionality.

"IF I DIE, THE CHILD DIES WITH ME!"

That must have struck a nerve somewhere, because suddenly the cargo door slid open and a gust of wind blew in. Without hesitation, she ripped the circlet off her head and tossed it across the cabin like a disc—and just like that, the icons and diagrams and alerts vanished, along with her mentor.

Far down below, the surface of the lake was choppy and steel blue. Fifty meters seemed impossibly high, but then she reminded herself that she had jumped out of a similar hatch before—from the edge of space.

Without another thought she stepped out the door. For a brief instant she found the horizon and fixed her eyes to it, squeezed her legs together tightly and wrapped her arms across her chest—and then hit the water feet-first with tremendous force.

The shock of the water knocked the wind out of her, and she struggled to swim back up to the top, gasping lungs full of air as she broke the surface.

Hovering above her, the shuttle made up its mind, broke off and flew in a wobbly path toward the intake hose, which appeared like a tower rising into the sky. Pennants of black smoke trailed from the gleaming ring of thrusters.

The shuttle approached the mechanical collar, and as it began to tip its nose up for the docking maneuver, something in the engine gave out. The shuttle began to tumble like a thrown rock and crashed into the side, tearing a deep gash in the metallic sheath covering the intake hose. A mixture of smoke, flames and water gushed out simultaneously.

Tory had bigger concerns. She was doing her best to tread water and get her bearings in relationship to the tall ships, but the wind-blown waves, which had seemed tiny from up above, now crested well above her head, slapped against her, filled her mouth and ears and nose with water. Her soaked clothes acted like weights, the cold water of the lake was a shock to her system, rapidly numbing her limbs and dragging her back down.

No no no, she desperately thought. *Not like this!*

Then a strong set of hands grabbed her by the shirt and held her head above the choppy water. She blinked into the rising sun, saw a canoe had pulled alongside her, and she weakly reached for the side. The hands adjusted their grip under her arms and she heard Tec's voice.

"C'mon Tory! I've got you!"

He was crouched in the center of one of the big Obijbwe lake canoes, Katya in the stern steering the boat, keeping it close to Tory with a sideways in-and-out paddle stroke that churned the water. One of the tall ships was behind them, only a hundred meters away, tacking in the wind.

Tec called out, "One... two ... *three!*"

On his signal both he and Katya leaned far over to the left at the same time he hauled Tory up and over lip of the right gunwale. She flopped down into the middle of the canoe, water pouring off her.

Then his arms were around her, pulling her into his lap, pushing her wet hair away, and she looked up at his smiling face.

"Tec," she sputtered. "Tec, I am so sorry—"

"Shhhh," he bent down and whispered into her ear. "I understand now. All is forgiven."

"I love you," she breathed. The water streaming down her face was mixed with tears.

"I love you too, Tory. You're back with us. You're safe."

Katya interrupted their moment, "Um, you may want to look at this."

The refill operation must have been aborted, because the intake hose was rising up and out of the water, rivers of water streaming down the sides. As it ascended into the sky, a single blinding bolt of lightning struck the nozzle—and a billowing explosion ripped through the mechanical collar.

A surging cascade of water gushed out, and the braided metal sheath around the intake hose began to unravel, working its way upward, spraying out jets of water in a spiral, some of which splattered on them in the canoe, nearly a kilometer away.

The wind rapidly peeled apart the metallic strands, which spread out like the roots of a tree. And then at the apex, a glowing dot appeared that increased in intensity until it was as bright as the sun. The shredded intake hose acted like an anchor dragging through the thick lower atmosphere, and the laden water tanker was not able to maintain its orbit. It skipped against the outer atmosphere and began to burn up.

There was a brilliant flash and the glowing dot fragmented into a cluster of meteors. An enormous boom—like the sky itself was cracking open—reached the surface, and the shards of the wrecked transport ship grew into fireballs that arced past and over the eastern horizon, leaving contrails of smoke behind, like a giant claw mark across the sky.

Katya pivoted the bobbing canoe and began to paddle back to the tall ship, while Tec held Tory tightly.

High above, the falling water from the tanker was lit by the sun and a rainbow appeared.

16

One afternoon during the Strawberry Moon, Tory sat in the shade of the front porch of the Anders' homestead. She gently rocked back and forth in the new chair that Tec had built in his workshop during the winter. Pickles loafed beside her. She read aloud from a worn leather book held in one hand, and spoke in a low hushed voice,

Forth upon the Gitchee Gumee,
On the shining Big Sea-Water,
With his fishing line of cedar,
Of the twisted bark of cedar,
Forth to catch the sturgeon Nahma,
Mishe-Nahma, King of Fishes,
In his birch canoe exulting,
All alone went Hiawatha.

From time to time, she paused to look down at the tiny sleeping child nestled in the crook of her elbow, and couldn't help but smile. She gazed out at the view from the porch. Bees buzzed in the wildflowers that bloomed along the front bank. The lush green of summer foliage rustled in a gentle breeze. The sweeping curve of the river sparkled in the sun, the hills were hazy blue in the distance, and puffy clouds drifted in the blue sky. She breathed in the fragrance and let out a deep sigh.

287

A canoe came up upstream carrying two people, and deftly navigated past the low-hanging branch at the bend. She waved, but they dipped out of sight below the front bank before seeing her up on the bluff. The bell at the bottom of the landing rung, and few moments later, Jace came up the front steps, carrying a leather travel bag over one shoulder.

Jace wore faded blue jeans and a flannel shirt with the sleeves removed, showing off the new bulging muscles he had put on since becoming Zeb's apprentice at the Forge. His long hair was tied back with a bandana, and he was covered head to toe with a layer of grime.

She hadn't seen Jace in over a moon, since last Market, now that he stayed in town with Suki and Zeb. Sadly, with the onset of winter, Jasmyn had decided to move on to warmer country, planning to travel even further beyond Falls-of-the-Ohio, down the Mississippi River. Jace had been heartbroken, but then began to realize, as Suki often reminded him, that there were *other fish in the sea.*

"Heya, Jace!" Tory called in greeting. "Is that a smudge of soot on your lip, or are you trying to grow a mustache?"

"Very funny," Jace said, then added, "We have a visitor."

Behind Jace, ascending the stairs, was none other than John Cornplanter. He was dressed casually, more in the fashion of the Ten Towns, with a flannel shirt, blue jeans and high boots, and a straw hat in the Amish style, with an eagle's feather in the band. A woven Mohawk basket was tucked under his arm.

"John!" she cried out in surprise. Pickles leapt off the porch, tail wagging furiously.

"Tory, it is good to see you!" He bent to give Pickles' head a vigorous rub. "I hope it is okay that I'm arriving unannounced."

"Of course! You are always welcome here, any time. But what brings you to Flood Town?"

"More about that later," he said. "But much more importantly—how are baby and mother doing?"

"Here, let me introduce you to Laurel," Tory said. She came down from the porch and gently exchanged the swaddled bundle for the Mohawk basket. Cornplanter cradled the baby in his arms, grinning with joy.

"What a beautiful girl," he said. "And such a beautiful name! The mountain laurel is one of my favorite flowers." He nodded to the basket, "A gift from Soon."

Just then Sara came running around the side of the house, and stopped in her tracks upon seeing the visitor.

"Sara, do you know who this is?" Tory asked. "It's John Cornplanter!"

Sara's eyes went wide. "We have your book! Will you sign it for us?"

"Oho! I wish I could take credit for writing that book—but that's not me. There have been many before me who have carried the name *Gy-ant-wa-chia*, which means Cornplanter in our language. And I pray there will be many more that follow. The Cornplanter you're speaking of became a traveling preacher, spreading the Good Story of Creator-Sets-Free. I believe he was the last Cornplanter to pass through Flood Town—way back when your grandmother was a girl your age!"

Sara scrunched up her forehead, thinking about that.

"Thank you for this beautiful basket," Tory said. "Would you like a tour of our place? Tec is out back."

"I would be delighted."

The four of them entered through the front door. Tory placed the basket at the center of the dining table and took Laurel back into her arms. The baby had barely stirred. She showed Cornplanter around the main room and kitchen hearth, described the layout upstairs and root cellar below the trap door, all of which he took great interest in. He remarked upon the painting of Flood Town, and noticed the newest addition—a carved red False Face mask hanging above Tec's writing desk. Throughout, Sara was glued to his side.

As they cut through the back yard, chickens scattered out of their way. The donkey poked a head out of the shadows of the barn to see what the commotion was about. They crossed through the back gate and skirted the edge of the meadow, heading out to the garden, where they found Tec working, snipping various medicinal herbs.

He straightened upon seeing the approaching party and exclaimed, "Well if it isn't John Cornplanter!"

The men shook hands, exchanged greetings and congratulations on the birth of Laurel. Sara tugged at Cornplanter's elbow, "Come and see the Three Sisters!"

This season they had followed the method the Seneca used, planting corn, green beans, and squash together, not in rows but in a scattered pattern so the squash vines had plenty of room to spread out. Cornplanter examined the green beans hanging from the corn stalk and remarked, "These are about ready to harvest!"

"I know, right?" Sara said. She continued the tour, leading him through the orchard and proudly showing off the beehive. She fearlessly opened the lid—something Tory still was squeamish about—and he examined the inside of the hive with fascination.

Next they walked down to the workshop. Cornplanter admired the neat organization of canning supplies, and Tec delightedly showcased his fly-tying bench and all the various colored threads and feathers he used. Cornplanter ran the palm of his hand across the worktable and said, "Much good work has happened on this table, you can feel it in the grain."

Sara pointed to a deep red stain by his hand and said, "I don't know if that is from strawberry juice, or blood from Tory's first night here."

"Maybe a bit of both," Tec said with a smile.

Finally they found themselves back on the front porch. Tec brought out a few extra chairs, and Sara retrieved a bottle of root beer from the cellar and poured cups.

"Won't you stay with us for a while?" Sara asked.

"I wouldn't want to impose! It's a short paddle back to Flood Town and I can find lodgings there—"

"No, we insist, John," Tec said. "Please stay with us. Depending on how much time you have, we can do a little fishing on the Stoney Creek, and also hike up to Ninety-Three."

"I would like that very much, thank you. And I appreciate your suggestion of visiting Ninety-Three—it is something I am keen to do."

"Then it's settled," Tec said. "Sara, let's roast a chicken for our guest tonight. We can have the first green beans too."

Sara jumped up, "I'll go sharpen the hatchet!"

Tec said to Jace, "Help your sister out. But first, please go and wash up!"

"I did wash up already, back in town! Grandma wouldn't let me come before I did."

"Well it didn't stick! Please go take a bath out back. Use hot water."

Jace grumbled as he stood up, and carried Cornplanter's travel bag inside.

"Teenagers," Tec said in exasperation.

Cornplanter chuckled. "I had a wonderful visit in Steel Town," he said. "I met Nicodemus at the Library. We discussed his book, and he lent me an anthology, *The Essential Debate on the Constitution*. I have been thinking a great deal on that subject."

He continued, "While not everyone believes in the Good Story—and there are as many interpretations of it as there are people, it seems—it is hard to argue against the wisdom in the teachings of Creator-Sets-Free, of how a person should treat others with love and compassion, especially those less fortunate."

Tec nodded, "The Basic Rule: *If you don't want it done to you, then don't do it to others.*"

"Cornplanter the Preacher expanded upon the Good Story. After the long dark winters that followed the Blackout, his vision showed a way to organize our communities, while avoiding the dangers of Progress that tempted and doomed the ancients."

"The False and Simple Paths," Tory said.

Cornplanter nodded. "But what I find is still missing, is a way for *communities* to coexist with each other. With mutual respect, without one trying to dominate the other."

"We have Treaties and trade routes—what more is needed beyond that?" Tec asked.

Cornplanter didn't answer, instead asked a question of his own. "Tory, tell me. The Martians—do you think they will come back?"

She frowned, and glanced down at Laurel, who was beginning to stir from her nap. "I don't think they have any choice but to. Its a matter of when, not if. I'm sure AIs are running through scenarios as we sit here …"

"We saw for a fleeting moment at the Great Council what we can accomplish if we stand together," Cornplanter observed. "I think we are going to need more of that in the moons ahead …"

He continued, "I've admired the American Constitution as a way to establish a common government based on consent of the people—while the Bill of Rights, and the Amendments that followed, protect the people's liberty, resisting at every turn the temptation of tyranny. There is much wisdom there. But the things not addressed—banks, corporations, technology, bureaucracy—those had much to do with America's ultimate downfall."

"As Cornplanter the Preacher has warned us not to repeat," Tec said.

"Yes. Candidly, for some time, my brothers and sisters among the Onondoga and Mohawk—as well as the Huron, Ojibwe, and Cree—we have discussed reviving the Confederation of the Haudenosaunee. It served our ancestors well for hundreds of winters, helping them resist the advance of the settlers from Europe, until the American Revolution tipped the balance at last and they were overwhelmed by sheer numbers. I'm not even sure the ancient Americans were aware that their nation was based on the example of the *Great Law of Peace*, which united six nations under one common roof, much as their thirteen states formed a mutual pact in the Constitution..."

He continued, "What I am proposing is that we bring back the *Great Law of Peace*, and expand it to include not only the First Nations of the Great Lakes, but the Ten Towns as well."

"But how will it work?" Tec asked.

"We will have a Great Council that meets once each year to focus on two areas, common defense and mutual trade. Each Nation and Town will keep its local government, its boundaries, issue Writs and Permits, hand down Judgments, handle its own trade through its Agents—and in the case of the Ten Towns, print its own *dials*. It will be governed by consensus and courtesy—all members must agree before moving forward on any item. We'll change the location of the Great Council each year, so that everyone gets to know each other's people. Having a permanent place lends itself to the creation of bureaucracy, which must be avoided at all costs. Look at the American capital, how it eventually became the Belt Wall ..."

Everything Cornplanter said sounded reasonable to Tory, and Tec was nodding in agreement too.

"I propose we call this new union ... *Commonwell.*"

"Don't you mean Common*wealth*?" Tec corrected him.

"No, we already are blessed by the Creator, who has provided us in abundance. *Wealth* implies hoarding these gifts for yourself, and that thinking leads down the False Paths. Instead, we need *wellness*—health and protection. That is the mission."

Cornplanter said, "Before I came out here, I spent some time with the Flood Town Council. By the way, I met your mother, Tec, and she showed me around her wonderful Kitchen Garden."

"Now you see where he gets it from," Tory said.

Cornplanter smiled. "I asked the Council if they agreed with this vision, and they did—though of course they cautioned it would have to be put to a vote of the town residents. I asked who they thought would be a good representative for Flood Town, and they were unanimous in their selection—even Verna, who spoke her mind on the matter."

"I think Tec will be great!" Tory said with enthusiasm, "Though I will miss him and wish he didn't have to go. But this is too important—"

"I'm not asking Tec," Cornplanter said. "I'm asking *you*, Tory Flood."

"*Me?*" she said in disbelief. "But I'm not even from here!"

Cornplanter looked around and said, "Are you sure about that?"

"Tory, you know about Mars! You have traveled and met people from the Ten Towns, from the First Nations." Tec said. "You are the perfect person to provide counsel."

Cornplanter said, "My hope is that, when the Martians arrive, that we can negotiate a peace with them, so our peoples can coexist ..." He sighed, "I'm not sure that is possible—but it is worth the effort. And if diplomacy fails, we must prepare for our defense."

Laurel began to squirm and show signs of being hungry. Tory looked down at her, so tiny and warm and fragile, and made up her mind in an instant.

"I accept."

She stood up and said, "Now if you'll excuse me, I'm going to go in and feed the baby."

"I'll go check on the children," Tec added.

Cornplanter sat on the porch for a while and listened to the sounds of dinner being prepared inside, the bird songs in the forest, the river rushing past below. He packed his pipe and had a smoke, and watched as the red sun began to set.

SOURCES QUOTED IN THE TEXT

- *The Song of Hiawatha*, Henry Wadsworth Longfellow, 1855
- *Selling My Pork Chops*, Lizzie "Memphis Minnie" Douglas, 1941
- Ausbund quotations are reproduced from *Songs of the Ausbund, revised edition*, copyright (c) 2019 by Ohio Amish Library, Inc. Used by permission of Ohio Amish Library, Millersburg, OH. All rights reserved.
- Scripture quotations are reproduced from *First Nations Version*, copyright (c) 2021 by Rain Ministries Inc. Used by permission of InterVarsity Press, Downers Grove, IL. All rights reserved.

BOOKS BY STEPHEN E MEYER

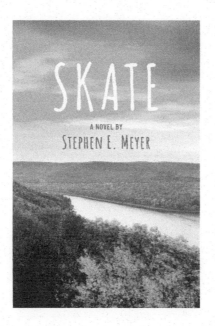

SKATE is a classic coming-of-age story set among the hunting camps of the Pennsylvania backwoods in the late 1980s. Stef, a young man on a quest to get his first buck, meets a mysterious young woman named Skate on his journey. A thrilling adventure ensues, with legendary hunters and fierce winter storms, as Stef risks his very life, determined to bring the buck in.

ABOUT THE AUTHOR

STEPHEN E. MEYER was born and raised in St. Marys, PA, where he discovered a lifelong love of the outdoors—hunting, fishing, hiking, canoeing—though he never has enjoyed sleeping in a tent. His stories are focused on traditional themes and forgotten places. He lives with his family in Philadelphia.